Arkborn

A Novel

Christopher Brown

Former Captain™ Press

*To my students, teachers, family, and friends.
I love you all.*

A Note on Prophecy, Promises, and Signs

After the dove returned with an olive branch and the Ark found dry land, God made a promise: *I'll never do this again,* he said. *And I'll put a rainbow in the cloud as a sign of this covenant.*

Later, human beings were packed onto ships and brought to America, where their stolen bodies built a new economy.

Their souls, though, remained their own. They endured. They sang. And sometimes messages were coded in their songs, most notably in *Wade in the Water.*

They sang the Bible, but the music and the poetry were their own. *O Mary don't you weep* blended together the sisters of Lazarus, Moses and the Exodus, and possibly the Armageddon of **2 Timothy**. These songs were handed down like the epics of Homer—by the human voice. And somewhere in that handing-down a new verse emerged, a new poetry:

> *God gave Noah the rainbow sign -*
> *No more water, but the fire next time.*

And earlier, in Bach's first setting of the Passion, when Jesus has been whipped and handed over for crucifixion there is this aria:

> *Ponder well how his back, bloodstained all over, is like the sky—where after the deluge from our flood of sins has abated, there appears the most beautiful rainbow, as a sign of God's mercy.*

The disaster foretold in **2 Timothy** is often interpreted as a spiritual one—the Second Coming, where the Refiner's Fire comes to purify the sinner. But there is another way of looking at **2 Timothy 3:10** and at that new verse in the spiritual:

> *No more water, but the fire next time.*

This *fire next time*, foretold and retold by Bible, slaves, and James Baldwin, may be literally true. Humankind's husbandry of Life on Earth may be found wanting. Life on Earth may be literally dissolved by fire someday soon.

Preface

The story of The Ark starts with its feet firmly planted in the earth of Spring. It is 2016, and God is pissed. This Earth part of her creation is at risk. She is looking at her options.

•

Way back then God said, let us make a human in our image, by our likeness, to hold sway over the fish of the sea and the fowl of the heavens and the cattle and the wild beasts and all the crawling things that crawl upon the earth. And he did, and he saw that it was good.

But it wasn't long before God had to reprimand those who looked like him, expelling them from the Garden, guarding the Tree of Life with a flaming sword, and condemning the woman to birth pains and the man to backbreaking toil.

For a while it seemed that all was well. But after ten generations God realized that the evil of the human creature was great upon the earth and that every scheme of his heart's devising was only perpetually evil.

Hence the flood. Nature, red in tooth and claw. And perhaps God felt a pang of regret, because he swore he would never again do such a thing.

Then all was well for eons. Or arguably OK. Apart, that is, from war, plague, persecution, displacement, and enslavement.

•

In the Spring of 2016, the time of Hope and Renewal, all is not well. Humans still hold sway, micromanaging those birds and beasts for profit and personal gain. They have taken on a loan that cannot be repaid. They give lip service to protecting the next generation. But the real problem is not that responsibility is being abdicated. The real problem is extinction.

Obviously the herd must be culled, thinks God. But how? Who? And how can I rescue some of my beautiful creation?

This time I'm not creating the hazard, she thinks. I'm not the one making this modern-day flood that threatens all life on Earth. But maybe I can do something. Maybe I can find a new Noah.

•

Odysseae Personae

Here are the people who take the leap. Who overcome their fears. Who set out on what will be the journey of their life. Their Odyssey.

- **Ahiga**, born 1997. He speaks English and passable Navajo.

- **Alex**, born 1965. He has loved trees since birth.

- **Andrew**, born 1960. He is a pilot. He speaks (or understands) English, C, Assembler, and just about any other coding language.

- **Ameerah**, born 1989. She is an engineer and a pilot. She speaks Creole, English, and French.

- **Art**, born 1952. He speaks English. He loves people. All people.

- **Ben**, born 1982. He is a musician, a humanist, and a brewer of beer. He speaks English, German, and Spanish.

- **Colin**, born 1984. He is a chef. He speaks German, English, and French.

- **Dominic**, born 1986. He is a baker. He speaks Italian, French, and English.

- **Eric** is Andrew's son, born 1980. Like his father, he is a pilot, and his languages are English and Computer.

- **Ferdinand**, born 1997. He is a pilot. His languages are Québecois and English.

- **Gopinath**, *born 1990. He is an engineer and a mechanic. He speaks Tamil, Hindi, and English.*

- **Isaac** *is Eric's son and Andrew's grandson, born 1999. He is a pilot and coder. It runs in the family.*

- **Latifah**, *born 1982. She is a midwife. She speaks English.*

- **Moses**, *born 1981. He is a visionary. He speaks English.*

- **Naveed**, *born 1987. He is an engineer, but also a humanist. His interests include mathematics, music, and physics. He speaks Farsi, English, and French.*

- **Niloofar**, *born 1988. She is a talented and ambitious engineer. She speaks Farsi, French, and English.*

- **Noah**, *born 1985. He is a visionary. He speaks Afrikaans, German, and English.*

- **Nurul**, *born 1990. She is a biologist, with interests ranging from robotics to fungi and bacteria. She speaks Javanese, Indonesian, and English.*

- **Omar**, *born 1988. He is an engineer and a pilot. He speaks Arabic, French, and English.*

- **Rachel**, *born 1983. She is a Medical Doctor and a musician. She speaks English.*

- **Sebastien**, *born 1990. He has always worked as*

a fonctionnaire, but he is a gifted humanist. He is fluent in French, Québecois, and English.

- **Wesley**, born 1951. He is a physicist and polymath. He speaks English but has a working knowledge of Ancient Greek, Latin, and Hebrew.

- **Youssef**, born 1998. He is an engineer and a pilot. He speaks Arabic, French, and English.

Recruits

Part I

I

Recruits

What is man, that thou shouldest magnify him?
and that thou shouldest set thine heart upon him?

~ Job 7:17 ~

The co-ordinates, and then the speck, gradually become the Ark. It is a cylinder, already bristling with stubby spokes, like the hub of a bicycle wheel. Youssef has a lock on the port and is flying, merging his velocity vector with the approach path. It is his first high-orbit docking.

It is also the Ark's – if you can call this assemblage of bits and pieces by its ambitious name – the Ark's first docking in high orbit. If Youssef could inspect it carefully, it wouldn't look much different from what he saw as he last docked with it in low orbit seven months ago. But he knows that since that day this pile of junk has moved, using the first and second burns of its main engine. That last docking was about 100 miles above the surface of the Earth. This one looks exactly the same – same piece of junk – but it is about 22,000 miles above the Earth. If you can call 22,000 miles away above anything.

Youssef remembers the stories some of his teachers told about young men going into battle in Spitfires and Hurricanes in World War II. They had minimal training. He feels like that now. He is using the Magic Carpet software, maneuvering toward a port on one end of the axis of this Ark that is to be. The software computes the orbital mechanics, translating the relative accelerations he wants into what will achieve the same in this high orbit. So far so good. The speck, the assemblage of junk, now the big bicycle wheel hub, is aligned with the symbol on his Heads Up Display. Youssef has to get the two vehicles' relative velocity to zero on schedule. He is flying by hand because he is good at it and wants to get better. Thirty seconds to Decision Point. He has to decide now if his trajectory is good enough. Can he continue, or must he abort, translating laterally so that he misses the Ark?

He is close enough now to see the real Port 3, lower right in the pentagon, merging with its symbol on the HUD. Deceleration is on track in the HUD graph. The grapple arm symbology appears in the HUD in his peripheral vision. That's it. DP. He's going in. In the cone of vision of the real world out front, the grapple arms – the real ones of the Ark – appear.

Youssef is enjoying himself. His ship's mechanical probe is dead in the middle of the target on the Ark. He is going for a ZET docking. Zero Energy Transfer. He tweaks the closing velocity slower. He wants this to last. He wants the first contact to be with the grapple arms as they embrace his ship.

Youssef has carried many pieces of the Ark into low-earth orbit. It was his dream to become a low-orbit shuttle pilot. Noah had decided that although the boosters were auto-landing successfully, with about a 95% retrieval rate, that wasn't good enough for his people. It's time to put someone's ass in the seat, he said. Youssef jumped at the chance. In two years he has had forty-seven launches, forty-seven first stage separations, and – praise be to Allah – forty-seven successful landings. Then he was tagged for high orbit. Beyond his dreams. In a blissful haze of high-energy learning for six months plus. Theory. Math. Video games about gravity and curved spacetime. The high-orbit shuttle in mind-numbing detail. The Simulator. Orbital Mechanics becoming his dreams, part of his natural environment. This morning Youssef was confident he could fly today's mission. Even without the Magic Carpet.

•

It might have been the election that turned Noah. Or not turned, exactly – because as far back as he can remember, Noah has always believed that stewardship of the Earth and learning to live in space are essentially the same problem – operating a closed system.

So what was the turning? It was more a decision to act after a long simmering of possibilities. It was a small step toward recognizing that one man cannot do everything. Although Noah is not yet old, his was an old man's calculation – what do I do now in order to be most effective in the time remaining?

The electric cars, the batteries – these could be seen as Earth stewardship. Or not. Perhaps the technology is just as useful on the way to Mars? For a few years now Mars had been the ostensible destination. The answer to why are you making rockets, Noah?

The turning was inward and silent, as all great works must be in their tender moment of birth. Tender, vulnerable, and yet violent as a storm. Noah saw that it was not up to him to decide the destination. Mars, up to now, had been an excuse. If indeed it was God speaking to him, Mars was not what He meant. No – God, or whoever, wanted Noah to gather together what he could of Humanity for the simplest of reasons. Survival. It was all of God's purpose in one word. It was Nature, Evolution, and the History of Mankind. God had done this before, way back in the beginning. He had sworn never to do it again. But God – if She were a large, black and beautiful humanoid – would smile as She thought of Einstein. How large his vision. How curious his faith. How close he came to recognizing Her as She threw the dice.

•

The shuttle is hovering in the target zone, barely translating. With his fingertips, Youssef kills the relative motion. The ship's mechanical probe hasn't touched the Ark. The new high-shuttle pilot concentrates hard. If he can keep his ship in the 10cm spherical target for 10 seconds, the secondary docking trigger will fire. The union will be consensual.

•

The original Ark was 300 cubits long, 50 cubits wide, and 30 cubits high. It had three stories. Since a cubit is the distance from a man's elbow to the tip of his outstretched middle finger, and taking a stab at the size of the man envisioned, that works out to about 150 metres long, 25 metres wide, and 15 metres high. Big, but perhaps not big enough for the new job.

Noah wants more than two of everything. Two is not enough for survival. He wants all varieties of human being. We don't have time for evolution, he says. He wants the sum and the history of man's knowledge. He wants curators. He wants trees and birds and bees. He wants light and air and beauty.

Noah is thinking more like a kilometre in diameter – even for the first Ark. The Ark is a flying saucer, but it will not fly in an atmosphere. Noah is aiming for that, but there are a few problems to be solved. How to use energy directly to navigate space-time, for example. He can be colourful in meetings, pushing a new idea toward derision. It's still propulsion. Throwing mass out the ass. Newton's Third. Hey – mass is precious. Remember Einstein? We don't throw shit away.

The Ark is a big wheel. It will rotate around its axis to make G. Its axis will rotate to make day and night. Naturalists are still working on thousands of details. How will phototropic trees and plants adapt?

•

It looks like one of those driverless cars. Behind it, at the light, tall thin Youssef suppresses a giggle. Ameerah is short. The light is one of those no-right-on-red outliers on the South Shore. The light turns green. Youssef can see a hand rise and tug the steering wheel for the turn. A pretty hand. Magically, the driverless car accelerates around the turn, as if a short leg has stabbed the gas pedal. But it rolls demurely down Boulevard Roland-Therrien toward Plant 1. The limit is 50kmh and there are speed cameras.

Behind her, Youssef is still trying to find her head. He can see the steering wheel and the back of the front seat. He has just met her – at the flying club at Plant 5. So far he knows they are both engineers. They are both contractors for Universal. She wants to be a pilot. They are going to see Lieutenant Sebastien at Badge Control. The driverless car seems to know the way. Trailing it at 50kmh, with cars passing them on the left, Youssef is as alert – as excited – as he was on his first solo.

●

Democracy was failing, and much of the trouble originated in the Net. Noah has been worrying at this for some time, but in the year after the election he began to act on the plans forming in his head. He bought a few Silicon Valley startups and trolled Human Resources, waiting for a strike. The vain, those interested in money and power – these he threw back. He was patient. Sooner or later he would find what he needed – young people who thought idealistically about the Net, the way its founders had a generation before. As his hooks gathered them in, he put them to work in new divisions of his companies, making tools. Tools for making the New Net.

The quality Noah looks for is seriousness. Not a person who never laughs, but someone who is serious about her work. Someone who has a thirst for new knowledge. Someone who can be questioning and critical about what he already "knows". These people are not the majority, but they are out there. Or rather, they are in here, in the companies Noah owns. When he comes across such a person he promotes her into a more challenging position and tracks her progress. These are his protégés. He has not met them, of course. But he knows that he will, when the time is right.

Noah has a knack for new ventures. But his success – why God looks upon him with favour – is that each of his ventures has a purpose larger than itself. When he is asked about another company – one of those beholden to the Harvard Business School model – he hesitates with one of his wan smiles. Then he deftly changes the subject. Maximizing return on investment for stakeholders is not his concern. His ventures are like his people. They are focussed on something larger, something beyond. They are stepping stones. Sure – he does step away from some, even though they are furthering societal goals, because he is one man and he needs his sleep. And yes – his ventures are at least partly aimed at capital formation. But already in his third or fourth venture he is flying space vehicles and talking about going to Mars. He doesn't hide his ambition.

•

At twenty-six, Sebastien was already Lieutenant Sebastien, head of Badge Control for Sécuritaire. A few years previously, Universal Technologies had spun off its security division to the contractor. Everything was being spun off. It was the Wall Street fashion of the day. Even in the core division, accountants began to outnumber engineers. If I had to start a clean-sheet engine today, said a senior team leader, I wouldn't have the people. Even so, after the purges and the carrot-on-a-stick retirements, the new engineer recruits were a good and diverse bunch. Ameerah, Gopinath, Naveed, Niloofar. Cheerful. Young. Smart as hell. And Sebastien. He never saw the job as meaningless bureaucratic paper-pushing. He saw it as a necessary control on thousands of employees and contractors as they came and went through Universal's plants and research facilities. Universal Technologies has a reputation for building and maintaining reliable engines. Part of Sebastien's responsibility was maintaining that reputation. He had the weight of generations on his shoulders. Like an increasing number of young Québecois(es), he made himself fluently bilingual. But above all he was cheerful and positive. He stood out because he had none of the grudging, policing aspect of the typical fonctionnaire. At twenty-seven, he made a leap untypical of the era. He jumped back to Universal, the spinner-off company.

•

In the second year after the election Noah's car company scaled up, and with it grew his ability to wield capital. He worried quietly at the Canadian deal for a year, negotiating with two governments and one company – Trombone Aerospace. He wound up with control of the company and operational control of the huge and half-abandoned Mirabel Airport.

One advantage of the Canadian deal was people poaching. Trombone had a lot of young engineers, and there too most of them were immigrants, from just about everywhere. Noah likes diversity. That's our strength as humanity, he says. No two of us are the same. How else are we going to add to our collective knowledge?

In that same year there were rumblings that Air Traffic Control would be privatized. Noah had been waiting for it. A failing state will always sell to the Market, he said. So will a failing business, if there's a way to spin it.

He set up a group to prepare. We want to jump on it if it happens.

It came in year three after the election, when the next campaign was in furious motion. Sell ATC was one of the desperate promises, and yet in the eye of the media it was under the radar. Noah's companies snapped up eleven of the twenty Air Route Traffic Control Centers.

When Noah bought Universal Technologies, Sebastien was one of those swept up, and he was high among those whose trajectories had been flagged. Noah was far enough along in his plans by that point that he saw a need. Immigration was over. His people would be travelling freely on company aircraft through company-controlled skies. Records would have to be kept.

●

Like many others, Naveed has a history that includes both Trombone and Universal. At Trombone he was involved with composites. The new airplane used more of them than previous large aircraft. The new airplane also had a new engine. A geared engine. Perhaps not the first, but the first of that size. As an amateur musician, Naveed became fascinated with the idea of a geared turbofan. With the potentially destructive forces that could arise between those linked, whirling masses. With harmonics, resonance, phase relationships. It was not enough to just connect those masses together and hope for the best. The future of the new engine, and of the new airplane, depended on figuring this stuff out. He left Trombone for an opportunity at Universal. Figuring out the dynamics of these whirling masses. And on the weekend he read textbooks on Orbital Mechanics.

●

With the earnestness of the very young, Ferdinand tells his student about seeing a friend die in a glider. The friend misjudged the turn to final and crossed the controls. He spun in from 500 feet. Ferdinand and his friend were seventeen.

Someone else in the ground-school class has already spun, and Ameerah's competitive side has taken control. She wants to spin for the thrill. For the bragging rights. The now-nineteen instructor has learned the hard way about survival. He has to pass on what he can.

●

Now in year three the New Net is up, albeit in test mode. One of Noah's Silicon Valley startups already has servers connected via satellite to the Nevada and Southern California campuses. These links and prototype satellite-only smart-phones use the new protocol – Spread Spectrum Sequencing. Despite the high latency bouncing up to geosynchronous orbit, the protocol is solid. Noah is almost ready to switch over.

And the Human Knowledge Archive Project has been in high gear for a couple of years, using bots to troll the Old Net, stealing whatever they can and stripping away malware, even storing the latter in offline lockups for future reference. It is not that Noah wants to steal contemporaneous proprietary secrets. He is far enough ahead without having to resort to what he considers cheating. But the projects working away at digitizing Humanity's history – those are fair game. Considering book-burning throughout history, the Dark Ages, and the destruction of the great library of Alexandria, it is prudent to make sure some of our remaining knowledge survives. Indeed, this digital history is travelling between campuses, backing itself up, and testing the SSS protocol. SSS was designed to handle the 250ms-plus latency. It was also designed to have a very wide bandwidth. The test speeds are close to the design speed. The exchange of sequencing keys, however, is still a work in progress. The engineers have been using one of the frequencies to exchange handshakes with more traditional enciphering. Not good enough, said Noah. Find a way to do all the communication on the spread spectrum.

●

Ferdinand is the issue of an improbable romance – proud Portuguese mulher falls for radical Québecois separatist. When Papa was a boy, power oozed away from English merchants and the Catholic Church and lodged in a new secular civil service. For a change of that magnitude, very little blood was shed. The time became known as *La Révolution Tranquille*. Families of fourteen or more children gave way to families of one or two. Papa's generation still half-believed, but at least outwardly they pushed hard against all the teachings of the Church. They no longer married. They came together with hyphenated names in a civil union and produced one point seven young. They urged the unilingualism of the farms into the city. English power brokers moved to Toronto and used The Market to take separatists hostage. By the time Ferdinand Portance-Magellan came along, Trombone and Universal were paying their engineers half what they could earn in English in Toronto.

Ferdinand's world ended thirty minutes west of Montreal, where the Trans-Canada Highway, hitherto the Autoroute Vingt, becomes the Four-Oh-One. Somehow Papa had extracted a promise that no Portuguese would be spoken at home. Unlike his easygoing Italian friends, Ferdinand has no mother tongue.

•

Naveed was tapped in the late autumn of year three. I'd like you to help with our space projects, said Noah. From whirling masses to celestial whirling masses. Naveed was ready. He moved to the Southern California campus, but not to work on rockets. He pitched Noah the tether idea. As a generator. As propulsion. Maybe even draining some energy from the Van Allen Belts in the process. Noah listened and said just tell me what you need. And whom.

•

Aviation in Canada is a small world. Still, Youssef can't believe his luck. Is this your first trip on the Global, he asks. Where's the eye-height target, she says. Ameerah has run the seat adjustment up to the top and is looking around. Finally, satisfied she can see out, she nods. Yes. Know who's on board? Remember Lieutenant Sebastien? He's going to meet the boss. Yeah. He's our customs, our immigration, our badge control. Who knows what he's going to be doing for the boss.

Their destination today, out of St. Hubert, is the battery plant in Nevada. The route is not quite Minimum Time Track. They have to go through Chicago Center. The boss doesn't own Indianapolis Center.

They have been dating for a while, but Youssef doesn't know where he stands. He still has to push through fear when he dials her number. But he wants to be with her. Now, on the flight deck, his pulse is already abnormal. And he still doesn't know the whole story about who is important in her life.

They run the numbers for the flight. It is an easy stretch for the Global, the latest version of Trombone's long-range executive jet. It will leap into the air off this 7000-foot runway with Flex Thrust and climb to Flight Level 440 with a shrug. In five hours and eight minutes they will be touching down in the Nevada desert. It is a layover. They don't yet know the plan for tomorrow.

●

Another rapid, bloodless change is happening. This time it is aviation's sine wave shooting upwards into positive territory at maximum slope. Pilots are in demand. Ferdinand jumps at the chance to fly a sophisticated twin-engine airplane for $500 a day plus expenses. The rub is that the captain is a crusty 80-year-old who speaks very little French.

You don't want to work for BestJet? Why not?

They don't hire Francophones.

That's total bullshit. Who told you that?

My friend at Unlisted Air.

I guess he didn't tell you that BestJet's Chief Pilot is French. He graduated from the CEGEP de Chicoutimi.

No!

OK, then. Research it yourself. I'll give you his name. Why do you think your so-called friend told you that? No? To keep you stuck in Quebec. So he could pay you half. Or less.

•

Perhaps it was relief. The letdown after a successful flight. Emerging from intense concentration into its result. Or perhaps it was the result itself.

A young pilot like Youssef takes low orbit in stride. By virtue of his velocity, he is temporarily parked above most of the atmosphere. Soon he will slow down and go down, just as he used to from the stratosphere in the Global: pull the engines to idle. Glide at 300 knots. At 12,000 feet, reduce the rate of descent and slow to 250 knots. Glide. Maneuver. Deploy high-lift devices and slow some more, down onto the back side of the power curve. Bring in some thrust to catch and stabilize the speed. Flare. Land.

It is the same, more or less, from low orbit. Only there is a lot more speed to kill. Fire retro rockets to to initiate the deceleration, and then let atmospheric drag convert your energy to heat. Just not too much heat in the wrong places. Arrive back in the stratosphere and then fly more or less as above.

But here the result of *this* flight is something new. High orbit. The sky is black. The Earth – dear Mother Earth – is no longer a comforting floor, something you are over the middle of. She is – *out there. Over there.* You can point at her. She is a nerf ball, even a soccer ball. The blue wrapped around her is tiny, fragile, and more vulnerable than you can imagine.

Looking out the port in the transfer room, Youssef breaks down and sobs.

•

Don't worry about it, man, says Art. Happens to everyone. This is serious shit. Bigger'n love, if you can imagine. Did you dream? Maybe about someone special? Yeah. Me, too.

Hey – congratulations! There hasn't been a ZET docking like yours. You're it, baby. That was a work of art. One thing for sure – it got Noah's attention. Yeah, he's here. You'll meet him. But first you gotta get your G-legs. Takes a day or two.

No, man. It's not like low orbit. It's not a quick turn, sleep at home. You're already a citizen of the Ark. Even if you don't stay.

•

The battery campus sprawls on the desert beside the new runway. In the style of the Silicon Valley startups, there is everything you need. Spanish-style enclosed gardens with trees and flowers. Clean and bright accommodation. Restaurants with menus that make you feel at home. There is even a pub with good food and draft beer. Youssef and Ameerah don't drink. They go for a walk and have supper. Tomorrow is a longer day. An hour's flight down to Southern California. Then five hours back to Mirabel Airport and the Trombone campus. There are rumours Trombone is changing gear. The market for the new airplane has collapsed. The new focus is a low-orbit shuttle.

•

There is another Global on the ramp. The captain is coming down the steps. He recognizes them. Youssef and Ameerah, who had been speaking English, switch to French in their heads. It is Ferdinand. His French is rapid, excited, run together.

Know what they're going to do with Mirabel? Spaceport. Can you believe it? Inclined orbit. Forty-five degrees.

Yeah, that's true, apparently. No more Florida. Too expensive. Boss is building another, near Cancun Airport. For equatorial orbit.

You thinking about applying? Yes – for shuttle pilot. You too, Ameerah, Here – handshake with my phone. I'll text you the link.

Mars? I don't know. Maybe not. I think he's going to build something. Or some things.

•

Gopinath is good with his hands. He is an engineer, but recently he is spending more time on the hangar floor. The handsome Universal coveralls suit his lean, six-foot-two frame. He installs the latest iteration of the geared turbofan on the fifth pylon, then goes flying with the team in the B-747 testbed to make sure they're getting the data. I am in the loop for the whole loop, he likes to say.

He has already solved a number of tricky problems with the pylon installation, and one with the engine itself. The latter has brought him some attention, but he has managed not to be seen as a threat. His bright smile and shy confidence disarm his teammates. What do you think, Gopi? they say. Maybe we can make this work, he says. Why not?

•

Howrya doin, man? asks Art. Yeah. I hear ya. It gets better. Hey – you're moving around! Well, you're a pilot. You're adapting. G-legs? Yeah. I know. More like zero-G legs. But remember, the Ark is going to have all kinds of G. Zero G. One G. Or more if we want. And everything in between. And some really weird stuff as we maneuver.

You been looking out a little? I know, man. But it's good to look. She's out there. Mom's there, and we're here. That's why they call it SpaceBirth. S'OK. I'll give you some time.

Hey man, that's beautiful. They way your tears float. They hang around you. It's like a halo.

No, no. I mean it. It's good. Like I said, this is serious shit. Months here and there's a few still don't get it. That'll mean trouble down the line. We may have to send one or two back.

I'll tell you one thing – Noah's impressed. He got it right away, too, just like you, and that was less than a month ago.

Oh, he's fine. Same old Noah. Oh, that's right, you haven't. But you will, soon. This piece of Ark is still pretty small.

•

The tether work led naturally to thinking about Earth's magnetosphere and Earth herself whose molten, moving magma makes and maintains that magnetic field. We need a magnetosphere too, thought Naveed. If we're going to live out there we're going to have to protect ourselves from high-energy particles. We also need propulsion. If we make the ship into a magnet, maybe we can do both. Direct the high-energy stuff around us, like Earth does. And pit the sun's gravity against the solar wind. Our magnetic field is the sail in the solar wind, the gravitational pull of the sun the keel.

•

Niloofar has just pulled off a lateral at Universal, into turbine design. It's still airfoils, she says, just at higher speeds and pressures.

Her name suits her. She is funny, wilful, determined. She learned her engineering in Farsi and arrived in Canada fully formed and ready to compete. She does her design work in French and English and already has a few patents to her credit. Her attractiveness and wit allow her to forge ahead without seeming pushy. Niloo, however, *is* pushy. She smiles. She makes people laugh. But she will not be deterred.

So far all of Niloo's moves have been within Universal. Now, though, she has no time to stand on ceremony. Ferdinand has brought her the rumour of the low-orbit shuttle. Within a week she is installed at Trombone, on the aerodynamics team for the project. It's just high-temperature airfoils, she says.

•

Howd ya sleep? asks Art. Good. You're right on track, man. Welcome to day three on the Ark. I'm Art. Didn't wanna get in your face yesterday. Hadda give you some space.

Youssef. That's great. Got any brothers? Yeah, I like that! But wait – I hear you speak a few languages. Whererya from? I know the Canada part. Morocco – OK. You got Arabic and French and English? Fantastic!

Shit – sounds like I'm doing a pre-interview or something. Guilty as charged.

Noah? Yeah, I've known him for awhile. We go back to before the car company. And that's not really so long ago. But a lotta shit goes down in that time in this crazy world.

Oh, he was in that startup, whatsitcalled. I was in the Castro, trying to help kids. Yeah, San Francisco. There was a resurgence of the epidemic, particularly among the black kids. It was awful.

Ha! You get right to the point! Why would they trust a whitey like me? Don't know, to tell you the truth. But they did. Called me Uncle Art. By that time Noah was calling me Doc. I'm a doctor of fuck-all.

Hey, who's interviewing who here? I love it! Why'm I up here? Because Noah knows I love people. Pretty much all people.

•

Alex has always loved trees. As a toddler, crouching in the pine needles, he looked for cones and for saplings. His favourites were the red-barked two-needle pines that thrive on the Canadian Shield. Even then he had an instinct for the life-cycle. The saplings were young, like him. They were friends. His pudgy fingers would gently hold the needles. Pick up and inspect leaves. He would try to catch minnows as he sat in the shallow water.

As a boy Alex heard the call of the loon and the whippoor-will and listened intently to the crows, frogs, and cicadas in their turn. He celebrated the first flights, and occasionally the deaths, of birds. He tried to imagine where each creature lived and what he ate. Learning to read dramatically expanded his range. Now he could wander not just his Canadian Shield, but the whole world and beyond.

At university he remained in touch with trees. The controversy about climate change troubled him. He was equally impatient with deniers and with those who called shame on Humanity for burning fossil fuels. Did not our buddies the trees breathe carbon dioxide, fixing the carbon into biomass? Did not these very buddies breathe out oxygen, that brings our own blood to life? And what did we, in turn, breathe out, if not the very carbon dioxide vilified as a greenhouse gas?

•

You don't have to quit, Ameerah, says Niloofar. They're so short of pilots, they'll keep you part time. Yes, and promote you, too. You'll be left seat on the Global. On your schedule.

No. I don't blame you. Rocketing off into space. It's not something we have to do. Besides, if you want to contribute, why not just join the team?

Are you kidding? It won't be hard. I'm the team leader. Uh huh. Since last week. I know. Naughty Niloofar. But why not? Because I'm a woman?

Commute? I'm ten minutes from the Trombone campus, five minutes or less from the Autoroute 13. The Global is mostly out of Mirabel now, right? So come live with me. There's room. We'll get along. You still seeing Youssef?

•

Do you know the history of Hawaii, Youssef? asks Art. Noah is obsessed by it. I guess that's no surprise.

Why? The islands were settled by Polynesians, probably around the twelfth century. Yeah, that's right. They were sailors and navigators and explorers. They flourished alone in Hawaii for five hundred years. They invented surfing. Did I tell you Noah surfs? When he has time. Which these days is never.

What? Yeah, they sure did. They surfed and prospered. They invented a system of governance. Know what *Aloha* means? Me neither. But it's not hello goodbye. It's how to live. Live honestly with yourself and others and Nature. And it worked for five hundred years. Not bad, huh?

What happened? First Cook, then Bingham. Cook brought guns. When he tried to muscle them, they killed him. Hiram Bingham followed, bringing Christianity, The Market, and Disease. It was worse than the plague. Their way of life was destroyed. The population went from 800,000 to 40,000. They stopped surfing.

Noah wants to be the reverse of Bingham. He wants to be a Polynesian explorer. More like Moana.

●

That's the weirdest thing, says Wesley, before he even sits down. Houston. Then Florida. In what is it, ten days? Two weeks? *And the flood was forty days upon the earth; and the waters increased, and bare up the ark, and it was lift up above the earth.* **Genesis 7:17.** And we're here to talk about the Ark!

Oh, sorry, Art. I'm Wesley. As I'm sure you know. Here to talk physics. Astrophysics. Spacetime. Black Energy. Hey, we should hook up with some of that. It's seventy percent of the Universe, for heaven's sake.

What? Well, I figured that would be the question. Among many others, of course. But really – *the* question. Would I go. If you were to ask me, of course. Hell yeah, I sure would. Hey, if you look at it in a longer time frame – say, somewhere short of ten billion years – it doesn't make any difference. Either I get my ass out there, die, and my ashes or the atoms I'm made of are scattered among the stars, or I stay here and the sun becomes a red dwarf, incinerates Earth, and blows me or what once was me to the same place. Same deal.

Huh? Yeah. I guess so. Have to go back a bit. The last man of the cloth was Grandpa. Sure. We got along. He was kinda special in my life. Felt like we were connected, somehow. Maybe that's why I have the King James Bible in my blood. No, I don't mind. Don't mind at all. The people we love – they're part of us.

Yuh know, sometimes I just get a funny feeling. Houston. Florida. Under water. Good thing Noah's got Mirabel. *But the dove found no rest for the sole of her foot, and she returned unto him into the ark, for the waters were on the face of the whole earth.* Genesis 8:9.

•

Nurul was seventeen when her team won the robot contest. It was a last-minute miracle that allowed them to briefly set foot in America to claim the prize. One week visa. Then back home. Nurul was hurt, but not fazed. She expected nothing. Nor did her team suspect Nurul's real passion – insects and miniaturization.

Beetles, ants, bees – these were Nature's teams. But MEMS – microelectromechanical systems – also fascinated her. Magnetometers and accelerometers on a chip. And spider webs, although the arachnids were solo operators.

Nurul's vision was huge jobs being quietly dispatched by teams of small beings of natural and unnatural origin. The natural were Nature's blueprint, available for inspection and imitation, as well as being indispensable in their own right. She thought of her designs as homage to Nature. Mere imitations.

Graduating at twenty with an engineering degree, she felt she was just beginning to see the world and what she could do. She continued her education, intending to learn insect genetics, but soon branching out to include bacteria – teams of even smaller beings who could make molecules and materials and could store and reproduce data in their DNA.

Nurul was like a spelunker, exploring branching arteries as they became smaller and infinitely more numerous, capillaries leading to the essence of the living.

And the not living. Or the partly living. Her designs had forgotten to make the distinction. Potentially, they could exist anywhere, do or make just about anything.

●

The key to this is the frame of reference, thought Naveed. It is as Noah imagined – up here in the Ark you think differently. Mankind has always solved the problems at hand. Here, these problems are.

So why do you need energy? To accelerate mass. But why do you want to accelerate mass? To change its velocity in a frame of reference. Why? If a mass is alone in space-time, I could not care less about accelerating it anywhere. So it must be that I want to change my velocity vector relative to another mass. That mass becomes my frame of reference.

And if we want to think about LaGrange points, what are those? They are null points relative to two masses – the Earth and the sun in our case. And what about the moon? It is a much smaller term in the equation. But it is there. It wiggles the solution relative to the Earth and sun. With the relative movement of masses, spacetime is not static. And it has periodicity.

So there are multiple frames of reference. They have different periodicity. So the space-time landscape is like a 3-D – no, a 4-D – ski hill. A 3-D ski hill changing in time. But the changes are periodic and therefore predictable. Tease out the vector for the initial push – like when you use ski poles to start downhill – and then you will need a little bit of thruster here to turn, and then as the slopes and valleys change, a little bit of thruster there to turn and follow. Maybe you could get away with using thrust only to change where the velocity vector is pointing. Maybe the velocity vector can be increased solely by steering "downhill". But you have to know exactly when to start. There will be multiple solutions, some of them years away.

Then this transfer orbit, as it were, will take us where we want to go. But by then another mass will be in the equations. Perhaps we will do another set of calculations to ski downhill – or uphill? – into the orbit we want.

•

Howdit go? asks Art. Yes, true. Noah doesn't waste time. His or yours. So?

The moon. OK. And that shuttle you flew up? He show you the plans? Yeah. That stuff is here. We can turn it into a moon lander. He asked you, of course. You interested?

Sure. We'll be parked in orbit, so your bird will effectively be a moon shuttle. What? Yes – mining. Mostly water. How long? Until we get the job done. We gotta . . .

Sorry. Old Art shouldn't blab so much. Hey, take a minute. Feel the now. But look at its beautiful side. Your floating tears. The light. If we're lucky, as we rotate, there'll be a rainbow.

It's OK, you know. This is a big deal. I know I've said it before, but this not going home, at least for a while, is huge. No? That's not it? Look at me, Youssef. Show me those brown eyes. You do want the job, right? Of course you do. But . . . yeah. I can see it now. There is someone. You're not sure . . She's not here . . . You're in love.

Why do I say that? Look at the port. Over there. See the

rainbow?

•

Nurul couldn't believe it. A woman in Canada asking for help. How could she even know about her? And her name – Niloofar – could she be Muslim? It was the oddest of coincidences.

But she was drawn by the woman's humility. Here she was, half a planet away, managing huge projects, and saying to Nurul that she couldn't do it without her help. The call plucked Nurul out of her isolation into action. It was a powerful feeling she never expected to have. The feeling of being wanted, needed. Part of something. Packing her modest possessions the night before she left home, she sobbed with joy.

•

Andrew, Eric, and Isaac are blood; Andrew an unlikely paterfamilias. His wives were legion; the wreckage of these unions was the ground upon which he walked.

But it was fertile soil. Eric, his son, and Eric's son Isaac sprung from the same roots, and as many said, became in their maturity even more eccentric than Grandpa. All three pilots. All three engineers. All three genius coders, all the way down to machine language. And all three thrive on risk and the arcane.

Andrew, in particular, could hold two worldviews in his hands and examine them like baseballs or baby birds. Or perhaps one of each. There would emerge not conflict, but synthesis, which he would proclaim without embarrassment. The reaction was not universally positive. Some whose visions he shattered would turn on him. They hate me, he would say. I don't know why.

•

Ameerah is still flying the Global, Youssef, says Art. And working with Niloofar. She's been on the team for both shuttles. But you knew that.

Now? I think they just finished up the high-orbit conversion pieces. They've hooked up with a new girl, working in bots.

That's right. The mining will mostly be bots. But Noah wants a human presence. Maybe not 24/7, but significant. The nation-states are sending probes and bots to stake claims. Noah figures that's arguable. He plans to have people stake claims, especially near the south pole of the moon. Yes. Water. Mostly water.

Well, that's what I'm leading up to. You, of course. He'd like you to be team leader.

And Ameerah? That's not so far-fetched. The way Niloofar's teams are going, they'll have to come up. Sooner or later. Of course, that's their decision.

•

Why'm I here, you ask? says Wesley. Because my chances are better here than on Mother Earth.

Youssef's tall, thin body straightens out, taking up more of the zero-G compartment. You don't think Earth will survive?

It's just Nature, red in tooth and claw, Wesley continues. It ain't pretty.

Youssef's body contracts again, the straightening having been perhaps reaction to a blow.

And the Lord said in his heart, I will not again curse the ground any more for man's sake. That's from the Bible. First Book. **Genesis 8:21**. If you believe that, then sure, Earth will survive. And I'm afraid I don't know what the Koran says on the subject.

He keeps an eye on Youssef. But on the other hand, Wesley goes on, I'm here. So that'll tell you something.

What? No. It's not to save my ass. How sure are we that this

Ark-to-be will become functional? It's more what impact I can have. And if I've learned anything it's that for a change of this magnitude there isn't a system in all of human history that can handle it. Capitalism. Democracy. Feudalism. War. Forget it. Forget 'em all.

OK, I will. I see only one way to move ahead. Vision. A fully populated vision of where we want to go. And will. A certain amount of beastly will. Not in just one person, either. Lots of people. If not hordes of people. They all share the vision and are willing to devote their lives to it. Give their lives, if necessary.

What? Well, to answer your question, yes, I think I'm closer to that here than I would be down there. Must be similar for you, no?

Not at all. I'd love to hear your story. Take your time.

Wesley's smile has grown from amusement to something more. That's a wonderful tale, Youssef. If I can rudely summarize, you don't know what you're doing, but you like what you're doing, and one thing leads to another. You're an ace pilot, and before you know it you're doing Humanity's most important flying job.

Far from it. In fact, your story is beautiful. In the Bible, God speaks to his prophets. They don't know what they're doing, either.

That's right. I'm sure it's the same with Allah, Buddha, the Great Spirit, whomever.

Yeah – it really doesn't matter. You could ask who spoke to Noah. Maybe he thinks he dreamed it up himself.

Good question. Again – doesn't matter. At least not for our outcome. But . . . it's more for *his* outcome. Personally. What it's like for him when his vision is realized. ***But the meek shall inherit the earth.* Psalm 37:11**. Yeah, Bible again.

Me? No. Physics and astrophysics. I think about things like, oh, is that a force or is that bent spacetime? How much anti-matter do we co-exist with? What is black energy? We think it's real, but like some forces it may be a result of some more fundamental frame we don't yet understand. *There are more things in heaven and earth, Horatio, than are dreamt of in your philosophy.* No, that's Shakespeare. Hamlet speaking to guess who. But tell me about some poets who wrote in Arabic.

OK says Youssef I don't know who wrote it but my grandfather often quoted it:

If you strive towards a noble goal, do not be content with less than the stars/ For the life's blood you spend (on a lesser goal) will be the same life's blood you spend reaching for the stars.

Yeah, Youssef. You got it. That's us. Our life's blood.

•

Call me Niloo. Thank you. Yes. We've contributed to both shuttles. And the conversion kits. Thanks. That's nice of you to say, Art.

Right, mining Moon. That's the new project. Couldn't even consider it without Nurul. Have you met already? And Ameerah, of course. Ameerah's also a pilot, by the way.

You know, Art, you're right. We're just beginning to get a handle on what those bots will be doing, let alone the exact conditions they'll be operating in. Well, sure. We're doing thought experiments.

On site? That's funny! Our lab on the moon!

Jesus, Art. The girls are going pale! You're serious! I can feel my face going red! I never thought . . .

Whew! I can see it in your face, Art. That's exactly what you mean. And I can see why, now. In that way it makes sense. We're right there. Our lab *is* the moon.

But we're women! Aren't we supposed to stay home and make babies?

Oh, my god. That too. Holy shit, Art. I don't know. Holy shit.

Can we talk about it? Let you know? A week? Yeah. Girls? Yeah. A week's OK.

•

Transport hated me, says Andrew. That's what defined me in those days. They'd find an excuse to deny a permit for the show. I'd go into the regs, cite chapter and verse, and prove they were full of shit. I wasn't too popular.

You've been checking up on me, Art! Yeah, that was when Dad was still flying with us. Dad, me, and Eric. That lasted a couple of years. Three Pitts S-2's. Formation aerobatics.

Why? Dad just decided. I forget. Hell, he was eighty-four. Pulling G's at sixty-four is bad enough. I should know. Dad flew the CF-104 when he was young. Back in the day. You had to know what you were doing to survive that machine.

Right. Now *I'm* Gramps. Continuing the tradition. Me, Eric, and Isaac. Where? Well, we negotiated a box near Tracy, California. We practice in that airspace. It's not far from Livermore, where we have a hangar. Sure – an aerobatics box is good, but we'd much rather beat up an airport. That's why we're still doing shows.

Yeah. That's funny. Our offices are next to each other at the end of a wing. Every day someone says, hey, all of you down here have the same name. What kind of coincidence is that? Really? You're kidding me!

Oh, working for The Phone Company is great. It's like a grad seminar. Pay is great, too. Except I don't know what to do with it. Pay my exorbitant rent. Take care of the airplanes.

Yeah. Not as much as I'd like. Ten years ago my rent was zero. Lived in the hangar. Code all day, then just before sunset, when the air is like silk, pull out the Pitts and beat up the airport for an hour. Now that was living!

Andrew has become even more caffeinated than usual listening to the pitch. I'm going to introduce you to another pilot, says Art. He goes to the door.

I know this guy! Youssef! Good to see you! Yeah, Art. We did some instructor stuff together. Then went and flew the Pitts. Like a duck to water. This guy is good stick!

•

All life depends on dying, says Alex. I'm not sure I mean anything by that. It just is. I don't see the proposition as arguable.

Sure. OK, Art. Let's see . . . take a basic food. Like bread. Or beer! Starts with a grain. Seeds. The reproductive system of another being. So we humans harvest, then plant some, use some. But that doesn't take away from the fact that these seeds are life. Little packets of DNA with survival stuff built in.

So maybe we grind the seeds into flour. Probably we neuter them right away by removing the germ. That's so the flour won't grow rancid. Gives it a shelf life, so the remaining survival package can be distributed and become our food instead of the seed's food. Then we have to add life back in if we want to make bread. We use a bread starter. How do we make that? We re-hydrate the flour and leave it exposed to the air for a few days. Tiny things – yeast spores, bacteria – arrive and start feeding on it. They multiply until they run out of food. Then they sleep.

What? Oh, if we want to make healthier, more complex bread we add more life. Maybe freshly ground flour that still has the germ. Or we soak grains for a couple of days until they sprout, and then add them to the dough. Then we add the starter – all those little sleeping creatures. With the right temperature, food, and a bit of moisture, they wake up and start doing their work – converting the starch to sugar, which they eat, burping out carbon dioxide and alcohol. Also, awake and feasting, they reproduce. What we observe is the bread dough rising, as little bubbles of carbon dioxide increase the volume of the dough several times over.

What if we leave it there? No. The dough won't last long. The little guys keep going until they run out of food, then they sleep. Soon the carbon dioxide leaks out and the dough slowly collapses.

But if we catch it at the right point, loaf it, let it rise some more, and put it in the oven, it's like a miracle. Heating up, the little guys go into a feeding frenzy. The dough rises quickly, giving the bread what bakers call oven bounce.

What's my point? Well, at a temperature somewhat below what it takes to bake the bread, the little guys die. They have given their lives so we can have our delicious staff of life.

●

You want all three of us? Andrew wrinkles his nose. That's how we joined The Phone Company!

Oh. Of course. You knew that. But that was then. I'm pretty old, you know. I go up, I'll croak up there.

Oh. Right. Mind if I have one of those Red Bulls? Yeah. Like I said, working for The Phone Company is great. But, yeah. Now we can kill ourselves taking pictures and texting and talking while we drive. Point is, the stuff inside that allows all that is really cool, and *could* be used for something useful . . .

Sure, but . . . what? Moon shuttle flight control? OK, Art. You got me! And Youssef – you're team leader? Oh. Just for flying? So who's doing the flight control software? You're gonna need a good team for that!

Oh. Huh. Got another one of those Red Bulls?

•

You have to admit we've both been busy, Youssef, says Ameerah. What? No. With Niloo's projects, I've been barely able to stay competent on the Global. Not that they seem to mind. No. There's nobody. I get kids with 300 hours. Oh, they're nice kids. But I spend the whole trip teaching, one way or the other. Time goes fast. Then I'm exhausted.

Oh, yes, don't get me wrong. I really like doing both. Niloo's tough, but we work together well. Maybe because then I go fly and *I'm* the boss. So I didn't apply. Wouldn't have had the time to go on course.

Sure. I know. Ferdinand did. He's still on the low-orbit shuttle, right?

Yeah. We've got to decide. Oh, Nurul would go anywhere with Niloo. Me? I love Niloo, but to be defined only as her right hand? I'd miss the flying.

•

Know why it feels good, Wesley? To be surrounded by green plants? To feel the energy of the sun on your skin?

Alex gestures, as if at a surrounding forest with sun slanting through clerestory windows. It feels good because you are a part of life, a life that is whole because of the trees and plants. You are not breathing oxygen from a storage tank. Trees use their leaves to grab energy from the sun and fix carbon from the air. Together with water from their roots, they make fuel. They use some, and give the rest to you. You are making water for the trees. It's circular.

Is there more to the story? You bet there is. There's soil. Worms. Fungi. Bacteria. Birds. Bees. How much of that do you really need? Yes, exactly. Why do you think I'm up here?

•

I manage my own risk, said Eric. Sure. I do some things Dad won't do. I'm younger. Won't last forever. Isaac? Ask him. I'm his parent, not his . . .

Eric stops the thought as if it never happened. He looks up. Wrinkles his mouth in a genetic imitation of Andrew. OK, the project. Can we do it? Of course we can. That's why The Phone Company keeps us together. We speak the same structures. Don't even speak that much. Just make. Put it together. It works.

Yah, maybe. Dad taught me. We taught Isaac. There's no separation. Not in how we code. Or how we fly. Except . . . yah, I might do something Dad won't. Anymore. If I'm feeling good.

•

I don't know for sure, Youssef. Ameerah's soft, flute-like voice plays his strings, pulls him closer, mucks up his breathing. We tell her how we feel, of course. But Niloo decides.

No. I really don't think of myself that way. In the airplane I'm team leader. With Niloo she's team leader.

How long? Oh, I've felt that way for years. Sure I'm a person. But being, as you say, an individual? I'm not sure what that means, anymore.

No! I'm not lost! Not at all. I know exactly who I am. I am part of this team and of that team. I give exactly what I can. No more, no less. When I'm tired I sleep.

I don't know. I like you a lot, Youssef. If we decide to come of course I'll see you. I'd like that.

But it will be different up there. Of course there will be kids. And I hope we will both be parents. If we go, if we're up there, all that will be different. How, I don't know.

•

But I'm just a kid! Isaac looks around, from Youssef to Art, and back to Youssef. Why do I get to decide anything?

Art has asked the question, but Isaac is still looking at Youssef. He tears his eyes away. Oh, my Mom left. I was little. Don't know why.

What? Oh, years. I hardly knew her. She's moved on. Not interested in me, I guess. His eyes move back to Youssef. He finds Youssef's big brown eyes looking directly into his. He blurts so you're the team leader for the moon flying. Youssef nods. The eye contact hasn't broken. Isaac coughs. Art is asking another question. Yes, Art. I guess so. But probably not as wild as Eric. More like Gramps.

Oh! You're talking about going up there! No. No fear at all.

Good, says Art. I see Youssef has your eye. Why don't you give him your ear as well? Youssef? What do you think?

Yes, says Youssef. His gaze is more operational, but still there. We're going to train in place, he says. New pilots will skip the low-orbit stage. No simulator, either. Straight to live. And you guys are perfect. No need to train you on the software. You're going to write it.

•

Spin is a special case, thought Naveed. It is like a subset of attitude, but it is more than that. It has an axis. It has handedness. It is a property of the smallest particles we know. It is a fundamental property defining matter, and thus any mass, anywhere, that we can think of. And spinning masses on a larger scale – our scale – are described with gyro dynamics.

Oh – I have to remember to tell Noah. His one-kilometre Ark is all right, but a bit larger would be better, from a human point of view. There are studies saying two revolutions per minute is the maximum comfortable spin for astronauts. Astronauts! Well, here I am and just looking out the port I would say that

1RPM would be a lot more comfortable. So that's an Ark diameter of 1786 metres for 1 G. Or he could live with just over half a G with his 1 kilometre-diameter Ark. So I will ask Art to pass that on. Or see Noah if he wants.

You know, down at the bottom of Earth's gravity well, we cannot see the forest for the trees, or something analogous. Here we can think. We can see how the magnetic dipole moment of a particle has an Ark-scale counterpart, for example. Spinning or orbiting particles making a magnetic field. That is, accelerating charges making a force. If it is a force. I will discuss that with Wesley. I am not saying that our big world operates as particles do according to quantum electrodynamics. Still, there are some analogous behaviours. I will ask Wesley about that. And about entanglement.

●

Oh, I'm sorry, Andrew, said Niloofar. I'm so sorry. Of course you have to go. You have to bury your Dad. He taught you to fly, didn't he? Yes. You told me the story. And I hope you will tell me again. When we get back there. On the flight, maybe. But we have to get moving.

I have heard people say that things come in threes. But here it is sixes. Six people decide they are going. Six people have loved ones who are not going. Or who have died, Andrew. Six people have to patch something together, emotionally, before they can leave their loved ones. Or patch something together in themselves. And we have little time.

I was speaking to Naveed this morning on the spread spectrum phone. Great bandwidth. It was like when I was working with him at Universal. Like I was in the same room. For me, personally at least, talking to Naveed was what pushed the decision over the wall. I trust Naveed. If he has figured it out I know it's right. He explained how he and a man named Wesley are preparing the Ark for trans-lunar injection. It is to be a low energy ballistic lunar transfer. BLT, they call it.

Yes – I thought one of you guys would like that. But it takes months, not days. And there is a launch window. Or injection burn window. Whatever. It starts next week. That's why we have to get our collective butt in gear.

So – the Global is here in Nevada. Ameerah flew it down. She'll fly us back to Mirabel. Oh, I forgot to mention. There are seven of us, actually, because Ferdinand had already decided to come, and he's here too but he's flying the launch to low orbit. Then Youssef is flying the high-orbit shuttle. Yes. A new machine. When we get to the Ark that will be five shuttles up there for conversion.

So, Ameerah. I know you don't have a first officer, but you have five boy-pilots to choose from for the right seat. Two of them were even current on the Global not so long ago. And I have confidence in all of them. What, Andrew? Isaac's not going to the funeral? He and great-grandpa? OK, never mind. Another story for a quiet moment. And Isaac is going to be on the plane, because we launch from Mirabel.

That's right. The Ark started at 45° north inclination and has been adjusting further north. Better for our BLT injection for lunar polar orbit.

So here's the deal. We get on the plane. Ameerah and one of you boys fly us to Mirabel. We use my place as a base. Andrew, you and Eric take my car and go to Ontario for the funeral. With Ameerah's car and whatever, the rest of us can do what we have to do. Then back to my place Thursday PM. For our bonding party. Launch is Friday.

•

We can no more separate works from faith than heat and light from fire. Bible? Wesley looks up at Alex. Well, sort of. It's Luther. He translated the New Testament into Early New High

German in 1523. From Greek. Old Testament in 1534, from Hebrew. Quite a guy.

Oh, because Grampy so loved the King James. And he said Luther was the inspiration. *Der Herr ist mein Hirte.* Tyndale knew Luther's translation. He loved Luther's language. It was pithy and beautiful, and the townspeople could understand it. Now the Church couldn't tell people what the Bible said. They could read it for themselves. What? Oh. *The Lord is my shepherd.*

Tyndale did it for the English. So the Church couldn't tell them what to think. Didn't finish, because he was kidnapped and executed for his trouble. But much of his translation, an English echo of Luther's, made its way into the King James.

That's right, Alex. The we can no more separate is not Bible. It's Luther himself.

I was thinking about *light and heat from fire*, says Alex. Nurul and I have been talking about it. You know how mankind has always burned wood for fuel? Wood is mostly cellulose, a large, complex hydrocarbon. As it heats up the molecule thrashes about, comes apart, uses some oxygen from the air, and makes a bunch of fuel molecules – butane, propane, ethane, and like that. Gasoline, essentially. Then they burn, of course.

We need fuel. And chemicals, too. Nurul has some ideas about how to get all of that from plant material at room temperature, or nearly so. It's like the way we use the little guys – yeast, enzymes, bacteria – to make bread and beer and booze. From starch and sugar.

So what we're thinking about is fire without light and heat. Save the energy for later, in a rocket nozzle or something. Of course it is not really fire. It is more like the process that takes vegetative material and converts it to petroleum. Only faster.

●

Everybody! Niloofar stops the conversations. I said we were six. Then seven with Ferdinand. And of course Art has to come with us. Eight. But now it is nine. This is Gopinath.

You can call me Gopi. He smiles.

Gopi is coming up with us. He will help us with the conversions. Correction – he will lead us. Right, Gopi?

I very much like putting things together. Especially when they will work!

We engineers think we know what we're doing, because we design things, Niloofar says. But someone has to make them. Put them together. Make them work. Gopi is very good at that. And he is also an engineer, by the way.

So welcome Gopi and get to know him. Get to know each other. Because once we get up there we're going to be busy putting those moon shuttles together. That's what we will be working on during the month or two we're in BLT.

Isn't that risky, asks Eric. All nine of us on the same booster? Two whole teams. And Art. What if our booster fails?

Niloofar looks at Eric, the assessor of risk. We'll miss this BLT window, she says. Another group will make the next window or the window after that. Art? Is that right?

Yes, he says.

•

A religion must provide a path to redemption. Wesley looks up at Alex. I don't know why I said that.

They have been getting to know each other. The conversation has been wandering, a mutual stream of consciousness. They have been enjoying it.

Is that you? asks Alex. Wesley quoting Wesley?

Wesley laughs. I guess it came out of my mouth.

It reminds me of Yeats, says Alex. He said something about responsibilities having their origin in dreams. So it is our imagination that distinguishes us in Nature. It doesn't make us better than trees, God knows.

OK, this one is not me, says Wesley. It's **Genesis 1:26:**

And God said, Let us make man in our image, after our likeness: and let them have dominion over the fish of the sea, and over the fowl of the air, and over the cattle, and over all the earth, and over every creeping thing that creepeth upon the earth.

So we're the boss.

It came into my head because I think it's not working anymore.

Yeah. I don't believe we're the boss. Not for a minute.

But a moment ago you were speaking of Fox News as a sermon, says Wesley. That makes sense. People gather every evening. It's not 11 AM on Sunday, but it's a sermon. The interpretation of the Word.

And it's a sermon that doesn't work.

You are right, Alex, God forgive us. Religion is hard. Any comfort comes through trial and pain, not served up to us in a dish. This cable stuff is not religion. It is an idol, a false god.

So why doesn't it work?

Camel through the eye of a needle.

Is that another Wesley?

Wesley laughs. No. But let me put it another way. You ask why cable sermons don't work. They are, I think, money trying to redeem itself and its owners.

That's not gonna work.

No.

They sit for awhile. Life seeps back into the room. The subject changes, as if by magic.

Wesley listens as Alex tells how the Negative Carbon Emission people are way ahead of NASA in scrubbing carbon dioxide from the air. But they are still not talking about balance, says Alex. They want to remove CO2 and store it underground. As if there will always and necessarily be imbalance. How we have to plant fields to make fuel and then scrub the combustion. Then they do the math and see how much of Earth's surface that would take.

They've got a scaling problem, says Wesley. And if you believed it would work, you wouldn't be up here. Am I right?

Alex nods, a small smile forming as he thinks about what to say next. And all this time we haven't talked biology or physics, he says.

Oh yeah, physics, says Wesley. I think about that too, every once in a while.

•

We'll back up all the way to electrical. Hell, to mechanical if we have to. Andrew pauses. Niloo has struck a pose. It takes his breath away. He clears his throat and presses on.

Noah was right to put pilots on the shuttles. Get a human butt in the seat, was what he said.

Having made his case, Andrew watches and listens as Niloofar presses hers. She wants robot authority and secure comm links as backup. We have to be able to help you, she says.

Andrew looks her in the eye. He has to work at it. Remember the Columbia disaster? You're young, but you're not too young to remember.

Niloo's pose softens slightly. I remember. It came apart on re-entry. It was awful. I don't remember why.

Tiles came off during launch. They had some clues. The crew wanted to do an EVA and check. Tell me, Niloo – what do pilots do before every flight? A walk-around. The pilot in command is the final airworthiness authority. If a fuel truck has hit a wingtip he scrubs the flight.

But they probably couldn't fix it, says Niloo.

That's what she said. Flight Control Houston. She was a girl, by the way.

You're going to get all man on me now.

No, just stating facts. They wouldn't let them do a fucking walkaround! They wouldn't allow the people whose butts were in the seats to use their incredible human resourcefulness to try to save their own asses! They wouldn't let them choose how to die!

Huh.

Two of the crew were girls, by the way.

●

With five shuttles in dock, the Ark is an odd collection of shapes. We can't help it, thinks Ameerah. We think sleek, like the Global. But there is no air in this ship's mission. It is all about the G vector. The docks and shuttle are designed for four G's in the axial direction, just to be safe. Naveed says they are planning a one-G burn. So for a while we will have a floor, and the shuttle docks will be the penthouse. I am not looking forward to climbing those ladders on the wall. I am going to stay put, as near as possible to the assembly bay. Gopi is not planning to assemble until until we are ballistic. But we are floating around the modules we designed, trying to get to know them in the flesh, in an operational way. The coder boys are seeing it all for the first time. They have a lot to think about. Soon we will be crawling around these modules, not floating. But not for long.

Funny about SpaceBirth. Gopi never stopped smiling. Isaac was in tears. Nurul's eyes were like oysters. Niloo looked harder, like a beautiful porcelain statue. I probably will never eat an oyster again. But you never know. For now we have to put up with this package food. It is like we are on a camping trip, Niloo says.

Alex and Nurul are already growing stuff in their lab. But to do it on Ark scale and have us all sustain each other, the structure will have to be there. That will take many, many shuttle flights. Noah and Niloo are thinking mine, manufacture, and assemble on the lunar surface. Then lift only finished modules, water, and fuel. We'll see.

Funny about SpaceBirth. I kind of like zero G. I'm going to spend more time in low G. Here, or on the moon. Later, I'll try to work and live near the axis.

I miss good food the most. I will talk to Niloo. We will need chefs and bakers. And to Art. We should eat together and socialize. Maybe they will talk to the boss.

●

We have to find the numbers for balance, says Alex.

Or find how to meet the numbers we have, says Nurul.

Alex looks up. It is as if he is seeing Nurul for the first time.

Yes, of course, Nurul.

They sit, looking into each others' eyes. Who knows what passes in a gaze?

●

It was good, Noah saw. Not perfect, but that was for another life, another time. Now was good enough for survival. But he would have to keep moving. From one step to the next never entirely sure what the next step was going to be. Or even if this step would work. The first time. Although some *have* worked the first time. Not many. But that hasn't stopped us.

Next is the moon. Mines, smelters, factories. On a small scale, of course. Then lifting structural parts, materials, soil, water. All out of Moon's gravity well, not Earth's. From Earth we lift life. Seeds. Fungi. Bacteria. Insects. Birds. And people, bless them. We will let life be fruitful and multiply. Until they are at home in their new garden. Made from mass lifted only from Moon.

•

Moon

Part II

II

Moon

Who believes not only in our globe with its sun and moon,
but in other globes with their suns and moons,
Who, constructing the house of himself or herself, not for a day but for all
time,
sees races, eras, dates, generations,
The past, the future, dwelling there, like space, inseparable together.

~ Walt Whitman ~

OK, decel burn, says Andrew. Zero-point-eight G. Feels about right. Isaac?

Yah. Zero-point-eight-oh-one. Right on. Passing one thousand metres.

Good to have a radio altimeter again. Feel like we can actually land on something. Landing lights on.

Roger. Landing lights on, says Isaac. Vertical on sked. Azimuth OK?

Got it manual. Gonna find a flat spot in the crater. Gimme a running on the vertical.

200 metres at 20 per second
150 metres at 16
100 at 11
50 at 6
10 at 1. There ya go.
5 at 0.

I'm scooting left a bit. Avoid that rock.

3 at point 5

2 at point 5

1 at point 4. Yer good. Down. She stable?

Like a rock.

Att's within 5.

Huh. OK. Shutdown.

Andrew looks around. Hey. Easier than a Pitts at Livermore. And I got a night landing in this thing. Now we get to work.

•

I figure we'll put the shelter igloo over there, says Andrew. I think we can keep the landing spot, too. Whaddaya think?

Yah. Didn't stir up too much dust. We could see all the way in. The legs found good placement.

Hey, *we* found good placement. The legs are dumb.

Not *that* dumb, Gramps. With a load I can find C of G and set up ascent angle.

Yeah, yeah. And now the pilots turn into ramp guys.

•

It's Niloo. She wants you. Isaac passes the sat phone. Except the satellite is the Ark, visible from their lander about one-third of the time.

Yeah, we're fine, says Andrew. We're lounging in the igloo with our suits off. Taking a break.

•

So, Art. You were saying you have misgivings? About the choosing?

Not exactly. More like should I have misgivings. Or should Noah.

Wesley nods. God told Noah what to do. What to make and who to take. Genesis 6, et cetera.

So the prophets, you're saying, are conduits?

Yes! That's a good way to put it. It's not Noah or Isaiah forcing apocalypse upon the world. It's the Word of God.

So, Doc, as he calls me, shouldn't worry too much about Noah.

Yeah, well. He's got a lot on his shoulders. And I don't know how he thinks about it. You'd be a better judge of that.

Using the handholds, Art propels himself through a full circle, keeping his Leonardo man in a single plane. He is getting quite good at it. Almost graceful. Your Genesis 6 was a long time ago. Very soon after Adam and Eve.

So?

So the body of knowledge had barely begun to advance.

And already there was trouble.

Now you're the one who would know, Wesley.

Yeah. Genesis 3 – Adam and Eve in the Garden. Genesis 4 – they reproduce. Genesis 5 – the generations of Adam. And then – sure, it's a lotta years, but not far in the story. *My spirit shall not always strive with man, for that he is also flesh.* Genesis 6.3.

That he is also flesh. Meaning, in modern terms, this is gonna go for shit.

'Fraid so, Art. Genesis 6.4 – giants fathering children, men of renown. Then Genesis 6.5 – *And God saw that the wickedness of man was great in the earth, and that every imagination of the thoughts of his heart was only evil continually.*

Jesus.

Yeah.

So God makes man. Man fucks up. God starts over.

Yeah.

Except now there's this huge body of knowledge. That's our Noah's concern. He can't bear the thought of it disappearing. I've told you about the Hawaiians?

Yeah.

They're good for five hundred years. Then they stop surfing and die back like plants in a plague.

Noah – our Noah – wants to save something from the wreckage. That about it?

Uh huh.

It is Wesley's turn to think upside down. He stops his turn 180° out of phase with Art. It is enough to let his mind work without severing the connection. We tend to think of the Greeks – Socrates, Plato, Aristotle. But there's also the Tang Dynasty, Egypt, the Romans, India. And the flame of balance guarded by indigenous people all over the world. He whips himself around into phase with Art. But there's more. Your misgivings, if that's what they are. You are looking for a new morality. Or trying to find an old one. All this has to make sense in human terms.

Uh huh. And it's not just me, Wesley. We all need it. Or we're going to hurt. Hurt so much we can't function properly. We have to be human together. Could you help?

●

A dumbbell would be OK to start with, thought Naveed. Art says Noah is fine with the 893-metre radius, but it will be a long time before we get enough matter up here to build a saucer that big. So we will build two spokes with elevators built in. The counterweight will perhaps be the elevator in the opposite spoke. Somehow or other. All this will serve as proof of concept. I am thinking, design for spokes every thirty degrees, and start with one outer ring. So the ring segments, the dumbbell weights as it were, will be just under 500 metres long. Let us say 100 metres wide and high. There, at one G, will be our first agriculture experiments. I will call them parks, because they will be that to us. As much for us as for the trees and crops that will allow all of us to survive. Alex and Nurul are talking about how they will hasten the turning of Moon rock into soil.

So that will be our goal for this Moon trip. Two spokes. Two 500-metre parks. The base on the Moon's south pole. How much water, we don't know. We will hope it is enough for this phase at least.

And energy. Some we could get when we are in movement relative to Earth's magnetic field. We would store that in Noah's batteries. But most will likely come from direct solar radiation. How much will we need for photosynthesis in the parks? And we will have to be mindful of the tradeoff when we move. For example, if we want to continue by mining from comets or the asteroid belt to minimize the delta-V required, that must be balanced against the much smaller energy density available. In the asteroid belt the solar radiation flux is only 14% of that in the vicinity of Earth's orbit around the sun.

●

Sink rate!

In a second, concern ramps up into terror.

Youssef! SINK RATE!

Isaac scans the panel. Main engine failure? Fire the emergency solids?

Huh, I . . . Youssef begins.

Isaac finds the much-too-subtle **auto-decel** light/switch.

Shit! He punches the switch.

Are you manual in azimuth as well? Fuck, are you even in there?

No. Yah, I . . .

> 10 at 2
>
> 6 at 1 point 5
>
> 3 at 1
>
> 2 at point 6

Shit! Attitude!

Uh . . . not responding . . .

At least one leg is down! Shutdown! Youssef! Shutdown now! She's going over!

In moon-G slow-mo, the shuttle diverges from the vertical. There is a barely detectible acceleration in the motion before it crunches to rest on its back. The landing lights stare stupidly across the crater floor.

Shit! The door! The port! It's . . .

In truth, the vehicle has chosen, and the options for its pilots reduced in number.

Goddammit! We're here for the duration. Youssef! Shutdown checklist! We don't want this to get any worse!

Like a trained dog, Youssef calls the checklist. Isaac is making damn sure they don't fuck it up. Landing lights OFF! We don't need the power drain!

Isaac takes a minute to look around the cockpit.

OK, now. ECS – scrubber fan. Heat source differential temp and pressure. O_2 pressure and flow. What's next? Get help. Right, Youssef? C'mon, gimme a hand here. Fuck. We've missed the end of the window. The Ark is behind us now for six hours. Shit.

They sit. Youssef has been struck dumb.

Didn't you ever . . . ? says Isaac. Didn't you ever fly a fucking two-pilot operation? He looks over. It is like back in that interview with Art. He can't look away. He stops trying. Instead he works on keeping his head in the operational moment.

We're going to be alright, you know? It's just going to take awhile.

How could I . . . Youssef begins. How could I have thought that I knew what I was doing?

You *do* know that in a two-pilot crew you *always* verbalize what you are doing. Everything.

The first tear is sliding sideways down Youssef's cheek.

And you never, and I mean fucking *never*, touch a goddamn control or a piece-of-shit switch or . . .

I know.

. . . any fucking thing without telling the other guy. I mean you just don't, asshole.

I know. The tears are streaming, those from the left eye running over his nose and dripping onto the right cheek. Youssef's arms act alone, extending across the cockpit. It is as if remaining unforgiven is not a possibility in this life.

We're going to be alright, you know.

Hold me, Isaac. Please hold me.

●

Andrew!

What?

I got some data just before they went into shadow. I don't like it.

But you're not going to say I told you so.

Niloofar wrinkles her nose. No. Now get dressed. We have work to do.

By now Andrew is awake enough to feel a stab of fear. What's wrong? What did you get?

Descent profile. Doesn't look normal. The decel wound up acceptable, but then the attitude at touchdown – I don't like it.

What do you mean?

I think they might have tipped over. On their side, or something.

●

It's funny how fast things change, thought Ameerah. I knew I had been tapped to fly, but I thought of it an an honorary future perk, an add-on to my work with Niloo, just like before. I guess we just like things to stay the same.

And then something happens. Isaac says they're fine, but hints that Youssef is taking it badly. So Niloo and Andrew are managing the rescue mission. Or, rather, Niloo is. Andrew is commander. Wouldn't Niloo hesitate to send off someone she is suddenly close to? No, that's me. I'm the one who would feel that way. And Niloo is sending me, too. I can't deny that hurts a little.

But maybe she's right. After our briefing just now I feel Andrew is a good commander, not a swashbuckler. And we're taking Gopi, with a bag of tricks he is putting together. Also, Niloo says the samples from the first landing show promise. She wants this to be a rescue mission first, followed by work as usual, including bringing back Youssef's ship, if possible. Unclear who would fly it, if we get to that point.

Well, girl, you better get going. You've got one hour to go over your procedures. Even though Andrew briefed it will be **auto** all the way, you never know. Andrew also said it's as dark as the inside of a wolf down there. You'd better know your stuff.

●

First we have to roll her over ninety degrees, thought Gopinath. Isaac says the port is down in the moon dust. So we will need a fulcrum, an anchor point, and a purchase. Since the mass of the vehicle now is just under four metric tonnes, the tension on my cable will start at – let's see – with the lever I will fix to the third and seventh spars and lifting the centre of mass over the fulcrum with an arm of 2.1 metres, just over one tonne to start. Of course that is on Earth. On Moon that would be about one over six, or 167 kilos to break away. The initially vertical lever will incline toward me, diminishing the lever arm. And that will be balanced by the lever arm of the centre of mass from the fulcrum, which is also becoming smaller as the centre of mass lifts over the fulcrum. So it will be controllable unto that point. Then of course it will just fall onto its new side, so I will be needing a cushion. How about one of the small igloos? I will calculate exactly how much pressure to put it it to make a soft fall with no bouncing.

We will get Youssef and Isaac out. Then the problem is how to lift the vehicle back onto its legs. I think we will simply retract them, then repeat the roll maneuver in the other dimension. But I might have to retract the two that are free before the first roll. We will see. Then with the machine vertical I think we can simply extend the legs again. I will look at the hydraulics and calculate the load.

●

Are you a pilot?

Art laughs. Me? No. I have no credentials whatsoever.

Andrew smiles. What about Noah?

Not as far as I know. No. Used to surf, but I've never heard him talk about flying.

Niloo tosses her head. Where's this going, Andrew?

Rehab.

Rehab? You mean for Youssef?

Yeah.

The exchanges silence the room for a few breaths. Wesley and Naveed are both nodding, but the silence persists.

Well? Says Niloo.

OK, says Art. As you know, we are here because Youssef is taking it badly. Part of our response must be engaging him individually, of course. But for us here the task is to shuffle the seats, at least temporarily, because our work has to go on. Andrew, you said *rehab*. I'd like to hear more.

There is work, alright, says Niloo. And Youssef's shuttle is still down there. *I'd* like to hear why the four pilots came back in one vehicle.

Sure, says Andrew. Experience.

You're all experienced pilots . . .

Not being a pilot, I'd like to hear more. Art looks at Andrew. Raises his eyebrows as if conducting an upbeat.

Yeah, OK. First of all, you don't ask a pilot who has just survived a prang to fly home. It's not get back on the horse. At least not right away. Second, I left their machine there because it's a test flight, and on a test flight you don't risk passengers' lives. Or the vehicle, if you can help it.

Sure, OK, says Art. And you said experience and rehab. Bottom line, we need Youssef and Isaac.

I'm old, says Andrew. I've had a lot of experience, both teaching, and checking myself out on new types. That's something that's not taught, by the way.

I was amazed, says Naveed. You just jumped in the shuttle and landed on the moon. Then came back and docked in orbit.

I didn't just jump in, says Andrew. I crawled over every inch of that ship. I memorized all the systems. I rehearsed in my head every fuck-up I could think of. And I was shit-scared in a respectful sort of way. Shackleton Crater is a black hole. It's like a low approach in fog.

Youssef should have had more training, says Niloofar.

Yes.

Why? Her question hovers, weightless.

Because he's young and he's team leader and I went and did it. I should have thought of that.

If there have been currents of fault or blame in the the room, they are now still. There is a hurt realization of how lucky they are. The hurt varies from person to person, but all realize that the loss these two young pilots would have been . . .

His great granddad might not have liked the way he's wired.

Andrew's observation floats in this change of current and eddies around the room. Isaac and Youssef, although not physically present, are making waves of emotion and affecting the breathing of those who are.

Finally, Art breaks the silence. So how do we rescue Youssef?

He's already rescued, says Niloofar.

OK, then, let's call it rehab. Andrew?

Sure. I can't do it all, but I can do the training part. Isaac and I can make a roster for the next flights. We'll get Eric going. Finish up Isaac and Ameerah. The five of us will have seminars every day until we're all on the same page. New missions will go through us so we can train.

Sounds good, says Art. Niloo?

Yes. I get the training thing.

But it doesn't fix the human thing. Wesley looks around. I get the training thing, too, but the human being has had a blow. He feels worthless.

Experience, says Andrew again.

Art leans forward. Explain.

There is a pilot question: do you have ten thousand hours, or one hour ten thousand times? In other words, experience is important, but it's not measured in hours. It's measured by how much learning happened.

Hence the seminars.

Yes, hence the seminars. We are just five, right now, and we've done three flights. OK, two and a half. So every bit of our experience counts. We have to share it. We will go over every landing and every docking, second by second. The data, the video, and the first-hand experience will all meld together and become part of our dreams. We won't remember if we were really there or it was someone else.

Yes, says Art. He looks at Andrew. I don't know how to bring this up, so I'll just do it. We have a love triangle. In the pilots.

I know. And d'ya know what? It's good. First, no committee like us is going to have the slightest influence. So we'll welcome it. All of it.

Andrew flashes his bright smile around the room, lingering for an extra nanosecond on Niloofar. Love is good. Right? So what if it goes for shit? Or it isn't returned. Or it fades. Or we love another. Down on Earth we cry and moan. Or call for justice. Or start a war. If we do that up here we'll all die. So let's just love whenever we can and damn the torpedoes.

●

Andrew's seminars are an eye-opener, thought Ameerah. When I wake up in the morning I am still in a dream of a moon landing, or a docking – usually one where I was not part of the crew. On a good day I am not re-living Youssef and Isaac's landing.

But what is it – three days out of the last ten? Something like that. I awaken in the middle of their approach.

How close they came! I still shudder, going through those fifteen seconds after Isaac calls *Sink Rate!* He prioritizes amazingly quickly, getting the vertical back on **auto** so they don't crash. No time to argue about taking over control, though. He calls the vertical like he did for Andrew. But Youssef is still not there. In over his head, poor kid. Andrew is right. It is dark down there. And it *is* like a low approach in fog. You have to be on instruments and visual at the same time. We don't yet have a Heads Up Display working for landing. Dumb in retrospect. But Andrew says that's the way we've learned everything in aviation. So until the HUD development is finished, we're going to use our variation of the PMA, the Pilot Monitored Approach. In our version one pilot flies down to ten metres and remains responsible for attitude. The other pilot can slow or stop the descent and displace in azimuth if the real world in the lights doesn't look like the plan.

In truth the autoland the three of them wrote is pretty darn good. I don't wake up in a sweat when I dream Landing 3 with Andrew and me, although I can still feel how behind the vehicle I felt.

We have learned so much in the ten days of seminars. So much about each other, too. We are a tighter group now. There are no secrets.

Eric is a cool one. But sandwiched between his father and his son, the cool one becomes part of them, a perfectly functioning piece of the puzzle. That was on display as the three of them in three days wrote the software to run the lander in simulator mode, complete with the trajectories and data from all three landings and both dockings. For the last five days our seminars have been sims. We have all been in both seats and have watched other teams work.

Andrew was right to stop all operations. But tomorrow we're back live. We are all going. Isaac is commander for the descent, and Youssef for the ascent and docking. I'm second-in-command for both. Andrew and Eric will fly the other ship back.

There are no secrets among us. Three of us are related, and three of us are – well, involved. The last time I woke up in Landing 2 it was after the shutdown check and after Isaac had finished shouting at Youssef. The recorders were still running. It was a happy ending.

●

How did I get involved with a nuclear reactor? asked Naveed. I have never been even remotely interested in nuclear devices. No – that's not true. I have held weapons in abhorrence, and been afraid of radiation. Now I think of Madame Curie and how she followed her mind not knowing that high-energy neutrons were re-arranging her DNA. But here I am in the same position. We cannot do everything at once, so the Ark's magnetosphere is not yet in place, and we are being bombarded. The flux is not immediately fatal, but here we are in exactly dear Marie's situation. Ameerah is quite right to worry about our reproduction. And she is right also that without reproduction our entire enterprise has no point. But I will take courage from dear Marie. Her radium killed her, but not before she understood and documented radioactivity.

And so why should I be afraid of a reactor? We need power. And we will need a lot more when we go to mine the asteroid belt, with its 14% solar energy flux.

Also, I find that I am coming to admire many of the design ideas in this reactor Noah has steered me to. By using heavy water as first stage coolant and moderator, we can use natural uranium and skip the enrichment stage. Which stage, by the way, is the process required to make bombs. With its extra neutron, the heavy water absorbs fewer of the emitted neutrons, so the reaction can be sustained with if you like weaker fuel. And with the calandria design we can refuel continuously without shutting down.

We will have to scale it down, like admiral Rickover did for his submarines. And like his submarines our operations will be under the surface. Gopi is keen to help make the project work and to calculate how far away from the moon lab we will put it, balancing radiation risk against energy loss in the steam pipes. But since we will need cooling as well, the whole transmission setup can work to our advantage.

I believe we will be able to make the fuel pellets. But it is like the cart and the horse – we will have to find water if we are to make heavy water.

Noah is right. Our first ideas will not always work. But neither is there any point in going back, in retreating, even if we could.

●

Almost none of it is going as I thought. Alex shakes his head as he looks up. If Wesley hadn't been watching closely, he wouldn't have registered the shake. He nods. Tell me more.

We're scientists, Wesley. We're taught to be sceptical of

received wisdom.

Yes.

And I think we are. We know who put this theory forward and how she and others tested it. We know which others confirmed the theory and how and when. And when we ourselves get an idea we sometimes spend years figuring out how to test it. We conduct the experiment . . .

Alex trails off, looking at nothing outside his head.

Wesley waits. He is expecting the old science joke about the experiment not turning out as planned.

So the results are surprising, he says. We are learning something. That's the whole idea. Right?

Sure, says Alex. But it's out of control. My foundations are rocked, pushed around. It's as though I have walked into a new room – a new world, even – that I did not know existed. Huge questions present themselves. Questions I never could have conceived, let alone planned to answer. And we have to choose which threads to follow first. Thank God for Nurul.

Wesley waits. He can feel Alex's excitement.

It is like going down a rapids in a canoe. Dangerous. I don't know why. Because we'll miss something, and then we'll all die? Maybe that's it. Thank God for Nurul.

She's not afraid?

No. That's not it. We're both pretty excited. It's more that when we move into that new room, or whatever it is, I'm standing at the threshold, looking in. She's already inside, looking back. She's holding her hand out to me. She can see the whole progress of science leading up to where she's standing. She doesn't know where she is going, either, but she knows she is on solid ground. She's holding out her hand, saying, come on in. It's OK.

Wesley waits, but the exposition has stalled. Sounds like you and Nurul are on a tear. That doesn't work. He tries again. I can see how exciting it must be. Scary, too. Still nothing. Alex is caught inside his head. Wesley takes a breath. How can I help?

Alex finds Wesley's eyes, and something lets go inside him. The air rushes out of his lungs like the river rapids he was describing. There are no tears, but his mouth is open, giving vent to the unfamiliar emotions he has been struggling with.

I don't think I've ever had less confidence in my knowledge, Wesley. The more we find the stupider I feel.

Wesley holds Alex's gaze, nodding slightly. The words in his head are from First Corinthians 8 – *if any man think that he knoweth any thing, he knoweth nothing yet as he ought to know –* and *knowledge puffeth up, but charity edifieth.*

The scientist in Wesley is excited for Alex. For the flood of new knowledge coming at him and Nurul. But Wesley's inner teacher urges caution. A parable, perhaps.

I went to Corinth once, he begins.

Grampy wanted me to go. Get a feel for where one of the great apostles preached, he said. I was young. Grampy was the only person in my life who took me seriously. So I went. Close to sixty miles on the autoroute from Athens, although it's more like forty-something west as the crow flies. MacDonald's. A waterpark. All the modern bullshit stuff. But still . . .

The lay of the land is still more or less as it was. Corinth is at the narrow part of the isthmus joining the almost-island of Kalamata to the mainland. There is an ancient canal through the isthmus. I could picture where in Paul's day they would drag ships across from the Saronic Gulf, which connects to Pireas and Athens, to the Gulf of Corinth, the almost-captured part of the Mediterranean north of Kalamata. Like portaging a canoe.

In his own words, Wesley summarizes the rest of First Corinthians 8, with Paul's parable of the meat-eating. Of the responsibilities of those who have knowledge. About how love is a piece of the puzzle.

Love, thinks Wesley. That's part of what's going on with Alex. He's falling in love with Nurul.

●

My heart was in my mouth, thought Ameerah. Of course I knew it would be me, taking over for the final ten metres of the PMA. We practiced it. And the plan point was almost good. Even so, I scooted a couple of metres further from Youssef's ship. Didn't want a repeat. Or the risk of involving his ship if Heaven help us we fell over.

Now the shutdown checks are done and the boys are all out there. Being ramp rats, Andrew says. Two more igloos are going up. And our front-end-loader robot is hard at work. Looks like a big Tonka Toy. But serious, with brains and power. It is designed to clear an igloo-sized area and dig down until it runs out of loose stuff – dust and soil. We'll take all of that we can back with us. Alex and Nurul want to get started on making it alive. It will go up on the test-flight ship. Ballast, Andrew calls it.

Then one of the core robots will go in and drill. We're hoping to take back the first ten metres of core. So the boys will be riggers, swapping in the new two-metre sections of drill pipe for a couple of hours. They're faster than the robot riggers who will keep working once we're back in orbit. Or so they say. Then they'll get the bit back down the well and supervise the robot riggers' first few swaps.

I realized I just called the robots *who*. Maybe it's because I can hardly distinguish them from their parents – Nurul and Niloo. Like when I use the flight control software I feel I'm talking to Andrew and his boys. Because I am, effectively.

•

It always seems to come back to energy, thought Naveed. And energy in this world still proceeds from the sun and stars, as far as we know. I have a feeling I will not be the one who makes the breakthrough into the world beyond that limitation, so I will live within it and do the best I can.

Take heavy water, for example. We need it for the reactor, so we have to separate it out, and that takes energy. We are back to the chicken and the egg again. Our best bet is to charge Noah's batteries up here in the sun, and shuttle them down to the dark crater. Heavy water, D_2O, is as I remember one in 3200 H_2O molecules, but we can use its different physical properties – boiling point, for example – to separate it out by successive distillations. And we have a natural vacuum on the moon. That may help. Also, if we find enough water, we may want to separate it into its elements and use those as rocket fuel.

I know there has been a lot of work done on this. I have not read enough on the subject. I will read more.

•

There has been a launch from Satish Dhawan, says Art. Noah is pretty sure the payload is the Japanese rover.

That mission plans to return samples, no? Niloo looks around the room.

Anyone know we're up here? Just a question.

And a good one, Andrew. No. Not as far as we know. And, Niloo, we're not sure. Once we get a good look at it we'll know if it is a return mission. Art nods in a circular motion, as if to rein in the assembled to common purpose. And the fact is, as far as I know we haven't given much thought – collectively – to what our response should be. To other missions, that is.

They could – I could even say they probably will – come in

and land almost beside us in Shackleton. Andrew pauses for breath. Do we know when their reconnaissance was? Could they have seen us already?

Noah thinks not. As far as he knows, their last orbital mission was before we got here.

Is Noah thinking about using force? Niloofar has taken on her porcelain sheen. We could be subtle, of course. Cover up cameras. Bend antennas. That sort of thing.

Right now it is very dark, says Naveed. They will have to illuminate everything their cameras want to look at. Unless they have infrared, of course. But in a month or two it may be brighter as the sun reaches the crater rim. The problem is that we don't know the reflectivity with much accuracy, so it is a guess to say how much light will reach our operations on the crater floor.

After a moment, Art steps into the silence. The Indo-Japanese collaboration isn't the only one with moon plans. There's the Russo-Chinese entente, supposedly. And NASA. And Europe is still a possibility, although they have tended to keep out of races.

Would you mind, asks Wesley, if I reframed the question slightly? We were speaking of a response. And of course a response is what it will be, unless we act pre-emptively. But don't we have to ask about our goal? Unless I am mistaken, what we want is to continue our operations.

Well put, Wesley. And I forgot to mention – Noah says he thinks they all will be bots. For the moment, anyway.

So whatever we do, we're not hurting humans, says Niloofar.

Continue our operations. That's pretty reasonable. Andrew looks around at the group. And these missions have no people, but we do. We're running all over the place down there and building stuff. So we don't have to hurt their bots.

You're going somewhere with this, Andrew. I can tell.

Yes, Niloo. You know that green, white, and orange thing with the cyclotron in the middle?

What?

Or the white with the red sun in the middle.

Staring at Andrew with wrinkled brows, Niloofar is breathtakingly beautiful.

Flags, Naveed says. Andrew is talking about flags.

●

Wesley they say you can help with matters of the spirit.

Well, Gopi. They may exaggerate.

Oh, you know, it is Art and Alex and they do not exaggerate.

Thank you, Gopi. You are very kind. But looking at your background – you were brought up in Hinduism, were you not? And there I am far from being an expert.

As far as Hinduism goes I know there is a sacred cow, and that is all.

Gopinath smiles. It is a radiant, captivating smile – perfect white teeth and sparkling dark brown eyes. The irises are almost black. Wesley can see why Gopi gets along so well with everyone.

Wesley laughs. OK, got me, Gopi. I'll do my best. I hear you are doing a fantastic job. Is there something bothering you?

Gopi grabs a handhold with his left arm and does a slow, levered twist. It is as if he is doing a delicate mechanical assembly, being careful not to over-torque his wrist and elbow. I am overwhelmed with learning, Wesley. It is giving me a humility. Not that it is a bad idea. He flashes his smile again.

And in the meantime am I being useful enough? I have heard you have much wisdom and can quote from many of the works of human beings.

Wesley laughs. He doesn't hold back. It is a deep, supported, baritone singer's laugh. And he has no fear that Gopi will feel he is laughing *at* him. Gopi's presence has incontrovertibly communicated that assurance. The laugh persists to its natural cadence. Leonardo, he says, catching his breath. Leonardo da Vinci. He can be your model.

The Mona Lisa?

Yes, that's the guy. But he was a lot more than a painter. He invented things we are still inventing today. And that was five hundred years ago.

How can we invent things he invented?

Because he didn't have you. Someone like you, I mean.

But I am not an inventor, Wesley.

You don't give yourself enough credit, Gopi. Let me explain.

Please, Wesley.

Leonardo was the supreme, lifelong autodidact.

Excuse me?

Meaning he taught himself. And I know you do it too. Every day of his working life Leonardo would come up with new questions about the world. Then he would set to work to find the answers – researching, experimenting, thinking, and drawing pictures and diagrams in his notebooks. About five thousand pages of his notebooks still exist. You can look them up on Noah's new net.

Five thousand pages! That will take me a very long time!

Well, and it would be even longer, because Leonardo wrote backwards, in mirror writing. In Italian. But that's not the point.

What then, Wesley?

The point is comfort and inspiration. You, Gopi, are a lot like Leonardo. Each day you puzzle out new problems. You teach yourself. Then you make something work better than it has ever worked before. If you lived back then, you could have helped Leonardo get his flying machine in the air.

●

It's me, thought Ameerah. I'm the one who has to do it.

She has just left Andrew's morning briefing, and is making her way toward the bot lab.

I had a feeling even before we came up here. It's going to be different.

With her schedule these days, Ameerah has little time to think her own thoughts. The bot lab is exciting. The small bots are already at work, leaving human scale behind as an irrelevancy. They are designed for the job at hand. Most of them are smaller than a baseball. It is amazing how much energy can be saved by avoiding strip-mining. Move only what you have to move. And the mini-bots are better yet. Insect down to microbe in scale, they cheerfully do their job a few molecules at a time. But that's OK, because they can replicate like yeast cells in rising bread.

Replicate, thinks Ameerah as she makes her way, using handholds and slo-mo glides along the familiar pathway. What is survival without replication? It is not. It is nothing.

With the lab and flying the moon shuttle, I am more than busy. I am exhausted at the end of the day. But still – I realize these thoughts have been there for months, just under the surface. I have been resisting them because I don't want to be vain.

But Art and Wesley are men. And only a woman can carry a child. And as Art points out, just as we all must decide how to use our gifts, only a woman can decide how to use her femininity. Our bodies are no longer slaves to men.

Of course that puts the burden on us. But we have always shouldered that responsibility when we had the opportunity to do so. Art and Wes, and, I presume, Noah, are all adamant that they have no right to a dominant role, as of old. They are, with our permission, supporting cast.

Ameerah is nearing the lab. Art and Andrew have taken to calling it *The Women's Room*. It's the three of them.

But Niloo and Nurul are – well, they're not humanists like Art and Wes. And Art and Wes are men. So that leaves me.

•

They'll have to do the orbital entry burn tomorrow. 11:47 Zulu. Naveed figured it out.

Unless they go direct to a landing decel burn, says Niloofar.

True, but that would be stupid, says Andrew.

Yeah? Why is that, Mr. Smartie?

Feedback lever. Closed loop.

Feedback lever. You just made that up! Niloo purses her lips.

OK, gang. Art raises his eyebrows the way he does, like a baton on the upbeat. I'd like to hear about the feedback lever sometime. But their entry burn is less that twelve hours away, and we're still working on our response.

Sure, says Andrew. No harm if they land right on top of the lab. It's underground. Or if they land on one of the igloos. That's their problem. But I don't want to risk one of our landers. Let's tell Eric and Ameerah. Get them back up here by 0700. And we'll have to track the rover's approach. They're not quite in the same polar plane as we are, but it could be close. We'll have to analyze everything by, oh, 0900. To make sure we don't have to do a burn for collision avoidance. *They* sure as hell aren't going to.

Andrew's analysis acts like a mild stun gun on the group. There are a few audible breaths as they digest the consequences of insufficient attention to detail.

Yes, Art finally says. Let's do all that. Everyone?

I am already working on the trajectories, says Naveed. Wesley says he will check my assumptions and my math.

Let's bring up Nurul and Alex too, says Niloofar. I think we should all be in the same boat.

Done, says Art. Anything else? He looks around. Niloo is looking him in the eye.

I'd like Andrew to explain his feedback lever.

●

It won't be marriage, Wesley. I have known that for some time.

I'm sure you're right.

OK, I am going to start again. Maybe not from the very beginning, but from where I was certain ... Ameerah's voice trails off, a perfect full-tone glissando. She looks at Wesley.

He smiles. I believe you, he says. Because you're a woman, and you're talking about ...

Yeeess. Womanly things. Wesley, I am going to bear children. I have felt it for a long time, and worried about finding a man. But now we are up here I see plainly that it is up to me.

Wesley can hear it. With a few chords from the continuo and a little tweaking, Ameerah's musical speech would become a recitative from an opera or an oratorio.

Not just me, of course. There are other girls here. But I have decisions to make. Those are up to me. What I didn't realize before is the urgency of it.

The urgency of reproduction? he suggests.

Yeeesss. The sibilant slides up a fourth. Our Ark cannot continue without reproduction. Without babies we will have failed, Wesley. Do you know male fertility is fading fast? And women have only so many eggs. We don't have much time.

That is true. Women are measured in months and eggs. We men are millions or nothing.

But Wesley even though I am certain other doubts nag at me. First, doesn't all of our moral history condemn me in advance?

Condemn you, Ameerah? I should hope not. Tell me.

The commandments, Wesley. Adultery. 'Till death do us part. Things like that. What if he is infertile?

Wesley exhales. Yeah. I see what you mean.

We don't have enough time, Wesley.

Yeah. You got me thinking about it. Starting with the marriage service.

I don't think marriage is going to work for me, Wesley.

I agree with you. But it is a starting point. For example, the service speaks of children issuing from a couple if it is God's will.

See? That's the other thing that bothers me. That makes me sound puffed up.

Yes, but maybe you aren't. I am thinking of the covenants. The covenant of marriage, but also the other covenants in the Bible, starting with God and Noah. Ameerah, may I take some time to put my thoughts together and get back to you?

•

We'll let them land first. Andrew smiles as if he is the most agreeable guy around. Then we'll take a few flags of different sizes. Both rising sun and cyclotron. We'll set up their photo op.

What if they photograph our lander?

It'll have one of their flags in front of it, Niloo. They can make like it's their lander if they want. We can't tell them what to do, but we can dangle a photo op and see what happens.

Andrew, what's your feeling about that? What if they . . .

. . . don't go for it? No biggie, Arturo. They tell their people, hey, here's somebody's lander. Maybe their head shed even authorizes release. They acknowledge they have competition. They might want to rush to catch up. But that takes money. And talent. And will.

And they don't have any of that, Mr. Smartie? Are you going all white guy on me?

Well, I suppose you could accuse me of that, Niloo. But that's not what I'm saying.

Soooo . . . you're saying?

I'm saying that if all they want is to keep their jobs, then our photo op is pretty tempting.

•

A covenant?

That's what I have been thinking about.

Marriage is a covenant. I thought . . .

. . . that isn't going to work for you. I know. That's why . . .

Ameerah can see Wesley's eyes beginning to focus inside his head, exchanging the external world for that of the written word.

. . . why I have been looking at the history of the word. Covenant. Middle English and Old French. Fourteenth century. To agree, be suitable, meet. But in my mind it is as close as makes no never mind to the Latin: convenire – to come together. Con and co. With and both. And they still suit our purpose. In marriage the couple's community comes together – convenes – to witness their vows . . .

Ameerah's eyes open wider.

Bear with me. Let me take you through my thinking on this. Not marriage. But a covenant could still be a good idea. And covenants are not as fixed as we tend to think.

Soooo – marriage is a covenant, but a covenant is not necessarily marriage.

Right. There are lots of covenants, starting with **Genesis 8:21:** *And the LORD smelled a sweet savour; and the LORD said in his heart, I will not curse the ground any more for man's sake; for the imagination of man's heart is evil from his youth; neither will I again smite any more every living thing, as I have done.*

Then God promises the same thing to Noah and his sons: *and I will establish my covenant with you; neither shall all flesh be cut off anymore by the waters of a flood; neither shall there any more be a flood to destroy the earth. God said, "This is the sign of the covenant that I make between me and you and every living creature that is with you, for all future generations. I do set my bow in the cloud, and it shall be for a sign of a covenant between Me and the earth.* **Genesis 9:11-13.** It goes on for a few more verses. God emphasizes that the rainbow will not only make mankind remember the covenant, but will also remind God Himself.

Then He promises Abram: *And I will make my covenant between me and thee, and will multiply thee exceedingly.* **Genesis 17:2.**

None of these are about marriage, exactly. But that last one is most definitely about reproduction. And Abram is 99 years old at the time.

Ameerah sighs. But what about now? What about the rainbow promise? Is God is breaking his covenant?

The gentle sigh of circulating air is, for a few heartbeats, the dominant sound in the compartment.

Well, Ameerah, says Wesley. His mind roams Genesis, Isaiah, Jeremiah, even Hebrews.

I think no, he finally says. It is not God breaking the covenant. Really, it never is. It is Humanity that is changing, advancing, retreating, screwing up. But God keeps trying. He will always try. He makes a new covenant, by which **He hath made the first old. Now that which decayeth and waxeth old is ready to vanish away.**

What's that?

New Testament. Hebrews.

Ameerah hangs her head. She can hear her heartbeat and the faint whoosh of circulating air. She looks up at Wesley.

Do you think our Earth will vanish away? Is it that bad?

I don't know, Ameerah.

I'm sorry I blamed God.

In her head Ameerah replays her reluctance, her conviction, and Wesley's stories about what has gone before.

Even if it's us, she says. Even if it is our fault, Humanity's fault, not God's . . .

Wesley waits.

. . . We're up here. We can adapt to a new reality.

Wesley nods.

. . . because maybe the people are sort of in slavery or maybe they are not taking care of God's Creation or . . .

Yes.

. . . there can still be a new covenant. We screwed up, so maybe it's up to us to make a new covenant. Something that keeps trying. Like God, whoever She is, keeps trying . . .

●

They're down. Position is landing pad. Close as makes no never mind. Andrew seems mildly pleased.

What? says Niloofar. What are the chances of that?

I understand, says Naveed. But if you go back over our calculations, over why we decided to land there . . .

OK, they can figure, too. They're after water, like we are.

But holy smokes . . .

It does look like things are unfolding the way Andrew thought. Art nods at Andrew, but his eyebrow upbeat is not taken up. The orchestra is silent. The pause lengthens.

Maybe it's time for Short-V. Now the pause is stunned silence. Eric's observation makes no sense.

Short-V? Niloofar looks at Andrew, who still looks mildly pleased. What's that? Another of your inventions?

That's Gramps. Heads swivel to find Isaac, who, up to now, might not have been in the chamber at all.

Yeah, says Eric. That's what we call Dad when he goes into command mode.

Short-V? Andrew? Niloo shakes her head. Why?

It came from one of Isaac's bad dreams.

It wasn't a bad dream, Dad, says Isaac.

Eric continues the story in his usual dry manner. Well, it was a dream. Isaac woke up calling him Short-V, and it stuck.

OK, Eric. Maybe you're right. Maybe it is time for Short-V. Art looks at the assembled. Anyone?

•

I asked the boys.

Ameerah looks up at Art and Wesley, leaving her sweet musical declaration hanging in the air. Neither man is eager to burst the beautiful, iridescent bubble.

Finally Art raises his eyebrows.

And?

They said yes. Should I feel bad?

No.

Wesley's response is soft, but immediate and decisive. We're breaking new ground here, Ameerah. We will all have doubts. But you have thought it through. And so have we. Sure – it's a covenant we haven't tried before, but it's still a covenant.

Are they OK with their part of it? asks Art.

You mean as dads, Ameerah says. It is not a question.

Yes. Because you will probably know who is whose anyway, but it's just a matter of a saliva swab and Nurul can confirm it. So yes – it's the boys' responsibility I'm thinking of.

Well, they're not going to run out of town.

Wesley laughs. Hearing Ameerah deliver the line in her fruity mezzo, he can't help it. He realizes he loves this girl. His face reddens.

Are you OK, Wesley? Ameerah's soft eyes are examining his face.

Dear Ameerah, I love you. I love you as if you were my own daughter. And you should not feel bad. We are all in this together. We are family now.

●

Wesley I have some exciting news! Gopinath's eyes are wide with delight.

Wesley is always taken with the way Gopi can adjust his body's orientation with a slow twist of one wrist on a handhold. He opens his own eyes wide and nods. He is aware only of the nod.

Yes, Wesley. We were all excited at the ice we found in the core at ten metres. And of course then disappointed when the vein turned out to be small and local. But as you know very well at least we had some water to test and to process.

Wesley nods. He is also beginning to realize that his eyes are as wide as Gopi's.

And of course we made that vein into our lab as we mined it.

Yes.

And at twenty-three metres another vein of ice which we are still mining and it goes on and on.

Yes, sure, Gopi.

But you are wondering why I am telling you all this that you know already. Gopi is nodding, flashing his beautiful smile.

Well, ah, yes, Gopi.

You see it is the amorthite!

Wesley is searching his considerable database. He comes up dry. Amorthite?

Yes, Wesley. I have just had a talk with Naveed, and we are

both excited.

Wesley has been enjoying Gopi's bubbling, but now he is feeling a touch of impatience. He frowns and nods. And?

Well you see it is not bauxite. There is none on the moon as far as we are knowing . . .

You're talking of aluminum?

That seems to puncture Gopi's tease.

Yes, Wesley.

The punctured one goes quiet. In an effort to re-boot the narrative, Wesley borrows from Art and nods, trying to conduct an upbeat. He smiles.

Yes, Wesley. Aluminum. Of course there is much aluminum on the moon and it is amorthite. The highlands are bursting with it!

And amorthite is . . .

$CaAl_2Si_2O_8$.

Ah!

But we were not expecting to find any in the crater.

No.

But there is, Wesley! Just below the twenty-three metre water!

Really?

Yes! Naveed thinks maybe somehow when the crater was formed. He wants you to help him with his thoughts . . .

He has a hypothesis?

Yes yes. He would like to figure out which direction to dig. You see because then we could do it all here. Everything, Wesley. We could print aluminum and glass and solar panels and chips and get oxygen and rocket fuel and Heaven knows what Wesley and all right here at our moon lab and base!

•

Dear friends, we are here today to bear witness to a new covenant.

Wesley looks around at the assembled group, the entire population of the Ark. They are too many for the space.

We have become a tribe through an accident of history.

He leaves room for the assembled to wonder if all this is indeed an accident. He is thinking that so far the Ark has no large chamber, no meeting room, no church. It would be a good idea to plan for such a space, because he has no doubt most people here are feeling hemmed in, rather than inspired by community.

Tribes have survived by working together. We are no different. Our hope lies in pooling our resources, our knowledge, and our experience.

Wesley looks around again, buoyed by the depth of character behind the faces before him.

We are doing good work. We are solving problems. And we are making progress toward our goal – finding a balance that will allow us to live without Earthly support. It is, and will be, a long, hard road. But as you know, Ameerah has identified an urgent need. Something we must address now. As a tribe.

Wesley pauses and looks around yet again. He is channeling Grandpa in the pulpit, moving to his rhythms, using his vocal inflection.

Without children, our tribe is barren and will not succeed in making a new home.

Conceiving, bearing, and raising children brings enormous responsibility. Traditionally, mothers and fathers and their community are bound together in this task through the covenant of marriage.

Love – lodging your hope and belief in a person other than yourself – has always had an enormous role in meting this task.

Wesley extends his arms toward the flock. Hands rounded, palms inward, the gesture is the gathering in, the big hug.

Today we have before us not two, but three people who love each other: Ameerah, Youssef, and Isaac. They are proposing that between and among them they – Insha'Allah – can conceive, bear, and raise children.

I said a few moments ago that we were gathered – convened – to witness a new covenant. New because it is not marriage. Covenant, because we are pledging our hope and our love. And we are not witnesses only. We are also parties to the covenant, pledging our support.

I know we are breaking new ground. I am not taking this lightly, nor am I suggesting it is easy for you to sign on in support. Ameerah, Youssef, Isaac, and I have had the benefit of more time – separately and together – to think about this new covenant. We have pondered it and slept on it. We were not without doubt. But as we considered together, the doubts began to fall away. Yes, there will be toils and snares. Yes, doubts will come and go. But we are of one mind with Ameerah's vision: we must not be barren. Our goal – and this is not a new thing for humanity – is too large, too grand to be achieved by one person, one generation, or even one tribe.

Ameerah has pointed out to us that reproduction is an essential part of that goal, as it is an essential component of life and of survival. Indeed, it is perhaps their very definition.

The crowded room breathes out, a collective sigh. Wesley jumps in with Grandpa's timing, surfing the sigh.

If any one of us can see a reason that this new covenant

cannot work, she must speak now, or forever hold his peace, and pledge to support this new covenant with all her heart.

It is a sobering moment, even for a group as close as this one. It is not that Ameerah's vision has been a secret, or that the boys' closeness has gone unnoticed. It is the growing sense that her vision has immediate effect on their collective effort. Her vision is the lever, not the stone being moved.

The boys and I have no objections.

Ameerah smiles up at Wesley. There are a few titters and giggles. The tension is broken.

Wesley extends his arms again, wider this time, making clear that the big hug includes the whole flock.

Shall we make our new covenant?

●

Sebastien

Part III

III

Sebastien

~ St. Thomas Aquinas ~

Moses sells stuff. His Aha! moment was putting together the internet and nationwide package delivery. The infrastructure was in place. Forget big box stores. I'm going to write software to move stuff!

There have been many naysayers along Moses' path. You're not making money and you never will. Et cetera. But Moses is a hard worker and a quick study, and he has followed the footsteps of the late and beloved Hungarian who ran the Chip Company for so long. Like him, he has made himself into one of that rarest of managers, a scaler – someone who can make a small operation huge.

But today, so far, has been distinctly abnormal. This kid Sebastien was pretty good at working his way through the layers and getting his attention. And he says he is acting for Noah. And that Noah wants to talk. But he can't come in person. So he will bring in a black box of some sort that will plug in to my videoconferencing setup and the net, So Noah and I can speak. And when I ask him about security he's ahead of me, answering every question, calling me Sir, briefing me on what the black box does. He says that if I want he will leave the room while I talk to Noah. Since it's their encryption, I'm not sure I see the point.

●

We think of each other as respectful rivals, says Noah. Am I right?

Yes. True. Moses is distracted by the background. It doesn't look like an office. But tell me – why couldn't we meet in person?

Noah smiles and does the wheeling Leonardo Man maneuver he learned from Art. He stops inverted. At least he looks inverted from Moses' point of view.

The two men stare at each other for awhile. Moses can't help it. He smiles. OK. Got me.

Noah swings right-side up.

You've been keeping a low profile, says Moses. And meanwhile, NASA has an operation going on at the south pole of the moon. India has planted a flag there somewhere. And China. Where are you, if I might ask? Obviously not on the moon.

In orbit. Moon orbit.

So you're right there. In person! And you're not doing anything?

Noah smiles. I shouldn't tell you this. But those flags? We put them there. All of them. In person. A man or a woman.

Jesus. Moses starts putting it all together, including reporting in his own newspaper. There had been a recent article called Moon Race, about how all these parties had competing moon operations. So you're telling me those operations are . . .

. . . are ours. Yes. But this was not a planned deception.

But you have this Potemkin thing going . . .

Yes. So it would appear. But when you're there already and you see a launch, and you track it . . .

. . . and it comes in and lands, almost literally where you are standing . . .

. . . well, yeah, more or less. And it's a rover. A bot with cameras and a digger. The Chinese one is a bit more sophisticated. It looks capable of sending samples back. We thought about what to do . . .

OK . . . Moses' mind races back through the recent history. Or what his paper and the rest of the media had reported as history. So NASA is full of shit. And China. And India.

Yeah. It was a long shot, but it turned into a three-pointer.

Jesus. Don't I know it. He looks at Noah. The camera has zoomed back, showing him floating free. But that's not why you called. Or whatever you call this.

It's a high-bandwidth link through a number of relays, including an earth-orbit geosync. No. I called because we need help.

•

By the third quarter the score was lopsided enough so the crowd was beginning to lose interest. They had come to watch this high-school water polo team in an exhibition game. Expectations were high. The team was 9 – 1 for the season. Ahiga called his teammates into a brief huddle.

As the fourth quarter got going there were gasps, then surprised exclamations, and then outright laughter. The score did not change during the quarter, but the crowd got their money's worth. The ball handler was always upside-down, catching and passing the ball with one foot.

Ahiga is a striking youth. Mom is full-blooded Navajo, Dad a white guy from the Bay Area. Although most of his schooling has been here in Silicon Valley, Ahiga has spent summers in the Navajo Nation and returns there for ceremonies. When he can. Without missing too much school.

Moses was in town for Ahiga's exhibition game at Stanford. He was laughing with the crowd, but he came away with an indelible image of Ahiga's exuberant physicality and his utter fearlessness. During the summer they corresponded. In August Ahiga accepted Moses' offer: a four-year scholarship if he would come to work for Moses after graduation. The project: company-wide community health. Moses called it *Soul Security*.

•

So why the change of plan? I thought you were going to Mars.

I didn't get it until I got up here. Noah is on the hookup again, appearing in Moses' office. I don't want to sound melodramatic, but it is a life-changing experience. You think differently.

So Mars is not a good idea?

Sure it's a good idea. But it's not the first problem. It's not *this* problem. And this problem, I am beginning to see, could be my *last* problem. Which is why I am asking you to help.

You don't know if you are going to finish? Solving the problem, I mean.

Oh, I'll finish, the various gods willing. It's going to work, somehow. Perhaps in a way we can't foresee. Noah pauses to do a spin on the vertical axis. Slow motion, as if he is looking for something. I know that now.

Moses is out from behind his desk, walking around. It is odd. Here he is, rooted in 1 G, breathing air that was recently outside, delivering almost anything you can think of to almost anywhere. But his head is out there. Unconsciously he tilts his head to align with Noah, who has rotated slightly since he last looked. You're going to make a closed system work. You're not there yet, but that's what you're going to do.

Yes.

You need more lift. You need more mass, especially water and, at least for awhile, organics like polymers. And some heavy water? Uranium? Maybe already in pellet form?

Yes. But we need you too. What you can do.

Moses laughs. Make money?

That helps.

Moses can feel an emotional Noah leaking through the network of links. These huge projects, these giant leaps, do have an emotional component. And Noah is dressed in what could be the same black T-shirt he had on that Florida afternoon when the first heavylift went up.

So why do you really need me? he asks.

Scale, Moses. You're a scaler. We need more of everything if the Ark is going to grow from a dumbbell into a disk. And we need people. More people.

You haven't done badly at that yourself. Moses can see Noah is glistening in the light. He has colour in his cheeks, as an athlete might.

Thanks.

You're up there, as you have to be.

Precisely.

And you're saying use all your assets.

Yes.

Universal, Trombone, SN Lavallée.

Uh huh.

Mirabel, Cancun. The boosters and shuttles.

Yes.

You need more of everything. And you said you had a list of crafts and trades, as well.

Noah nods.

I'm beginning to have some ideas, Moses says. You're on.

●

Dominic dusts the flour off his hands. The starter has been fed. Over the next eight hours, it will double in volume. He has just finished mixing what will be tomorrow's sourdoughs – starter, flour, and water. It is a slack dough, goopy and sticky, more hydrated even than ciabatta dough, which parks at the slack end of doughs. The big bowl is covered and will sit for four hours or so at 26° C., until it is active and bubbly. Then it's into the fridge overnight, at 4° C. Some people call this delayed fermentation, thinks Dominic. Really, it is giving all the tiny creatures – yeasts and bacteria – a chance to do their thing at their different speeds and climate preferences. And also about letting me get a night's sleep. Bakers are slaves to their dough, but we all gotta live.

Tomorrow that slack dough will become loaves of different types as flour and salt are added. It will rise some more as the yeast feasts on the new flour. Different hydration and development makes for different breads. Molded loaves can have slacker doughs. Free loaves need a slightly stiffer dough and more folding during the rise for more gluten strength – the goal being that open, chewy *crumb* which marks the best baguettes.

Another baker might be frustrated at the interruption. Perhaps it is the bread itself that has rendered Dominic immune to such time-based irritants. Today's ciabatta and batards and rounds and baguettes are on the shelves. The starters and tomorrow's prep are rising. He can deal with the pizza dough a half-hour from now and not be behind for the lunch crowd. The small creatures and organic molecules who who are doing the work are comfortable. With a final swipe of his hands on his apron, he emerges from the kitchen. An eager young man awaits him in the eating area of his patisserie-traiteur.

I'm Dominic. You wanted to see me?

Sebastien nods. Yes. I hoped to meet you. Thank you for taking the time.

You want to sit somewhere? Outside, perhaps? Would you like an espresso? Latte? Something to eat?

Sure – outside might be nice. Sebastien is thinking about the street noise covering their conversation. Inside, it is a bit too echoey.

Dominic senses a faint accent. Or is it just the way the young man says *might be nice*, as if it is a phrase he just learned? Although he still thinks in his mother's Italian voice, Dominic effortlessly switches to Québecois.

Latte and croissant? I just took them out of the oven. For once I caught them right at their peak, before I overcooked them. They are like peaches. Their moment is not long.

Sebastien flashes a smile. Like many people with unremarkable features, the smile transforms him. Yes, please!

•

Of course, says Ahiga.

Moses sighs with relief. In the last year Ahiga has made himself indispensable. So much so that Moses cannot see this new project with Noah going forward without him.

But I have to take the dogs.

That startles Moses. The dogs?

You've met them, Moses. Turk and Juno.

Indeed he has, he remembers. Not being a person who grew up with dogs, he found them fearsome. Perhaps he has partly blocked that meeting.

Yes.

They are huge. Turk and Juno are mastiffs. Turk tips the scales at close to 100 kilograms. His female companion is a svelte 78 kilograms. And come to think of it, the three of them – Ahiga, Turk, and Juno – are together everywhere. Recently, when Moses has been aware of Ahiga at work, the dogs have been there.

Moses' mind is racing. It has gone involuntarily into overdrive. Normally that only happens in the morning, when he is alone doing his exercises. But here it is again now, sitting with Ahiga.

Where are they?

Seb's sitting outside with them.

You want to bring them in? I think I had better get used to them. Ah, get to know them, I mean.

Ahiga nods. OK. He goes to the door and opens it partway. He makes a small whistling sound by inhaling through almost-closed lips and teeth.

Somehow in Moses' mind it is as if nothing has changed. But the dogs have materialized out of nowhere, sitting at Ahiga's right and left hands. Moses' vision at that moment is that this trio is more than a team. It is a unit of purpose, a trio indivisible, a three-in-one. The dogs are extensions of Ahiga, and he of them. Moses is no longer afraid.

Hold out your hand, says Ahiga. Open, palm down.

Moses does so. Ahiga releases a little tuk sound. The dogs stand and, in turn, come to sniff the proffered hand. Moses breathes deeply, willing calm. He feels the softness of those enormous muzzles. He feels a kindness welling from them. As they circle back to Ahiga, they brush by Moses on his straight chair, nudging his thighs with their great bodies.

Moses' mind has raced ahead, building a new base on the moon. In the highlands. Mining amorthite. For aluminum, fuel, glass, oxygen. Building the asteroid belt explorer ship. Sending it into the dark with an inexperienced crew. Seeing how the dark can bring out the worst in people. And seeing now, in front of him, the keeper of order. This irrefutable physical presence which is Ahiga and the dogs. He holds out both his hands. Soon each one is stroking a great head.

Of course, Ahiga.

•

I hope I'm not being indiscreet, but where is your wife? Or significant other?

Sebastien reddens. He knew this wasn't going to be easy.

Well, you see, it's a bit of a story.

You know, I love a good story, says Latifah.

Sebastien does his best. How he knows Ameerah from his days working for Universal in Montreal. The story moves along to where Ameerah is now.

Oh my goodness oh my God! And now you're going to tell me she'll be needing a midwife before long!

Um, yes.

Latifah smiles. A big, toothy, cheerful smile. And you're asking yourself how you're going to break it to me that she's not coming down here to meet me. Not ever.

Sebastien feels the rush of warmth emanating from Latifah. Her femininity stretches his imagination. He feels he could be completely contained by her, enveloped, content.

He smiles. Yes. You're right. She's up there and she wants to have babies up there.

She sounds like a nice girl.

Yes. Everybody loves her.

Are there other girls up there? Do they want children?

Yes, two more. Niloofar and Nurul. And yes, I think so. And we are recruiting more girls.

You know, Sebastien, I have some things to arrange. But I'm thinkin' maybe you might be able to count me among those girls.

Thank you, Latifah. Basking in her presence, Sebastien almost forgets his secondary mission. And, oh, is there an, um, physician that you like to work with?

Huh – OK. Latifah smiles. You sayin' we should be a team.

Yes, I . . .

And probably I should ask him or her if she would come too.

●

We're scaling up the shuttle by an order of magnitude. Remember the Guppy?

I think so. Noah inclines his head. Flew airplane parts around. The guppy swallows a whale.

That's the one. So far our shuttle even looks a bit like the Guppy. The plan is to carry fuselage sections into Moon orbit. Of the belt ship, I mean. And modules of the Ark, as well.

Moses is enjoying the new project. And talking with Noah over this link. He is in his office, at one-G, but part of him is already out there.

And thanks for the data streams, the designs. Starting with the cybersecurity stuff. We implemented it all and then some before we started to decode the rest. How's it going with the zero-G group?

Hey, we're a one-G group as of an hour ago. Got enough of the dumbbell in place to give it a spin. See what I mean?

The camera zooms out to see Noah – is it the same black T-shirt? – standing, legs apart, on what looks like a floor.

I feel a little unsteady, to tell you the truth. And this is only about half a G. Amazing how fast you forget how to handle gravity.

Maybe the T-shirt is a ritual for the big milestones, thinks Moses. Congratulations!

Thanks. If I fall on my ass, try not to laugh.

Moses laughs. OK. What else you got?

We have six gardens at different G levels. Sprouts are up. We'll see how they handle G, light cycles, and a zillion other things. Makes my head spin.

That Nurul and Alex?

Yes, but among many. Just about everybody signed up for a gardening shift a week. What about you?

What about me. What *about* me. And of course not me really but our enterprises.

Moses' mouth has been on autopilot. His mind is racing again.

Well, Noah, the common thread is something like *We're outa here*. Out of Florida, for a start. Everything we could truck out has gone. Mostly to Cancun. Some to Mirabel. All this thanks to you, of course.

Noah coughs. Yeah. What about the paper?

Well, that's people. I said I wouldn't interfere, and I haven't. But I did say, at the last meeting . . .

What, Moses?

It wasn't even . . . you know. I think it was the climate guy who triggered it. There was an article in the other paper. You know, one of those thirty-year anniversary articles. How a generation ago this dude stood before Congress and made predictions. How they came true almost exactly.

Almost?

Yeah. The Montreal Protocol fixed the refrigerant gases. And today's computers can model the upper atmosphere better. But aside from that he was spot on. And I mean spot on. Right up the middle, between his upper and lower bounds. Can you imagine? If the world had acted on that?

No. Given today's politics, that's hard to imagine. Noah is getting interested. He has never seen Moses so worked up.

Fuck, Noah. I know we've both swallowed a lotta shit in our time. But I've had it. I see you out there and I'm jealous. I'm coming too. I'm outa here.

●

I thought you guys might know each other.

Sebastien puts on his most correct French, mediating between Ferdinand's rapid, slurred, and sometimes incomprehensible Québecois and Omar's mix of Algerian and Continental.

Yah, yah. Universal, Trombone, don't know where else . . . long time . . . not well . . .

So, Ferdinand, you know Omar is an engineer . . .

Yah.

And also a pilot . . .

Well, didn't know. Possible? Sure, at Universal . . .

Yes, and you're an engineer too – mechanical, graduate of École Avion Technique.

Yah, well . . .

And you've probably heard about the project Omar is working on. Moses' new shuttle.

I heard tell it's huge. Ten times mine.

The shuttle comparison floats over the physical presence of the two young men. On the bell curve of human size, Ferdinand occupies the flare of the bell on the tiny end. Omar is dead in the middle, where the handle would be attached. Ferdinand still has *muscle building* on the young end of his Curriculum Vitae, right after *Air Cadets*. Omar is fitter by an order of magnitude. Muscles show clearly in the spare panes of his face and on his powerful neck.

So I thought I'd bring you guys together, says Sebastien. You might be the ones to work out what happens next, after . . .

What? Ferdinand's expression is even more intense than usual.

I think Sebastien is talking about Moses, says Omar.

What!

He has abandoned his booster. Left it sitting on the pad in Florida. Shipped out anything that fits in an eighteen-wheeler.

What?

Yes. What with pressure from the top, NASA has been making things impossible for Moses. He is already out of the country.

Top?

Top of government, I mean. Not top of NASA. But it's

impossible to tell the difference any more.

Hostie de con.

Ferdinand's comment stops the exchange.

Sebastien steps in. Yes. That's why I bought you two together. The new shuttle – they call it the Guppy – is already in production at Mirabel, using both Universal's and Trombone's facilities. Omar has calculated we can get an empty Guppy into low-earth orbit with Noah's heavylift. Ferdinand, you've already flown two heavylift second stages. You see where we're going.

But it's not the weight, says Ferdinand. It's size, drag. We're already limited at max Q.

You're right, says Omar. But I've been looking at the data Noah provided on the engines. Actual data from every launch. And by combining what has already been demonstrated – in terms of throttling back – and changing the profile – basically, ionosphere before pushover – we can reduce max Q and push it up to the exosphere, where we're worried more about temperature than dynamic pressure.

That possible?

We think so, yes.

You can lift a Guppy. But – what about our hostie de con?

Noah was already trucking engines out of California. So there's nothing new there to attract attention. And he has set up production near Cancun. And in Montreal, at Universal's South Shore plants. Canada has the steel and aluminum. And a lot of it has already moved down the St. Lawrence and through the Caribbean. South of Cuba.

Hostie de con.

But it's a different *hostie de con*. Ferdinand has become emotional and the man-veneer has dropped away, revealing the innocent, concerned for all humanity. The words, though, are still practical.

He is where, Moses?

I don't know. Omar casts a glance at Sebastien. Maybe Sebastien does. We have been communicating through a link he set up. Using Noah's technology.

I don't either, says Sebastien. Could be anywhere. The last signal link is an Earth-geosync satellite.

Ferdinand looks around at the others. There is a plan.

Yes, says Omar. We fly. I want you to train me.

Can I talk to Andrew through Noah's link?

I don't see why not.

Because I haven't flown a Guppy either. For us this is a self-checkout. I'm going to need Andrew's advice. And . . . it is what, the plan?

Three Guppies into low-Earth orbit. Each with a second heavylift launch with fuel and supplies. Sebastien pauses to let Ferdinand catch up. The Guppies can be stacked. The fuel-and-supplies second stages can be joined, like heavylift boosters.

We are putting this all together?

Don't worry, says Omar. We'll have help.

Hostie.

Ferdinand smiles. Though he has just turned twenty-one, he looks younger when he smiles. We're going to build. And then?

That's why Noah sent me to see Moses, says Sebastien. Getting more people. Making the whole operation bigger. Moses is good at it.

And then?

You're going to fly it all into Moon orbit. And the three Guppies and cargo second stages are just the beginning. The proof of concept.

We're going to integrate the teams, Omar says. Make a much larger Moon base in the highlands.

I'll get to see Andrew in person!

Yes. He and Eric and Isaac are still tweaking the flight control software. We'll have a chance to do a lot of sim training before we land our first Guppy on the Moon.

Ferdinand nods. He doesn't care about what comes after that. He has already signed on.

I have a lot of recruiting to do, says Sebastien. After that, I'm coming up. With Ahiga and the dogs. And then we're going to crew the belt ship.

●

I'll start with a draft cream ale and a carpaccio.

Sebastien is exhausted. He is looking forward to a good meal and sleep. He remembers the waitress, a solid, womanly girl with a no-nonsense air.

Oh, I'm sorry, sir! I remember you started with those last time! I'm afraid the carpaccio is no longer on the menu. And we have Guinness on the creamer. But we do have the St. Ambroise IPA.

That sounds good. I'll have the IPA.

And . . . the plat de crudités?

Um . . . no – I'll have the calamari.

I'll put that in for you right away.

She goes off to her touch-screen terminal, and Sebastien studies the menu and the chalk-board on the wall. It is still a nice room. But he doesn't see anything that really tempts, and he is too tired to explore. There is a bavette with pepper sauce glaze. It will be a steak/frites night.

She is back with the IPA. It looks wonderful.

Did you change chefs?

She looks at him for a moment, her eyes big and intense. Colin. Yes. You met him last time. He has gone back to Germany.

•

Rachel, honey – play me something, would you?

Tifah – you down?

No, Sweetie. But I feel like cryin'.

Rachel picks up her violin, tweaks the tuning of the E-string. Does a rolling triple-stop D-minor triad with the other three. That sound about right?

Oooh yeah. Just a bit of it, to loosen my tears.

Rachel leans into the Bach Chaconne, the bow magically making more notes than the violin is capable of producing. By the third variation, Latifah is sobbing.

•

You still current on the Global?

Yah. It seems not probable. But I do one launch a month. I have a couple of weeks free to fly.

OK. Leipzig. Sebastien pulls out his iPad. I looked it up. EDDP. Can we get in and out of there?

Ferdinand nods. No sweat. Parallel twelve-thousand-foot runways.

When can we go?

Now, if you want. I just finished breakfast. Gimme a half-hour to grab a reserve F/O and file a plan and load fuel. See you on board.

Sebastien grabs his backpack and heads into the hangar.

Welcome, Lieutenant! It is this one!

A dark-complexioned man gestures at a new Global. This one for once has a flattering paint job.

I'm sorry – I must have forgotten your name. But you do look familiar …

Do not worry. We have not met. But I am Gopi's cousin. My name is Aarav.

Sebastien holds out his hand. Pleased to meet you, Aarav. Thank you. He climbs into the cabin and settles in, setting up his laptop and protocol translator. The latter is more than an encryption box – the emerging packets in effect piggyback on the old net. Through conspiring servers worldwide, Sebastien can do untraceable searches. Still, it is not as secure as Noah's Spread Spectrum Sequencing protocol.

Sebastien sits back in the seat and closes his eyes. Carpaccio. It was a surprise and delicious, but that wasn't the point, was it? It was Colin himself, who brought his creation to the table unasked and on the house, to follow or crowd out the calamari. It was Colin who cautioned Sebastien – you'll want to eat half a loaf of bread with it and have another beer before dinner. And it was true. It took self-discipline to leave room for the steak he had ordered. And it was Colin who, on a polite query, explained his craft modestly and succinctly.

Sebastien had finished the evening pleasantly stuffed, but not uncomfortably so. The character that was Colin, however, had remained. Last night's forgettable meal was receding, but Colin himself had been strongly re-awakened in Sebastien's imagination.

An attractive young girl with three stripes on her epaulettes steps into the galley and glances back at Sebastien before disappearing into the cockpit. Close on her heels is Ferdinand, waving a sheaf of papers.

Six hours twenty-two.

What's the time change?

Six hours. GMT minus two.

Good. We might be in time for a late dinner at the Brauhaus.

•

You want to go, don't you, Tifah?

I'm scared, Sweetie.

But you want to go. I can see it. Rachel's big brown eyes do have an air of seeing more than the spectrum of visible light.

I have this feeling of life ending. I can't see it going on. And I can't see it going on without you.

But the babies . . .

Oooh, yeah. Latifah is crying again. It is one thing that keeps them together. They both cry after a birth. For some reason this seems like a birth. But Latifah is sobbing too soon.

•

Ben is a friend I can't afford to lose. Colin is explaining his return to Germany.

They have made it to the Brauhaus Thomaskirche, a couple of hours before closing. Ferdinand has tagged along, hungry for beer and supper. Suzette, the F/O, has pled a tough week on reserve and gone to bed.

Can you stay for the staff meal?

Colin has taken a ten-minute break to meet them in the small office. Sebastien has already dangled the gist of the proposition. He has honed his approach so the seed is planted unobtrusively, like a cottonwood tuft drifting on a summer-evening breeze.

It is more tapas than platos, Colin explains. We'll take a corner table with Unser Herrscher. That's Ben. Scot by way of England and America. English, Spanish, and German. Not much French, I'm afraid. He's the bartender. Here in Leipzig for a double major in Bach and beer. Singer, keyboardist, conductor, brewmaster. I think you'll want to meet him.

●

But the babies . . .

Yes, Rachel. They are going to be born out there, whether we go or not. It will be the foundation of a whole new . . .

World. People. Tribe.

Uh huh. And we have been tapped. We have an opportunity.

Go on, Tifah. Take your time, but go on.

It's huge, Sweetie. It's overwhelming. It's a bit like birth, but compounded . . .

Yes.

I'm balancing babies. Babies that we know will arrive here, against babies we hope will arrive out there.

OK.

Rachel, honey – do we want to leave the womb? Labour our way past the dilated cervix and down the birth canal?

You're talking Earth. And launch.

Uh huh. Born into Space. Red, wet, and crying.

Rachel smiles. The slight severity of her angular face melts. Her short dark hair frames her long face and dark eyes. She is beautiful.

I'm game, she says. You gonna come too?

•

Ferdinand is close to nodding off. He has not refused the beer and tapas that keep appearing in front of them where they sit at the cosy bar. Sebastien has been enjoying himself, watching Ben work and Ferdinand fade.

The latter jerks awake.

Sorry, Sebastien. I fly, then beer, then . . . He is semi-coherent in Québecois. It is OK if I go back to the hotel and miss the meeting?

Well, sure. No problem. Thanks for getting us here today.

We fly tomorrow?

Don't know yet. We'll talk in the morning.

Ferdinand steps down carefully from his barstool. Waves at Ben.

Thanks, Ben.

Now it is just watching Ben work. Sebastien gives him his full attention. Seb's German is rudimentary, but he gets enough to follow the drift, mostly. His German is getting better by the minute. Ben makes his work look effortless. He makes it seem as though he is doing nothing else except pay full attention to each person at the bar.

Another beer? More tapas?

Danke. I had better wait a bit. Ben smiles and moves on.

Time passes, but Sebastien does not notice. Unser Herrscher. It sounds familiar but Seb can't quite get there. Scot. Multilingual. Sebastien, initially lured by the brewmaster angle, wants to know more about the music. Not a musician himself, he is vaguely aware that he is sitting in the middle of musical history. Thomaskirche, next door, is where Bach was kappelmeister for most of his career. Bach, he is also vaguely aware, is a musical kingpin – a pivot-point between the Renaissance and the Classical Period, a one-man definition of much that is music. And Unser Herrscher Ben is an apprentice, though the master is almost two hundred seventy years gone. No – gone in person, but very much still with us. Even non-musician Sebastien feels a tingle, as if Bach's presence lurks in Thomaskirche, in the Bach Museum next door, and even here in the Brauhaus. Sebastien has heard stories. He can imagine himself stepping outside, drunk, and saying something discourteous to the old guy with the wig. He imagines Bach the street fighter taking him down with a nose-twist. He hopes Ferdinand got back to the hotel OK.

●

Now we gotta go, Tifah. Now there's no choice.

Sweetie, you're upset! What's wrong!

I can't, I can't . . . Rachel sounds like she is choking.

My God, honey! Can you play something? To calm down? The Adagio from the G Minor?

Rachel looks down and away and shakes her head no. She is sobbing.

Latifah enfolds her in her arms and pulls her close. What is it, Sweetie? Come to Mama. Tell.

It's not just the kids. Rachel is struggling to catch her breath. Words come out, but through racking sobs. They found one little one . . . mother already deported . . . how could they . . . and now . . . and today . . . breast feeding . . .

What, honey? Breast feeding? There's nothin' goin' on about that . . .

Rachel is nodding, now furiously.

There is? No! Tell, Honey. Tell.

... trade organization ... threats of retaliation ...

For what, Honey?

... if anybody promotes breast feeding.

Jesus. You shittin' me.

Rachel shakes her head no. Latifah imagines tears flying off her like water from a wet dog.

No Tifah it's true.

It's true.

It's true.

They would rather sell their fucking formula than let a baby survive.

Than let a baby survive.

Than let the whole fucking human race survive.

●

The neon out front has been extinguished. The staff meal is over. The food is back in the refrigerators. The staff have cleaned up and said goodnight.

The three of them have moved to a cozy alcove table with a U-shaped bench. Standing before each of them is a very dark alt beer with a head so substantial that Ben had to shape it carefully with a small wooden paddle.

Instant moustache, says Colin, smiling.

Sebastien laughs and takes a sip. Or tries to.

The three of them have been together for an hour. Sebastien has been trying to take their temperature. Yes – their temperature as a group. The three of them. How is this working?

But particularly these two. Colin the laconic chef. No – not laconic. Reluctant? And Ben. Unser Herrscher. Our ruler? There is something powerful between them. Colin said as much. That's why he came back to Germany. Are they an item?

Sebastien almost giggles as he realizes he has thought this modern thought in English. But he thinks not. His radar is pretty good. Well, flawless so far, he admits. His security work and recruiting have exposed him to a stream of humanity and he hasn't been wrong yet, as far as he knows. Are they in love?

No, not that either. In the flush of falling in love the self is subsumed in the loved one. The world's centre moves to the other, at least temporarily. There is no sign of that here. They are two of the most self-possessed men Sebastien has met. But there is a mutual respect – Sebastien imagines a solar system with two suns which orbit in a careful pas-de-deux.

Whatever it is, it is intoxicating. He doesn't want this to end.

Ben – Unser Herrscher?

Ben smiles and inclines his head toward Colin. Ask him. He made it up.

Colin looks mildly hurt. Where do I start?

At the beginning?

No, Ben. Genesis is too far back. At the concert.

Ah.

OK. Ben is teaching voice and organ as part of his practical – I should say his performance – experience for his degree. Oh, wrong again. It is the conducting that is the performance part, not the teaching.

Ben is smiling and nodding yeah it could be.

So I went to a concert last month. Youth orchestra and youth chorus. A few excerpts from the St. John Passion. Ben is conducting. The opening chorus. That's the text: Herr, Herr, Herr. Unser Herrscher.

He could be conducting right now, thinks Sebastien, watching Ben's nods.

It's beautiful, continues Colin. We're in Bach's church. He's still there. You can feel it. When those chorales – the hymns – come along, you can feel those townspeople still singing along, lustily and from memory. A lost congregation whose voices still shake the timbers.

You know, you're right, Colin, says Ben. Bach knew how to get to his congregants. You get them singing, and you've got 'em.

And then, in the middle of the concert Ben . . . Colin is looking at Ben, re-living the moment . . . did something weird. I mean, I don't know the score, but I knew this was a way-out interpretation.

Ben laughs. Smiles.

He stops. Then he turns to the audience. And waits in silence. Ben, what was it, twenty seconds?

Ben nods.

Then he sings the part of Pilate. The Roman Prefect. Pilate is actually sympathetic with Jesus.

You won't speak to me? Do you not know that I have the power to crucify you, and I have the power to set you free?

I can hear Ben singing that. It still gives me tingles.

Ben laughs. Just as Bach is a pivot-point in musical history, he says, so is this moment the crux of The Passion. Will he be crucified, or won't he? What's going to happen?

Yes, says Colin. What's going to happen now?

Unser Herrscher pushes his chair back, beaming. We're

going, he says. Right, Colin? Just like that. Back to Tempo Primo. Tomorrow we get on board and fly back with you.

•

Into the Dark

Part IV

IV

Into the Dark

The unbidden thought is like an unexpected blow. Art shudders under the force of it. Where did *that* come from?

He looks out the port again, moving his neck slowly to cancel the rotation of the Belt Ship. Yes, it's different all right. He thinks of Youssef arriving in high orbit. About how we all adapt, one way or the other, to seeing Earth *over there*. And how being in Moon orbit was different in degree, but not in kind.

Out here something more fundamental is changing. Sun is becoming a star.

It was weeks ago that first Moon, and then Earth, became points of light. Moon has since winked out.

Art waits for another rotation to bring Sun into view. Yes. It's subtle but it's there. Or rather, not there. Sun is fading, smaller. I can plainly see what Naveed meant about needing more energy. Hence the reactor.

Art closes his eyes. He is not afraid, but something is gnawing at him.

He opens his eyes again. Sun is gone. Just stars remain. Stars and the odd planet. Sun will come again, he knows. In a minute or so at the next rotation. But the unbidden thought has returned. Death. Whose, he is not sure. But this, plain as day, is a dying of the light. And Art is no longer sure that this – whatever it is they are headed for – is a good night.

●

Turk and Juno have been having tough time with zero G. Mercifully, the slow spin of the belt ship is enough to ease some of their transition, pushing them gently to the circumference where they can lie down and not worry about floating into something.

The poopenplatz, as Ben calls it, has also been a good thing. A patch of grass and timothy and a maple sapling that might someday provide shade, it has become a place to lie down, nap, and live, at least while they are not on duty or resting with Ahiga.

As they are the only dogs aboard, marking behaviour has almost vanished. Human scent, however, is everywhere, enhanced by the limited hygiene schedule. The background smells of structure, moon dirt, and re-cycled everything have almost become normal.

On duty they make the rounds with Ahiga, often accompanied by Ben or Sebastien. At the latter's direction they visit at least the entry of every compartment on the ship, charting the universe of scent.

Ahiga has been teaching them by example as he pushes off explosively from a handhold or a wall, and rockets down a corridor. He can do a roll or two and a one-and-a-half summersault en route, landing with his feet or with a rapid hand-over-hand pivot on the handles. The dogs do their best, but so far are better at takeoffs than landings, which sometimes elicit yips of pain.

Ahiga comforts them, putting an arm around each big chest and pushing off gently to the axis of the ship. They float free together, nuzzling each other.

For the last few weeks the dogs have been pooping at the far end of the poopenplatz, on a patch of moon soil. The spin of the ship has kept the valuable re-recyclable in place until Ahiga can collect it.

Yesterday, Ahiga arrived to find them not lying down in the grass, but floating together near the axis, each with the other's front paw held in a great, gentle muzzle.

•

Captain Omar pushes off and sails down one of the long corridors. This could be a breeze, he thinks, if it weren't for the dogs. His aim is excellent. Perhaps not quite as good as Ahiga's, but still excellent. He hasn't got the control Ahiga seems to get steering with his hands and feet – even his head.

He does a hand-over-hand decel approaching the four-way stop. He has seen Ahiga run it, but he doesn't dare, because of the dogs. They run stop signs routinely. He has spoken to Ahiga about it, but Ahiga just smiles and says Hey, they are our canine brothers and sisters.

That guy sure is fit. Not fitter than I am, because that's impossible. But maybe as fit. But it's the way he moves . . .

Omar breathes out audibly, pushing the thought away. He pauses at the intersection. No dogs. It is a second-gear stop. His inertia pulls him through to the opposite side and he does a two-arm accel, pulling hard even though he is not angry. He winds up in a tumble. Shit! How do you stop a tumble? Stretch out, like a twirling skater. The back of his right hand hits a hand hold. Shit!

He stops, massaging his hand. Comet 289P. Why not? Close approach to Earth in six months. Who is going to fly the Grapple Ship?

We are outbound to the belt, 289P is inbound to its Sun perigee. The Delta-V for the Grapple Ship's first burn is large. Long, and tough on the pilot. Then he's going to spend months tweaking with the ion engine before he lands and grapples.

He. Who is he? A pilot, obviously, and there are only three on board. I can't – I'm captain of this ship. Then there's Eric and Ferdinand.

But this lasso thing is a first. Maybe a first and only. It's risky as hell. And lonely. You are looking at a year away, minimum. And if the grapple doesn't work, or there's no water, or there are too many technical problems turning the water into fuel …

Ferdinand. Great pilot. Taught me everything, really. Docking the three Guppies and their supply ships. Doing the translunar BLT maneuver.

As Omar hovers, still holding his stinging hand, the image, the fact, of Ferdinand takes him over and blocks all other thoughts. Omar's chest hurts. He closes his eyes. He can see Ferdinand, small and perfect, a miniature of himself. A blush creeps up Omar's neck and into his cheeks. This time his exhalation, as he pushes away memories, is almost a snort.

Eric's older, he thinks. Got a reputation as a daredevil. Maybe he'll volunteer.

●

You probably know Wesley and I were working to …

Ben smiles, says nothing. But he knows where Art is going.

… well, it was Wesley who thought through the covenant with Ameerah and the boys.

Yeah. Wes knows our cultural history. A lot of it, anyway.

So do you, Ben.

Different stuff. But some, I guess.

What I'm trying to say …

Art looks up. Ben's eyes are not blue, he realizes. Or not just blue. There has been a change since the first burn, when the belt ship, under power for the first time, left Moon orbit and declined to be captured by Earth. Maybe it's the light out here, but those rays of grey radiating from the pupils have intensified and become almost silver.

You and Wesley were taking care of the human side.

Art nods. Ah, he says. Yes. I asked him to help. He has been amazing.

And he's not here.

No. And Ben . . .

Ben waits. In his head is the overture from the Bach Motet *Singet Dem Herrn Ein Neues Lied, Sing to the Lord a New Song*.

. . . I think out here it's going to be hard, says Art. No. I know it's going to be. So hard it will be completely beyond me.

Maybe I could help?

●

Did you bring your violin?

They have been talking music, having fallen into the topic as if by accident.

Your music?

Rachel nods. Yes and no. Only what I've memorized. She already knows Ben sings, and has a keyboard stashed away.

Maybe we can make some music together?

She blushes. I only memorized solo stuff. Mostly Bach.

Oh, terrific!

So – for the other stuff – no music.

Rachel, no problem. Do you know Sibelius? Not the composer.

Sure. The software. Composers and conductors use it.

Right. Me included.

You compose?

No. Well, not much. But I conduct. Was working on a degree. And I have used Sibelius, mostly to print out instrumental parts from orchestral scores.

You have anything on board?

Yes. The software. And files. Mostly orchestral scores. Mostly Bach.

So we might . . .

Sure. And if there's something else – anything, basically, that you can think of – we'll get it. I'll ask Colin. He can upload from the archive on Earth. I'm a member. Then package and send them to us.

. . . play together? Make music? Rachel lifts her face. Her brown eyes meet Ben's silver blue. Her long face softens into beauty.

Ben softens, too. There is even a bit of the brogue in his voice as he continues.

Yes, Rachel, and we'll be needing of it. All of us. We're gonna need everything we got.

•

Omar's proposed mission for the Grapple Ship has rattled the crew.

The disturbance has proceeded from Eric to Naveed to Art and to Ferdinand and Ben. Naveed is hoping Art and Ben will understand at least some of the orbital mechanics involved with the proposed mission.

The problem, says Naveed, is that we are 180° out of phase with 289P. Its orbit is a long ellipse, the apogee way out beyond Neptune and Pluto. It is speeding inward toward the sun, toward its closest approach. Our apogee is the asteroid belt. We're going the other way.

Yeah, says Eric. So the Delta V is enormous.

Delta V? asks Ben.

The change in velocity, explains Naveed. Imagine you're a policeman on the Autoroute. You see a car coming the other way going way too fast. To catch him you have to brake hard for one of those turnarounds through the median, then accelerate back up to at least 160 KPH. Say you were cruising at the 100 KPH limit before that. That's a Delta V of 260 KPH.

Thanks, says Ben. That makes sense. So Omar . . .

Omar is an engineer, says Eric. He can figure that out.

Naveed shakes his head in that Persian way that looks like yes and no at the same time.

Maybe his Orbital Mechanics is . . .

. . . Ouai, C'est-ce que je veux dire, says Ferdinand. That's what I mean. We flew intercepts together. He's a good pilot. But he hasn't done the mathematique.

Ferdinand looks up. He is beginning to understand how they got from Omar's proposal to where they are today in this chamber.

He asked you, Eric. says Ferdinand. Right? What I mean, 289P?

Yeah. Eric curls his tongue around his lower teeth and sweeps. Does the same for the uppers. He didn't ask you?

Red is creeping up Ferdinand's neck.

Why not? Says Eric. He knows you. You guys spent a lot of time together.

Red suffuses Ferdinand's cheeks and ears.

Yah. Too much, maybe. He . . .

Ferdinand looks at his feet. He looks like he is going to cry. I tell him, J'ai jamais craqué qu'pour les filles.

The silence is sudden and solid, like amber stopping time. If there is respiration in the chamber, it is silent and invisible.

Art is the first to take an audible breath. Until now he has been a listener, watching the emotions move among the others.

OK, he says. This is starting to make some sense. Ferdinand, would you say that maybe Omar has a crush on you?

Yah. Did, anyway. Don't know about now. Told him no.

Was he embarrassed? Art's question is gentle.

En hostie. Il rougeissait. Ferdinand sniffs. Shakes his head. C'est pas qu'il n'est pas bon gars, tu sais.

No, Ferdinand. Of course.

Art continues, pausing between each utterance, trying to make a story.

These things happen . . .

That's why he asked Eric maybe . . .

So what he asks of Eric doesn't really make sense . . .

It really doesn't, says Naveed.

It's a bunch of shit, says Eric. Worse. It's a suicide mission.

We all might be close to that at the best of times. Ben is not speaking loudly, or too quietly, but his voice fills the chamber.

So. Art. he continues. You were saying . . .

Art is uncharacteristically quiet. Ben looks around.

There are about 18,000 near-Earth asteroids, says Naveed.

That's our mission. To learn more about them. There are only 100 comets, more or less, we can consider looking at – or perhaps capturing with the Grapple Ship. They are our ambassadors from the Oort Cloud, perhaps bearing water. If we could grab one, that would be a huge step forward. A bridge to the future. We're getting some water from Moon, but it's no geyser.

Naveed trails off. No one seems ready to continue.

OK, says Ben. Bottom line, we're here to make sure our missions succeed.

That means risk assessment, says Eric. Taking chances, maybe. But not stupid chances.

Eric, we could get together, says Naveed. Make a simulation system. That way we can plug in any of the asteroids or comets. Run scenarios against our orbit. Or the Grapple Ship's.

Yeah, says Eric. Know what the fuck we're doing before we jump.

●

Ahiga, I just got an alert.

Art?

Sebastien nods. Ben and Art.

Yes, says Ben. I brought it to Seb. Just now.

I assume it's a conflict alert?

Seb shakes his head. Not yet. Tension, though.

Who?

Between Omar and the other pilots, says Ben. Eric and Ferdinand.

OK. Thought I sniffed something yesterday. Or the dogs did and they told me. Ahiga puts an arm around each canine chest.

The threesome floats free, toward the axis of the ship. Anyone demonstrably irrational?

Yes, says Ben. A bit of emotion all around. But Omar – he has asked – oh, directed, even, I guess – something Naveed assures me is irrational. And dangerous.

•

Rachel, I want to sing with you. I don't know why.

Tell.

And it's for tenor. I couldn't sing it.

But you want to. Or you need to.

Ben nods. I think so.

You know, Ben – I know about that. Sometimes, if something hits me hard, a piece will start in my head. Then, if I know the piece, I have to play it.

Tell me one.

Well, often it's the Chaconne.

The D Minor.

Yes.

Rachel, watching Ben, sees his eyebrows twitch. Within the first bar, she hears it, too. She watches, fascinated, as he conducts with his face and eyes. After the cadence in bar thirty-two his eyebrows stop. He sees her again.

OK, that was the Chaconne. But the one in your head before – what key is it in?

Ben reddens. Sorry. Yeah – F# Minor. Baroque F#. So in modern terms, say F Minor.

Rachel puts her hands before her as if praying. Her left and right are mirror images joined in imitation of cosmic handedness, except they are joined only at her fingertips. Her beautiful long hands set off her beautiful long face. Her conjoined fingers pulse like a beating heart.

So – say we transpose it down a third, to D Minor? What is it, by the way?

Ben's eyes are tearing up. It is Rachel's beauty or the music in his head.

Yes, Rachel, of course! D Minor. Like the Chaconne.

Rachel's eyes wrinkle. You still haven't told me what it is. I'll do the – what, orchestral part?

Ben nods. It's from the St. John Passion. Peter has just denied Christ for the third time. The cock crows. Peter is devastated. It's called, Ach, mein Sinn.

Oh, my sin?

Not exactly. Ah, my soul, some translations say. For me it's more like, *Oh, my twisted spirit, my very meaning and purpose, where are you? Will I ever find you again in this world, now that I have denied my Lord?*

•

They're talking about me? They can't! I'm Captain!

They mean no harm, Omar. They're worried. Art turns his head, his eyes seeking Omar's. What you have asked them is – well, it's not mathematical.

Of course it's mechanical. Mathematical. It's orbital mechanics.

Sure. You're right. But Naveed says we're 180 degrees out of phase.

Naveed? So he's in on this too? The rugged planes of Omar's face are softening, and not in a good way.

He has no right to go second-guessing . . .

Omar's temples are pulsing. Art waits. Will there be doubt? A second look? He decides to grab the moment.

It's not my field, Omar, as you know. But they were saying, I think, that the Delta-V doesn't work.

Sure. It's a lot. I know. I haven't run the numbers, but . . .

Art nods. They have, and . . .

And? It doesn't work?

It works, but there's no fuel left.

So? Make some more. 289P is mostly water.

Yes. That's the plan. Art pauses, waiting for Omar's eyes to engage. They say it's too risky.

They? Who is they? Naveed? And Eric?

Yes. And Ferdinand.

Ferdinand . . .

Omar's eyebrows go up and his breathing changes. Big breaths. Like sobs.

Art nods again. Ferdinand.

Omar shakes his head. I didn't ask Ferdinand.

I know.

Ferdinand. He . . . Omar looks sharply at Art. He . . . how much do you know?

Some.

Some.

It's OK, you know.

OK. OK! Jesus and Mohammed!

There's nothing wrong, Omar.

Nothing wrong? Jesus. Everything is wrong. Omar is not shouting yet, but it is getting close.

Shit, Art thinks, let's get to somewhere steady. He tries again for eye engagement. He has to work at it.

Omar, there's nothing wrong with loving someone.

Omar has turned away.

Or even, Art continues, just having a crush on someone.

Omar is shaking his head. Hanging his head. Banging his temple with the flat of his hand.

●

Remember how close we came to Earth?

Ben nods. Yes. I have never been more afraid.

Scary as hell. Eric smiles. You don't want to get it even a little bit wrong.

The way I look at it, continues Naveed, is that we were skiing downhill.

Eric nods as Naveed continues. Well, it's a metaphor, of course. A ski hill is essentially 2-D in terms of where you can go. Here in the solar system we are dealing with is 3-D. Four-D, really.

Yup, says Eric. Warped space. Warped spacetime.

Time! Ben seems to be inspecting Eric and Naveed as a strange object that is greater than the sum of its parts. I think that's what I haven't seen, up to now. Spacetime?

Actually, says Naveed, I think this is right up your alley. In a way . . .

The music of the spheres?

Yup. Naveed tests the use of a new word. Music has periodicity. Vibration. Frequency. So does space. And spacetime, when we start talking larger numbers.

So this death-defying downhill, buzzing Earth …

I like the way you put that, says Eric.

We're skiing downhill, getting energy, says Ben. Free Delta-V.

Yup, says Naveed, again.

And it's a bit like Lucy and the football …

Hah! Says Eric.

Earth thinks it's going to catch us, says Ben. But if we aim very carefully …

And account for the wisp of atmosphere we're going to brush through …

That's Eric, ever calculating risk, down to the small terms of the equation.

… the football is, metaphorically, pulled away. And off we go, energy almost intact …

Yup.

But Naveed – you're saying that by then things have changed. says Ben. The playing field has tilted.

Yup. Well, actually it is in constant flux. And it is even before we start. Before push off. Before first burn.

Right … we can't just push off any old time …

No, says Eric. That time is our aim.

So our aim, says Ben, is not just where we're pointing when we burn …

Well, it is that as well, says Naveed. But it is also when.

When we burn. Because space and spacetime have periodicity. Like music.

And you guys are putting together a what – I think you called it a simulator?

Yup. Eric's coding it.

Solar system sim, says Eric. 'Least that's how it started. We wanted to run scenarios . . .

But it's already changing! Naveed has almost cut Eric off, he is so keen. Ben watches with interest.

Now I am doing as much navigation as I am orbital mechanics. Mostly celestial. I feel as if we are a ship at sea and we set out without knowing how to navigate.

True enough, says Eric.

And now we are learning on the job. We are learning so much!

Ben smiles. How are we doing?

Not bad considering we didn't know where we were going, says Eric.

Don't let him scare you, Ben.

Ben's neck is getting sore from looking back and forth between them.

Eric has already modelled the solar system almost down to rock size, says Naveed.

Yeah, but the small stuff is really guesswork at this point.

Yes, but that's where the navigation comes in.

Ben had thought of Naveed as a thinker, almost a loner. But these guys are obviously making sparks together.

You see, Ben, it's at the point now . . .

Excuse me, Naveed – you mean the sim?

. . . yes, yes. Eric's sim is so accurate that we can run our own trajectory against it. So we looked at making our navigation more accurate. There's the math of orbital mechanics that changes all the time with our proximity to other bodies . . .

Complicated as hell, says Eric.

. . . and inertial is useful any time we do a burn or a tingle.

What's a tingle? asks Ben.

Ion engine, says Eric.

But basically, continues Naveed, it has to be . . .

Celestial, says Eric, the man of few words.

. . . Yes – Eric has that running too, Ben. Took him a day after we talked about it.

So wait, says Ben. You run the belt ship in the solar system sim. Then you increase the accuracy of our own navigation. And compare?

Yup.

That's how we found Ceres, says Eric.

Well, we sort of knew where it was . . .

We got hold of the data from Dawn.

Yes. The little explorer that died last year. It was in orbit around Ceres.

So . . . says Ben. You compare . . .

My first model of the asteroid belt was a torus, says Eric. Very rough. I have been putting lumps in it.

And the biggest lump is Ceres?

Yup.

How big? What I am thinking is, what is its gravity? Because it has water, right?

And iron. And carbonates, Ben, says Eric.

0.27 metres/sec^2, says Naveed.

Eric and Naveed are both smiling, waiting for Ben to get it. They seem confident that he will.

0.27 – how does that compare …

They speak. Synchronously, as if rehearsed.

One sixth of Moon. One thirty-sixth of Earth.

●

What is it, Seb?

Pressure alert. Ahiga is checking.

Where? You think it's a puncture?

Stores F. Don't know. We're isolating it.

This is a Sebastien Ben hasn't seen. Sebastien was working when they met in Leipzig, but this is different work.

Ahiga and the dogs – they should be here any minute.

Juno is the first to arrive. She floats in at a modest pace, twists around, and lands on her feet. Ahiga is next, doing a slow forward somersault. He plants his feet beside Juno, and puts one arm around her neck and head, scratching her chest with the other.

Where's Turk?

Comin'.

Indeed, the big dog has taken direct aim at them from somewhere far down the corridor.

Oh, oh. Look out! Ahiga pushes himself and Juno laterally into Sebastien, who pulls himself aside.

Turk looms into view butt-first and a little fast. Ahiga braces for the catch.

Whoa, that coulda hurt, big guy! Ahiga makes the rescue look effortless, like a ballet jump. But Ben can see his colour rise. There is a fine sheen of sweat that wasn't there before, and his breathing is deeper. Heart rate, too, thinks Ben, although he doesn't know how he knows that.

Got it contained, says Ahiga.

Stores F?

Yes, Seb. Just that one compartment. But . . .

Ben hears something in Ahiga's voice. Maybe the sweat wasn't just from catching a one-hundred-kilogram dog.

But? Sebastien hands himself around the dogs, getting closer to Ahiga.

The dogs tell me there's someone in there.

We'll need Rachel, says Ben. Where's Art?

Haven't seen him, says Seb.

The dogs want to move, says Ahiga. They're on to something.

OK, Ahiga. Seb – I'll brief Rachel. She may need time, and time may be critical. And Seb, could you page the team – Eric, Naveed, Ferdinand, Gopi – and get them here? Brief them. We have to find out what happened. And fix it.

●

Stores F? Only stores F?

Yes, Gopi.

And not zero? Lowest pressure 0.25 bar?

It seems so, Gopi. Last I saw. Seb raises his eyebrows. What do you think?

I am thinking not a puncture. Not a big one, for sure. Maybe software? Eric?

I'll patch into the logs, says Eric. See if whatever it was left a trace.

Then perhaps we will know how to fix it? asks Naveed. Bring it back to 1 bar?

Yes, says Seb. And temperature, too. It's already -40° in there.

Shit, says Eric.

But that has to be Rachel's call, says Seb. She's working it through. How to bring him back safely.

OK, we'll be ready, says Eric. By the way, do we know who's in there?

Seb looks around at the group. If Ben has found Rachel, that leaves Art and Omar.

Shit, says Eric.

•

Shit, says Eric. Where's Ahiga?

Following the dogs.

Shit, Seb. It's not only Stores F. It's Stores B, as well. There's a crude malware app on both controls. Stores B is already down to 0.5 bar.

Zero-point-five. That's not death. Or even unconsciousness, yet. Can you get control?

Yeah. Got the app contained.

I'm heading for B, says Sebastien. Ahiga and the dogs are already there. I'm sure of it.

 Arkborn

•

The breathing sounds like he weighs 1000 kilos, not 100. It is insistent, like speech. Turk is excited, and he is communicating. Juno adds small cries from the back of her throat.

The door's locked, says Ahiga. See?

Indeed, the door's touch panel shows red x's.

I can fix that, says Eric. And I don't think there is anything in there anyone could use . . .

. . . to physically – oh, jam it or something? asks Sebastien.

Yes. So if I take control of that panel . . .

OK, says Ahiga. Is Ben coming?

Ben, thinks Sebastien.

Turk is doing the best prance he can in zero G, rearing up on his hind legs like the Ferrari horse. He doesn't seem to care that it results in a back flip. The second time around he damps the rotation by planting his hind feet somewhere. This time it is Juno's belly. She squeals with delight and grabs one of his front paws with her gentle mouth. There is a bit of rotation left, but they don't care. A canine merry-go-round, hanging near Stores B.

Ben, thinks Sebastien. Ahiga is right. Something bad has happened. The dogs and Ahiga have figured it out. Something with Art and Omar, because everyone else is accounted for. The dogs have their force concentrated here, in B. So here, they are saying, is the perpetrator.

But we are just ten. Force doesn't solve the problem. Not the whole problem, anyway. We can't afford the loss of a crew member.

Let's ask Ben, says Sebastien. Which door do we open first?

•

Eric, can you warm him up? I mean, before we bring the pressure up.

Eric swallows his smart reply and allows himself to look into her eyes. He sighs, but it is more a throat-clearing. He tears himself back to the rational, systems Eric.

I think so, Rachel. Give me a few minutes.

And for now, says Ben, could you keep B at half an atmosphere? Warm it up as well, if it's below 20° C.

Sebastien nods as he thinks it through. Ben is answering his question. We're going to put the perp on hold. Keep him asleep or at least drowsy. Give Rachel time to try to save the other one.

Sorry to be picky and demanding, Eric. Rachel is thumbing and selecting her way through files on her reader tablet. I'm trying to – I remember something about cell necrosis. How it halts – or might halt – with oxygen deprivation. I'm thinking get him warm first, at 0.25 bar. Then we'll re-pressurize the compartment – not boom, but not slow either – and I'll go in and try to start his heart and breathing. Is there any way we can monitor his temperature from out here?

Eric dares another look at her. He was sure she and Tifah were an item. He was surprised she volunteered for the belt ship crew. Maybe she and Ben already felt a hint of something. No surprise there. Her eyes are as deep as a pool in Elysium.

Maybe, he says. Give me a few more minutes.

Rachel smiles. Super. I need a few minutes myself.

She's not just beautiful, thinks Eric. She's smart as hell. I think what she wants might actually be possible.

He pages through the storage bay systems. Fire Detection. Strips of MEMS narrow-view I/R sensors, walls and ceiling. Should be able to make a 3-D out of that. Get the co-ordinates of the strips in stores F.

Sebastien watches. Eric's fingers are a blur on the keyboard as he disappears into the world of code. That part Seb has seen before. What's new is the sheen of sweat on Eric's forehead. Eric has always maintained a no-sweat-supreme demeanour. That's gone. He looks younger, almost innocent. Seb has a flash of Isaac for a second. Still, he thinks, Eric is not as good-looking as either his father or his son. But I've never seen either of them as far into code as Eric is now. This is a new level of concentration. Maybe a new definition.

In a window at the top of Eric's screen a fuzzy image appears. Storage boxes, and a brighter mass. It looks like a crumpled, senseless, human body. Now, in the top right corner, a new window. In big numbers, 14° C. Now, below, two smaller sets of numbers. - 38° C. 0.26 Bar.

OK, thinks Eric. Peg the outflow valve at 0.26 Bar. Raise the input air to 30° C. There is also electric floor heat. Talk to Rachel first about that. Now Stores B.

A new sub-window appears, bottom right. Stores B. 15° C. 0.49 Bar. Peg outflow at 0.5 Bar. Input air 22° C.

He looks up, surfacing.

Is that . . .

Yeah, says Eric. Can't resolve who from the I/R. Not yet, anyway.

That's the body temp, right? continues Rachel. 14° C.?

Yeah. There's also floor heat, Rachel. I can tweak that too, if you want.

Let's wait a bit. See how fast he warms up.

●

Art. Can you hear me?

His eyelids flutter, troubled by light. Rachel . . . beautiful . . .

The eyes try to focus.

Hello, Art. Nice to see you.

Where? Am I?

Stores F. I haven't moved you. Rachel's soothing alto has settled a little, into the contralto range. I persuaded your heart to restart – oh, six minutes ago. She is still holding his right hand with both of hers, monitoring his pulse with her right thumb.

Was I cold? I had a dream I was cold.

Yes. Rachel is stroking the back of his hand with her left. You were very cold. She watches his eyes, now open most of the time. We took our time warming you up. Didn't want to shock you.

Thank you, Rachel. Art's eyes are exploring – first Rachel's face, then the compartment. Rachel watches, evaluating Art's return to consciousness. She knows the memory of trauma is not far away.

Art – would you mind if I called Ben? If he came in and joined us?

No . . . I would love to see Ben . . .

●

So, Ahiga. You and the dogs OK with guarding B for a bit?

Ahiga nods. Another nod. Toward Stores F.

Sorry, Ahiga, says Ben. Yes. It's Art. Rachel started his heart. He's conscious. Speaking. She's asking for me.

Go, says Ahiga.

●

Come in, says Rachel. You guys should talk.

She has put a pillow under his head. Almost unnecessary in the minimal G of the slow-spinning ship. Still, with the floor heat on, Art might be almost comfortable. Ben takes her place by his right hand.

Later, I'd like to move you back to your quarters, Art, says Rachel. Put a few monitors on you. And an I/V for saline. You're dehydrated.

Rachel pauses and feels Art's forehead with her long fingers. You're doing well. I'm going off to set up your place with my equipment. There is a fluid gesture, a graceful dance step, and she is gone.

Thank you for coming, Ben.

Ben squeezes his hand.

I want to tell you the story, Ben. I should have told you before. But I couldn't see it . . .

Another squeeze. Take your time, Art.

Thank you. But . . .

Ben waits. Strokes Art's hand as he saw Rachel doing.

But . . . it's like there's a window, says Art. I can see clearly. But the window is going to close.

I'm here, says Ben. We can look together.

Art sighs. Ben feels Art's pulse quicken. It is steady at the new rate. We have some time, Art.

Yeah. Another sigh. I don't know why I didn't see it all before. Especially after those years in the Castro with the black kids. The way their culture looked down on them. In their reasoning it was a dead end. No solution. My heart broke with each one of them. All I could tell them was wait. Time will change things. Not you, maybe, but the world around you. There will be a way ahead. You will love and be loved and it will be OK.

Art pauses. There is a tear rolling down his cheek. For some of them, that was true. Another tear. Some of them. Not all.

Ben squeezes his hand again. I know, Art. I have experienced that. Reason's impasse. Time's resolution.

Art's left arm moves, so his left hand can reach Ben's wrist. He squeezes. Thank you, Ben.

We'll let you rest. Soon. Can you tell me about Omar?

Another sigh. But the pulse is still steady.

Why didn't I see it, Ben? It is so clear, now. I told him it was OK to love. OK to have a crush on someone. It's human. But I didn't see the bind he was in. Didn't let him know I could see it and understand.

He's a Muslim.

Yes.

He's a human being.

Uh huh. Art is silent for awhile, gathering his thoughts. And his courage.

He is a young man, continues Art. Like young men the world over, he wants sex.

Ben waits.

. . . and like most young men, he worries. Worries that he won't get any. Worries the girls he likes will refuse him. Worries vaguely that even if a girl likes him, the sex will come with a responsibility he is dimly aware of but can't fathom.

Yes.

And that urge is strong. God help us, especially so with a physical specimen like Omar. He is what the Ancient Greeks would consider a god.

Sure.

But then, Ben – it's not his religion, it's the corruption of it that is out there, taking that human urge, and . . .

Art closes his eyes, as if the vision were too painful to look at.

. . . and promising, in exchange for killing, sex slaves in this world and virgins in the next.

Yes.

Problem solved. No wonder those groups recruit so successfully.

Ben waits. Reason's impasse is beginning to take form.

But Omar, Ben. What if he desires men? A man?

Yeah, sighs Ben. He's screwed.

Denied, says Art. And damned. In both this world and the next.

No way out.

No, Ben. No way out. I don't know why I didn't see it. It's a replay of the Pulse nightclub. Remember that?

I was in Germany. But yes – it made the news.

There was an opinion piece in the paper. Pushing back gently against the theory that the shooter had been visiting gay bars for research. To plan his attack. But anyone who has ever desired a person of her own sex understands the other possibility.

Art's face goes slack. Alarmed, Ben focuses on the pulse, the breathing. The pulse is strong. After a long exhalation, the breathing resumes.

Possibility?

More a certainty, in my book. The quote in the article was something like – that he, the shooter, was filled with so much secret shame that he would do anything to prove his distance from the gay world.

Shame. I don't know. Maybe.

The article says, I think, it was society that filled him with secret shame.

And denial? That he would do anything to deny the label? Gay?

Yes, Ben. Deny. Deny me.

Omar?

Yes. Deny me, his witness.

Art – did he lock you in here?

You know, it's not society. We do it to ourselves.

Fill with shame?

Not on purpose. No. We want to understand ourselves and each other. Know who we are. We put people in pots. As if that gives them meaning. Them or us. But it's not – accurate. Not at all . . .

It makes me think of Rachel. And Colin.

And Noah.

I heard he calls you "Doc".

The air in the vents sighs softly. The floor is a cozy 32° C. Just below body temperature. There is peace here, in Stores F.

Dear Rachel, Art continues. She will take me home, to my quarters. And take care of me. Bless her.

In the silence Ben finds himself thinking of pots and people. And about the window Art spoke of. And about Rachel.

You know, Art, I love her. And she loves Latifah.

Art opens his eyes.

She loves you, too, Ben.

And she volunteered for this crazy mission.

To take care of us.

Yes.

The peace of Stores F quietly intrudes. From far away, or so it seems, the sound of the two big dogs arrives, carried like scent on the wind. Breathing, panting, and vocal offerings of all kinds – small mewling cries, fragments of alto howls, low growls of pleasure, and the occasional deep-bass woof. No sounds from Ahiga, but he speaks to them mostly in body language.

Omar, says Ben. I have to go wake him up. Talk to him.

Art nods quietly, eyes closed, his head lifting slightly from the pillow. Yes. He will need . . . I don't know . . .

Redemption.

Art's head rests again on the pillow. His eyes are still closed.

Yes, Ben. Redemption.

●

This holding us apart from him has to break.

But why is he holding us away? asks Gopi.

Ben has been briefing the crew. How Omar is awake and confined to quarters, guarded by Ahiga and the dogs. How Sebastien has declared him *off duty* until further notice. How this briefing is a de facto reconsideration of how their mission will be guided.

That is the essential question, Gopi. Why is he holding us away? I can tell you what Art told me only an hour ago.

Please, says Eric.

He says Omar is incapable of engagement. Of any kind. With any of us.

Why? asks Eric.

Because he holds himself in contempt.

Il est bon gars, tu sais? murmurs Ferdinand.

Yes, and he's a good pilot and a great engineer, says Sebastien.

Yup, says Naveed. He does good work.

And I can tell you his designs are mostly working, says Gopi. Even the first time.

You say he holds himself in contempt, says Eric. In other words, he hates himself. And so he should.

In the silence that follows Ben can hear a new background noise – a hum but almost a note. It is a slightly sharp G above middle C. He knows it is probably a 400-hertz resonance, not surprising since the ship's AC power is 400-hz, like an airplane.

That hum, he says. That 400-hz?

Yup, says Naveed.

That's new, right?

It's louder. It's the frequency converter. For the ion engine. 'Course you can't hear the radio frequency being generated.

So it's like a burn? says Ben.

Yeah. A slow burn, says Eric.

Ceres?

Yup, says Naveed.

Sun and Jupiter are our first and second-order bodies, says Eric. We're adjusting our Sun orbit – bending our trajectory, if you like. This burn – or tingle, whatever you want to call it – is going to last about a week.

Ceres.

Yup.

OK. Ben nods. Well done, guys. Now . . .

Ben pauses, letting the 400-hz hum rule the chamber. So, Seb – is Ahiga pretty sure Omar locked Art in Stores F?

It wasn't any of us, says Eric. Art can't code for shit, and I couldn't code shit like that. That malware app was pretty crude. Has Omar written all over it.

Ben waits, nods. So Seb – what does Ahiga think?

Well, he's relying on the dogs, says Sebastien. They are operating in the universe of scent. But yeah – he says it's a slam dunk.

OK, says Ben. You have any idea why Omar, if it was Omar, locked himself in B? And why he programmed B for 0.5 bar?

You said it, says Eric. He holds himself in contempt. He hates himself.

And the 0.5 bar? asks Ben. That's not fatal.

Perhaps it is the tender and compassionate Krishna, says Gopi. Perhaps he is intervening.

Yes, says Ben.

He's a muslim, for fuck's sake, says Eric.

Yes, says Ben.

The religion doesn't matter, says Sebastien. He hurt, and he's hurting more now. Let's just say it's the Great Spirit. Don't you think that, out here, that makes more sense than ever? And we need Omar. Can't we try to rescue him?

Yes, says Ben.

•

You sing? Ben's face lights up.

I did as a kid. Rachel shakes her head. Not a lot in recent years.

Alto, right?

Yes.

Wonderful.

But Ben. I'm out of shape. I'm – it would be terrifying.

With just you and me? I can help you get your chops back. I'm a choral conductor, you know.

Of course.

Well, a student. An aspiring choral conductor. But I've done quite a bit of vocal coaching.

So Ben. This feels familiar. She smiles. You're thinking about something. Something in particular.

Ben reddens. Sorry, Rachel. Yes. I have been thinking about this for some time. A concert. Chamber music. Service. Attempt at healing. Remember the Chaconne? And 'Ach Mein Sinn'? In D Minor, at your suggestion?

Of course. Rachel looks him in the eye. And there's more. To the concert.

Yeah – I've been thinking about the D Minors that we love. Of course there's the Art of the Fugue. But that is an evening by itself. A spiritual workout.

Yes.

So I thought of the Shostakovich – the 24 Preludes and Fugues. The D Minor is a double fugue. A spiritual workout in miniature.

Yes. I know it. At least to hear. She sings, dah di di da da dah da da dah, di di da da da dah, di di da da da dah. Pianissimo.

Ben is nodding his head yes. His eyes are moistening because her voice is lovely and because she is on pitch.

The second theme! he says. Lovely! A-flat Major, which of course turns out to be F Minor. Beautiful!

Rachel smiles. So you're going to do the Shostakovich? Keyboard?

I was, says Ben. But now I hear you introducing the second theme. On violin. And with all the octaves, that second half is too virtuosic for me. I'm hearing you and me together, with you doing a lot of double-stop near the end.

That would be fun, Rachel says. I think I see where you're going, Ben. To the 'Ach Mein Sinn', lighting one spiritual candle at a time. Pulling at their hearts with one thread, then another, weaving them into twine, and then a rope and then a hawser. So they can't resist.

She looks up at him. So where are you going to start?

Mozart, he says. The Lacrymosa. From the Requiem.

Yes – D Minor, she says. But that's four parts! And orchestra!

I'm thinking two voices, violin, and continuo, says Ben. I'm getting some ideas. We'll put it together with Sibelius.

•

Ben, we are thinking, says Gopi. Of putting a reactor on Ceres. And leaving it there.

Ben smiles. It is another moment like the Eric/Naveed team, except now it involves almost everyone.

It was Ferdinand who just explained how the elemental Ark, in orbit around the moon, was the model for what they were planning to do here. Shuttles, going back and forth between the mother ship Ark and the base on Moon. Except now the Belt Ship would be the mother ship, sending a larger shuttle to Ceres.

Then Gopi outlined the process for turning the Grapple Ship, which had been one of the Guppies, into a Ceres shuttle. To a base on Ceres. Hence the reactor.

So – a permanent base on Ceres? asks Ben.

Yup, says Naveed. We thought, why not? With the data from Dawn, we're almost certain that Ceres has more of everything we need than Moon does. Or if not more, more accessible.

0.27 G, says Eric.

Eric is going to do the flight control software, says Naveed.

But we're only ten, says Ben. How do we man a permanent base?

We don't, says Sebastien. We set it up, mine all we can take home, and then let Nurul's bots run it.

So we're coming back?

Well, maybe not us, says Sebastien. Or not all of us, anyway. But yes.

●

The aft wall is a floor. Except for Eric and Ferdinand, everyone is lying down. It is a twelve-minute burn of the main engine. It will slow them just enough so that Ceres can capture them. It is time for a nap. Or contemplation.

The burn is about 0.8 G, enough to be uncomfortable after months of being essentially weightless. Ben tries to relax into his futon.

He is working the bar at Brauhaus ThomasKirche. Colin is in the kitchen. Except he isn't. Colin is on the Ark. Ben is on the Belt Ship, slowing for Ceres orbit. Colin is happy, Ben suddenly thinks. Colin is joyful. He is going to be a father.

Ben realizes he has broken out into a sweat. He shakes his head back and forth on the futon. That's a dream! Maybe I fell asleep. But no – I'm awake. I can feel the vibration from the main engine. He glances at the time on his screen. The burn is about half done. He raises a heavy arm to feel his brow. Damp, but not feverish.

I am awake. But Colin is still here, as if he were next door. In the kitchen. And he is delighted. He is going to have a child. Colin, a father.

The burn ends. No vibration. No 400-hz, at least that he can hear.

Ben slides gently off the aft wall into a sitting position on the floor. He has held on to the futon, keeping one end of it under his butt.

He is drawn to the portal. To look for Ceres?

Some compartments have portals. His is one of them. The portal, of course, is on the outside wall of the ship. Which, with the ship's slow spin, is usually the floor. Hence the window on the floor. Ben hands himself over for a look.

No sign of Ceres. But suddenly Ben's cold sweat is accompanied by a light-headed disorientation he remembers well. Orion! He is a boy again, on Shetland. It is a clear and cold winter night. He has walked to the harbour village and back on some errand, the importance of which has vanished from memory.

The stars were close that night. As he trudged to the harbour, an hour's walk away, they pressed down on him. They gathered around his ears. The Milky Way was like a sparkling black-and-white rainbow with its feet in the dark flatness of the sea on each side of the isthmus. Orion was rising in the east; his belt, as Ben already knew, pointing at Sirius, the brightest star in the sky and one of the closest. No Sirius. Not yet.

Had he taken that envelope to town? Or did he have it now, in his backpack, as he trudged home again with the stars on his shoulders? Ben remembers how he felt as if it were yesterday. His world not so much the beautiful rolling hills of Shetland but the dark and fathomless sea blocking his view of the stars underneath his feet.

He was almost home again when he stopped and turned to look east. That's when it happened. His feet on the ground were no longer his anchor. He was floating free of physical sensation, navigating by the stars. Earth was the dark flat sea, hurtling through space. Orion was two hands higher, climbing into the southern sky. His belt had flattened, trying to become more parallel with the sea. Ben stared. The three Marias? Ben's eyes swept east along Orion's belt, leaving the last star – Ainitak? – and crossing black space to Sirius. Bright. Unmistakeable. Two fingers above the sea. Ben's feet on a Shetland path were not just hurtling through space. The Earth beneath them was spinning. Like a top.

●

It is mostly removing the things we are no longer needing.

Gopi has been explaining the conversion of the Grapple Ship into a Ceres shuttle. Eric jumps in. The ion engine. The reactor. The grapple hardware.

We don't need the grapple hardware? asks Ben. I just calculated I would weigh 2.8 kilograms on Ceres.

Yes, says Naveed. And our roughly 40 metric tonne lander – metric tonnes of mass, that is – would weigh 1.08 tonne on the surface.

We don't risk bouncing off? asks Ben.

That would require a substantial impact velocity, says the unusually wordy Eric. We're pilots. And the software is proven. I'm just re-calibrating it.

You do have a point, Ben, says Naveed. Not bouncing off, but drilling. We'll need some weight to drill against.

Yes, yes! says Gopi. It is like the reactor. We will land it and leave it, the grapple hardware. We will use its calibrated anchor drills from small to large. Fasten a platform. Then leave it on the surface.

Yeah. Eric is back to his accustomed economy.

•

It is a different kind of orbit. Not mathematically of course, thinks Ben. Newton's value for G still obtains. But the big mass in the equation is a lot smaller. Even in Moon orbit there was a sensation of whizzing over the surface like an airplane in flight. Their engagement now, with Ceres, is more like a pas-de-deux.

I may never set foot on Ceres, he thinks.

Ben has reclined near the port in the floor. He has a pillow and has oriented himself so he is looking forward along the flight path. Compared with Moon, this is a slower airplane at a lower altitude. Perhaps an airplane on approach, although he and the belt ship are not, he knows. But maybe he can catch a glimpse of the real lander – the converted Grapple Ship. Eric and Ferdinand will have landed by now.

There will be many more landings, thinks Ben. The gods willing. We have to get Omar back in the seat. It's not as if we have too many pilots. Or even enough.

Many more landings. Gods willing. Maybe I will get to walk on the surface. Take a stroll on Ceres.

•

But why? Omar looks not just withdrawn. He looks terrified, even though he and Sebastien are lounging comfortably against the wall near the poopenplatz.

Healing, says Ahiga. He nods at Sebastien.

Guérison. Bien-être. Hoping to put Omar at ease, Sebastien has switched to French. Ahiga's people on his mother's side believe we are all connected. That Nature must be in harmony.

Yes, says Ahiga. There are many ceremonies. For celebration. For healing.

The people don't believe in – well, they believe that sometimes people can be out of harmony, Sebastien continues in rapid French. With each other or with Nature. The goal of the ceremony – usually the traditional one for the problem at hand – is to restore the harmony. Not just with each other but with all life. Their healing ritual is to keep company with the person in pain. To rub shoulders. To be close enough to hear others breathe. And not just humans.

He switches back to English.

And not just humans – right Ahiga?

Yes, says Ahiga. The Navajo rituals do not include dogs. Not real dogs, anyway. But . . .

. . . Ahiga believes that Turk and Juno can be healers, says Sebastien. That animals can be the best healers.

Juno and Turk have helped many people, says Ahiga.

How? asks Omar, looking around nervously.

You don't have to say anything, says Ahiga. Or do anything except let them be close to you.

Ahiga and I will be with you too, says Sebastien.

Listen to their breathing, says Ahiga. Breathe with them. He makes that small sound, inhaling between almost-closed lips and teeth. The dogs materialize, floating gently toward the group.

In slow motion the dogs and humans mingle, like merging galaxies.

Breathe, says Ahiga gently. You will feel your spirit loosening, taking more space.

Ahhh, sighs Omar.

Perhaps it is fear, but fear leads nowhere, Omar sees. And the dogs. As he breathes out he feels their enormous presence enveloping him. Not afraid. There is no point. They could kill him in a few seconds if they wanted to.

Yes, says Ahiga. When you feel that you like them, touch them. Let them touch you.

Galaxies are mostly space, the probability of collisions low. Nevertheless the enormous influence of mass affects all masses, altering each trajectory, sometimes subtly, and sometimes less subtly. Neither galaxy is as it was.

Somehow dogs and people have come together. Omar closes his eyes. He has never felt this way. There is no desire, no possession. Certainly no conquest. He reaches out with his arms. Soft fur on huge, muscled bodies. He strokes them. They snuggle closer. He wants to cry. Omar – a part of him he has never acknowledged – acquiesces.

●

Jesus!

What?

It's floaty as hell. I think my numbers are wrong.

Azimuth right on. Altitude holding. 100 metres.

Ferdinand! Can you take control?

I 'ave control.

Eric pulls himself over to a sub-panel. I'm going to adjust assumed G. Turn it down slowly. Let me know when you can hold a normal descent rate.

Got 2 metres per sec with full down.

Lemme give you a bit more. Don't want your control to be too biased up.

Got 4. No, 5.

OK.

Eric hands himself back into his seat and buckles up. He can see Ferdinand's concentration. You continue, he says. Do the landing. I'll call the numbers.

Ouai, OK.

70 at 5. Azimuth good. Middle of the crater.

50 at 4.

30 at 3.

20 at 2.

10 at 1.

5 at point 5. Attitude good.

2 at point 1. Careful. Don't float.

1 at point 2. Nice! Att good!

Yer down. Jesus, yer good!

T'anks. Shutdown Check.

The pilots allow themselves a few breaths, and look around.

Ceres. What the fuck. Nice job, Ferdinand.

T'anks. Ferdinand runs through the shutdown check again using his flow, where he remembers every item by its spatial relationship with the others. Satisfied, he looks at Eric, who is back at the sub-panel. So you t'ought G is more?

Yeah.

Eric has pulled out a small baker's scale and a metal weight marked 1 kg. He turns on the scale and waits for it to adjust to tare. It reads zero.

This should be just under 28. 2777 recurring.

Eric puts the weight on the scale.

26 point 5. No wonder. Holy fuck.

But . . . you put in the numbers from Dawn.

Yeah. Dawn did a real good mapping.

But . . .

Yeah. I think we got a good place here. Better than I hoped. I think the crust is thin. I think we're gonna take home some water.

•

Omar you see I will be needing your help.

Sorry, Gopi. My mind was drifting. What did you say?

Well you see we have drilled some and found ice. Very much ice, some of it very salty. Some even kind of squishy because of the salt.

That is good news, right?

Oh, yes. Very good news. Now we have to mine it.

But you are already mining, isn't that so?

Oh yes. You are right of course. But now we are wanting to set up a robot factory.

A factory to make robots? I don't know. I am not a very good coder.

That is OK. You see we have Nurul's robots and when we are needing new code Eric is stepping up. But you see by robot factory we are meaning a new factory run by robots. So we can go back to the Ark and let them do their work.

Omar nods. There is some colour in his cheeks and they have lost the frightening softness they developed prior to his crisis.

So you are trying to process this water.

That is it, Omar! We are wanting to purify, and to recover the salts, whatever they may be. Then to make fuel with some of it. We are leaving the reactor. For power.

Yes, alright. Omar looks at Gopi. Actually looks him in the eyes, at those almost-black irises. At those brilliant teeth and wide smile. They are hard to resist.

Yes, alright. Of course. You said you need help? Maybe I could . . . look at . . . some processes . . . for de-salting . . . and for separating the water . . .

Oh, that is wonderful, Omar! Thank you!

•

We're going to lose him, Ben.

What?

Ben looks up from his screen. They have been using Sibelius to adapt the ceremony music to their resources. Two voices, two instruments. If they can play and sing at the same time. The exercise is particularly difficult for the Lacrimosa from the Mozart Requiem, scored for SATB chorus and orchestra.

Lose . . . Art?

Yes, sweetie. There are tears on Rachel's cheeks. The necrosis. It . . .

She brushes the wetness from her cheek, but the tears are gaining on her.

It didn't stop. It just slowed. There's nothing I . . .

Ben pushes away from the screen and slowly docks with Rachel, hugging her. They are floating, as the dogs often do, near the axis of the ship. He whispers in her ear.

Sweet Rachel. You've done more – more than anyone thought possible.

She is sobbing, her shoulders shaking in Ben's arms. Ben reaches out three fingers to cushion their slow drift toward the wall. They nestle there, between the Sibelius screen and the port to the next compartment.

Did I tell you? he says. Did I tell you that Gopi reached out to Omar? And that he got through?

He is holding her gently. He thinks of the dogs – of how gentle Juno is as she holds Turk's front paw with her mouth so they don't drift apart.

Did you know that the Lacrimosa was the last thing Mozart wrote? So say the scholars, anyway. And that he only wrote the first 8 bars?

Mmm.

So I . . . I guess . . . we can take some . . . liberties. With our arrangement.

Ben. You're crying, too.

Rachel gently brushes his cheek.

Then Mozart died?

Ben nods.

Her two hands, her beautiful long fingers, cup Ben's face. Well, she says. Let's get back to work. Our ceremony is going to need a requiem.

●

How does the orbit look, Eric? Are we OK?

Hang on a sec. I think so.

Naveed sees Eric's fingers intermittently becoming a blur. He parks himself nearby and waits. I have to be careful, he thinks. We are counting on Eric's coding and navigation, and on how much orbital mechanics he has in his head. We are doing well, but we don't have a huge amount of redundancy. That's why Omar's – well, coming back, I guess – is so important.

Eric bangs a key with finality. OK. Got it. I think. Wait. Let me get an orbit sample here. Like a degree or so.

Naveed waits. Even having emerged from coding, Eric's brain is still going a mile a minute.

Naveed thinks about the line of people who got them here, and who are still informing their every move. He can feel their presence, even though they are hundreds – or in some cases thousands – of years gone.

Aristotle, who said it takes force to move an object. Galileo, who made a telescope and saw the planets moving continuously with no apparent force applied. Newton, born the year Galileo died, who quantified this apparent force and wrote equations that are still basic modules in Eric's software. Newton who also, at the same time as Leibniz, developed the Calculus, the mathematics of movement and change, the instrument of all serious science since.

I'm going to go two or three degrees to be sure. Then I'm going to write an orbit adjust module. For every time we bring more mass aboard. Like today.

Eric is back at his keyboard, having taken a couple of steps in his magnetic shoes.

I'm tracking our orbit with the Celestial nav system, he says. Gonna track our divergence from the calculated path. Get a difference vector. Kinda like WAAS GPS. He looks up, briefly.

Naveed nods. Celestial, he thinks. The sextant. Probably used in the 17th Century to colonize America. In wide use during the 18th. Appearing in Newton's writing.

Eric is busy again. Naveed knows him well enough now to see him disappear into his brain, into code. His eyes see mostly nothing, but take in the screen like we take in things in our peripheral vision. Movement, for example. Eric's touch typing is good enough he makes almost no mistakes. Still, he is aware of the syntax forming on the screen and usually has the syntax checker turned off. Too distracting, he says.

Naveed watches the code take form. It has a beauty, like music on the page. Like mathematics. Symbolism for beautiful thoughts. Maxwell. How he brought together the work of all the electromagnetic units, as he thinks of them: Volta, Ampère, Ohm, Gauss. Put their work together into equations. And what emerged was more than the sum of Gauss and company's work. There was a natural velocity. A vector. The speed of light!

The line of people who brought us here is an arc in Naveed's head. The end of the arc sits on the Ark, with Wesley, Nurul, Alex, and Andrew. And – well, here there's Eric and his math. And me, too, he modestly thinks.

•

We are gathered to mourn, to redeem, to honour, and . . .
and to survive. That possibility – larger than any of us – is what we hold, each one of us, in our hands.

Ben looks around, gathering in the assembled crew.

We are not large in number – nor are we, as Naveed reminds us, long in redundancy. We – nine now – have at least that many months ahead before we rejoin our sisters and brothers on the Ark. There is much to accomplish; much of that will be firsts. Things never before attempted.

Together, we have the talents and the will to do this work and to survive. First, though, we must take the time to mourn and to accept our loss. Only then will we be able to redeem, to honour, and to love one another.

For Art did love. He is the only person I know that really did love everybody. Truly. To the very end. That is a rare gift.

Rachel and I hope that today's music will help us play through our loss. We begin with the Lacrimosa from Mozart's Requiem.

Mozart died young. In December of 1791, at age 35, he was sick with what we think was rheumatic fever. Weeks before, he had started writing the Requiem for an anonymous commission; however, his wife Constanze believed (or wanted *us* to believe) that he was writing it for himself.

Requiem is Latin for *rest* or *peace*. The *Lacrimosa* – Latin for *tearful* – was the last thing Mozart wrote. And he wrote only the first 8 bars, setting only the first three lines of the text:

> *Lacrimosa dies illa*
> *Qua resurget ex favilla*
> *Judicandus homo reus . . .*

> *That tearful day*
> *When from the ashes shall rise*
> *a sinful person to be judged . . .*

We will play the *Lacrimosa* as completed by Sussmeyer and adapted by Rachel and me for the instruments at hand. The full text continues to say:

> *. . . a sinful person to be judged.*
> *Please have mercy on him or her!*
> *Gentle Spirit, grant them eternal rest.*

The music says . . . well, the music speaks for itself.

They begin. D minor, 12/8. Four triplets to the bar. It is the time signature Bach often used to express those facets of existence that are beyond the reach of reason.

The chamber is rapt. Music is a surprise. Reason is suspended.

It is not a long piece. Rachel, now pulling down-bow, sobs down a G-minor arpeggio.

A- men.

Their voices come to rest on D and A, an open fifth.

Ben looks up at the chamber, which appears to be stunned. He looks around at the seven people and the two dogs. Gopi catches his eye, smiles his captivating smile. Raises his hands in front of his chest in the posture of prayer. Begins to clap.

Oh yes! he says. Thank you!

The room joins him in applause.

More! cries Gopi. Oh I hope there is more!

Ben waits. Rachel checks the tuning of her E string.

If you can still hear those last notes, says Ben, you'll notice we're going to continue in the same key. He nods at Rachel. She drops her bow and pushes a rocking triple-stop D minor.

Ben smiles. D Minor. Everything we play today will be in D minor.

Bach, says Ben. Johann Sebastien Bach. He died in 1750, six years before Mozart was born. Bach is like Galileo, Newton, Maxwell and Einstein. What music is today depends on Bach's life accomplishments. He is one of those people who – as Naveed said to me yesterday – got us here.

Much of the music Bach left us has a teaching component. The Anna Magdalena Bach notebooks are one famous example, although they contain works by other composers.

But any pianist can tell you about the 48 preludes and fugues that make up the two books of the *Well-Tempered Clavier*. And of the last work Bach wrote, the *Art of the Fugue*.

This, I have to tell you, is also in D minor. If the 48 are written for the instruction of pianists, the *Art of the Fugue* is written for all future musicians and composers.

But there is more. The suites for solo cello and solo violin, for example. They teach the string player to do more with her instrument than anyone previously thought possible.

I am going to sit this one out and listen. Rachel is going to play the Chaconne from the wonderful D Minor Partita for solo violin. You will see how she makes an orchestra, and a whole musical world, out of her instrument.

The tablet screens Gopi has rigged for them go blank. Rachel closes her eyes. This one has been slowly engraved on her soul, like the dripping of water on stone. She will lean in and bow hard when she feels it. She will listen. Listen even more than play. She will let Bach sing to her. The open strings, when they come, will be just that. They will not, disguised by technique, blend with the fingered notes.

There are many of these open strings.

The Bach D minor Chaconne remains a mystery. For two-hundred-fifty plus years musicians and scholars have studied it, performed it, and transcribed it – and they are still at a loss to understand its power. For the musician, every performance is a new adventure.

Rachel's feet are fixed in her magnetic shoes, but the rest of her moves with the beat and the emphasis of the music. She is, in her own way, illuminating the music as she plays.

The room is slowly drawn in, hearing the music as Rachel hears it, as Bach made it.

Sadness. Not a passing selfish sadness, but a recognition. An understanding. How life is cyclic and there is loss. How feeling this universal pain and loss outside of the self frees us to weep for all life and for each other.

Rachel's bow speaks the harmonic rhythm, the pulsing of the spirit. The open strings vibrate and sing until silenced by a fingered note. Each variation whipsaws the heart.

The seven in the audience – no, eight, ten with the dogs – are kids on a swing. Rachel and Bach are the parent, pushing. They know how to reinforce the rhythm, to feed the resonant frequency, to push catchings of breath into sobs.

Racking sobs. Rachel can feel the room coming with her and she is glad. She feels the gladness as Bach and God intended, as a super-concentration as the swing amplitude approaches danger and she guides it just so, just short of climax, short of breakdown.

Rachel's lovely elbow is clawing the air as the last variations explore the range of the violin. Ben is so smitten, watching her, that the last note takes him by surprise. One note, two strings, one of them open.

Turk sings. Softly, head lifted, lips parted so his muzzle makes an *O*. An alto D. Juno gives a soft cry of appreciation.

The dam breaks. The humans applaud. The dogs pant-talk, the sound of their breathing readable everywhere in the chamber.

Thank you, Rachel, says Ben. His voice is breaking. Wasn't that wonderful?

He looks at the moist faces of the seven. Wipes away a tear.

Good, he thinks. We're at least up to twine. Maybe rope. We have lighted two spiritual candles.

I think you'll agree, says Ben aloud, the Bach is a powerful piece of music. Generations of musicians have loved it and have tried to understand how it works. But perhaps we don't have to understand.

Turk and Juno turn toward him. They are silent, but smiling.

Ben nods, acknowledging the dogs and the rest of the

audience.

I have said we are nine, says Ben. But with Turk and Juno we are eleven, and it is they who have just reminded me of the other reason we are gathered here today.

Of course we have to accept our loss and celebrate Art's life. But Turk and Juno – and Ahiga through his heritage – understand that there is something more. Those of us who remain must be brought back into harmony. With ourselves and with all creation.

Turk raises his head. Sings a short but sweet alto D.

There is low murmur of appreciation in the audience.

Ben laughs. Nice, Turk! he says. OK, Let's do another. Dimitri Shostakovitch.

For much of his life, Ben says, Shostakovich had an anvil hanging around his neck. Joseph Stalin. Writing music was a game of cat and mouse. Shostakovich relied on Stalin not understanding what he said. There were a few close calls. But Shostakovich survived Stalin by twenty-two years, and wrote wonderful music.

Out here our perspective changes. Stalin fades into insignificance while Shostakovich lives and grows. He is another of those people who *got us here*, as Naveed says. In homage to Bach, and in unabashed imitation, Shostakovich wrote a set of preludes and fugues in every key. But the structure of his work was slightly different: whereas Bach charged chromatically up the scale from C to B, Shostakovich started from C (no flats or sharps) and moved up the sharps and down the flats. One sharp. Two sharps. In the middle are six sharps – F# major – followed by six flats – E-flat minor. And so on down to one flat. F, and D minor.

So you see where we're going, Rachel and I. The last prelude and fugue of Shostakovich's set of 24. The D minor.

The prelude is short but dramatic. It foreshadows the theme and hints at the theme before, well, almost stating it. The theme plays around the intervals of a fourth and a fifth, coyly refusing to reveal if it is major or minor.

A movement catches Ben's eye. Ferdinand, who had been with Eric, is drifting toward the dogs.

Shostakovich loves that ambiguity, Ben continues. So do musicians who play and sing the blues. Well, so do all musicians, because music is ratios of pitch. An octave is defined as 2/1; a fifth as 3/2. Also ratios of time, of heartbeats to breaths.

Ferdinand has drifted just beyond the dogs, and is behind Ahiga and Omar. He slides between them and puts his arms around their shoulders.

Enough, says Ben. We'll let the music speak for itself.

3/4 time. Definitely D minor, at least for the first bar. But then the ambiguity Ben mentions takes over. There are hints at C, A minor, and F, and then an open C chord on the first beat of bar ten. From the C, the start of a D minor scale leads nowhere – except a crashing octave D deep in the bass. *Fortissimo*. It is repeat of the first bar, except what had been solemn has become aggressive. And this six-bar exposition, seeming at first like a repeat of the first eight bars, is going somewhere else, and faster.

There are audible gasps in the audience as Ben and Rachel land on the downbeat of bar 17. An A major triad, doubled in the bass. *Fortissimo*. The dogs' heads are chin-up as they emit passable alto A howls.

Ben catches Rachel's eye and she nods, waiting two heartbeats. Without lifting her bow she repeats the A major triad on up-bow.

They have acknowledged their audience, both human and canine. We played bar 17 with five beats, not three, thinks Ben.

But that's OK.

As the Prelude ends, Rachel glances up and catches the action. Omar has turned his head toward Ferdinand. He tilts his head left until his ear and cheek caress the forearm of the young man with no mother tongue.

The musicians are working hard, well into the development of this complex double fugue. As with any endeavour that requires intense concentration, time slows and almost stops. A dream thought half-forms, timeless, in Ben's mind. We are in the nether regions of equal-tempered tonality where tons of sharps turn into tons of flats and come back down to none. Or one, in this case. It is a miniature of the structure of the entire work, the whole of the twenty-four preludes and fugues.

The first subject. First entry, just like it was at the beginning of the fugue. Only it is an octave higher – or two octaves, with the doubling. And the tonal ambiguity of this first subject is suddenly made plain, taking on unambiguity. The brilliant sun of F sharp. D major.

For the first time the two subjects are playing at the same time. And this is the first time Ben's voice has been heard since the Mozart. He is not a tenor, but his supported upper register has shivered spines. The dogs lift their heads. Were it not for the *fff*, gasps would have been audible. Ferdinand has drifted behind Omar and has both hands on Omar's shoulders.

Another dream-like construct flits through Ben's mind, taking an instant but covering multitudes. C-flat *is* B, at least with the slight fiddle of equal temperament. The ratios are imperfect but the function, and the inclusion, open up worlds. We are imperfect. We are unique. Maybe our imperfection can bring us together. Can allow us to be together. Allow us to love.

Here is the second *fff* climax, and Ben sings again, this time with words:

> *for-give-ness of sins*

It is a stretto, with the first subject imitating at a two-bar interval. Rachel, sings, an octave above:

> *for-give-ness of sins*
> *and re-demp-tion of wo-men*
> *and of men . . .*

Ritenuto. The last bars. They sing in unison. It is back to the beginning of the beginning, the first subject:

sol	*do*	*do*	*sol*	*do*	*do*
Re-	*demp-*	*tion*	*of*	*wo-*	*men*
Re-	*demp-*	*tion*	*of*	*men*	

Rachel's lovely alto is solo as she arrives on *-men*, a beat after Ben. The instruments are fading away on octave D's, as are the voices.

Gopi holds his prayer hands on his chest, shaking his head. Ferdinand has his arms around Omar from behind, squeezing life into him.

Gopi nods, clapping, shaking his head. Oh, my goodness, oh, my goodness!

The dogs emit two little crying noises and are silent.

Thank you, says Ben. We have one more piece. I have to tell you I have taken a liberty with it.

I desperately wanted to sing this piece. For me it completes the spiritual story we have been sharing with you. The problem is, it is too high for me. It is in F# minor, and the line peaks at a tenor A.

You don't want to hear me sing that note. But if you will

permit me a small digression . . .

Bach loved B minor and F# minor and used them explicitly for wrenchings of the soul. You might ask why, since we have just heard Shostakovich as he works his way around the flatted circle of fifths that is equal temperament. How, you might ask, are these keys different from others, when all the intervals – the ratios – are the same in any key?

Well, they weren't. Not in Bach's day. His two volumes of preludes and fugues is called the well-tempered, not the equal-tempered, clavier. Bach didn't use split keys, so his tuning was a compromise, just as ours is today. But the compromises weren't equal. So each key still had its own character.

What we did – at Rachel's suggestion and my necessity – was to transpose this piece down a major third, to D minor, the key we have been in all day. It is an aria from the St. John Passion. The singer is Peter. He has just denied Jesus for the third time. The cock crows. In a breath his heart breaks. He feels as though his soul has broken in two, that in some way he has ceased to exist.

I will sing it in German, so that at least will be as Bach wrote it. When Bach set words to music, their meaning expanded. His settings render the whole greater than the sum of the parts. You will hear me sing, *Ach, Mein Sinn*, which sounds like Oh, my sin.

Well, sort of. The German *Sinn* has a larger meaning.

I am not going to attempt a literal translation. Instead, I will tell you what Peter, in words and music, sings to me:

Oh, my twisted spirit, my very meaning and purpose, where are you? Will I ever find you again in this world, now that I have denied my Lord?

Ben looks at Rachel, whose violin and bow are poised. With an eyebrow and a nod, he conducts them in.

In sixteen bars the music is defined; the stage is set for Peter's voice:

Ach, mein Sinn	*Ah, my soul*
Wo willt du endlich hin	*Where will you end up?*
Wo sol ich mich erquicken?	*Where will I find relief?*

Where? Omar's eyes are wide with fear. Where can I find it?

Ferdinand has his mouth close to Omar's ear. Sebastien, who knows the kid so well, is a few feet away. He can lip-read: *Art t'aime, Omar. Toujours. Toujours.*

Bleib ich hier	*Do I stay here?*
Oder wünsch ich mir	*Or do I put*
Berg und Hügel auf den Rücken?	*The hills and mountains of this Earth behind me?*

The music is briefly in C major. Ease. Comfort. There is a sweetness in this option of death.

Bei der Welt ist gar kein Rat	*In this life there is no help*
Und im Herzen	*And in my heart*
Stehn die Schmerzen	*Lives the agony*
Meiner Missetat	*Of my misdeeds*

There is no help in this world. But I cannot leave.

Weil der Knecht den Herrn	*While the servant*
verleugnet hat.	*denies . . .*

I long for the sweetness of death, but it is denied to me . . . even as I have denied . . .

. . . the Lord

. . . my people. My purpose. What is within me. Oh, Allah, help me!

The music ends. The audience, including the dogs, are mute – incapable, as yet, of reaction. Omar's silent weeping breaks into sobs, solo in the silence.

Ferdinand hugs Omar with a strength suited to the hard, bruised body in his arms. His embrace denies Omar solitude. Denies him permission to leave.

•

Spring

Part V

V

Spring

we cannot leave
this land of our ancestors
on this earth

we are being killed by the monster
on this earth

shuku shuku (the sound of the train)
i want to get on the train
to get on to the train in the morning
i want
oh, mother, it's leaving me behind!

~ "As'kwaz'ukuhamba" traditional Xhosa anti-apartheid song ~

(translation by Patisa Nombona and Mollie Stone, 2003)
(2017 musical setting by Ted Hearne)

Today he can see it. Sun is brighter, perceptibly bigger. He remembers Spring on Shetland. The tiny blue and white faces of Spring Squill, the Sea Pink dotting the clifftops.

He doesn't need the solar flux data. He can feel it on his face, through the port. Light. Energy.

Warmth. Sun is the unequivocal one. The knowledge – if that

is the word for it – less so. That Colin is going to be a father – it is not that he doubts it. No. It has, somehow, become a certainty. But Ben cannot reconcile this certainty with objective data, with what his scientific training would take as truth.

Could Colin not have told him – in a note accompanying the Sibelius scores, perhaps? Or had the scores arrived before he knew? Why does he have the strong sense that it doesn't matter?

Rachel.

He knew she knew before she told him. He knew she knew something, as he knew about Colin.

Latifah. Pregnant.

With Colin's child?

He had not thought of Latifah. That knowledge had come only to Rachel. But he and Rachel had shared this – knowledge. Almost without speaking. And there is the timing of it all. Pregnant? With Colin's child? Perhaps.

We're getting energy from the shield!

Oh, sorry, Ben. Naveed hesitates in the doorway. I didn't mean to interrupt your thoughts.

No, no. Come in. Tell me. The shield. You mean the shield on the ice block.

Yes. Exactly. You know how we didn't want our enormous mass of ice behaving like a comet.

Like a comet?

Yes. Sun-side melting and blowing away in the solar wind.

Oh – of course.

So we made a sun-shield. For the Sun side.

Yes. I remember now.

So Omar and I were thinking. We had to insulate the ice from the shield. There is a temperature difference.

Yes . . .

So Omar said, let's use a Carnot cycle.

A what?

It's the way a refrigerator works. Or an air conditioner.

Sure, OK. But don't you need a refrigerant gas?

Yes. We're using water. Water vapour. And steam. Omar got some – what do you say – he cannibalized some parts. Turbines. Compressors. Generators. We are making enough electricity to power the ion engine full-time if we want.

I thought I heard more 400 hertz . . .

And now we are melting the ice block. Heating the water sun-side. Then re-freezing it on the deep space side . . .

You're using change of state. Wait – two changes of state?

Yes! Exactly! Solid, liquid, gas.

That's just like our Earth's atmosphere! That's why they have all those terrible storms now.

Yes! We imitate climate change. Hot air can hold so much more water vapour. So we have introduced a new turbine stage. Ahead of it very hot compressed air is introduced to carry the water vapour. In the turbine a very great deal of heat is released as the vapour condenses.

That's the other sound. The turbine.

Yes. Turbines, actually. We are running what amounts to a jet engine, compressing air, fuelling it with water vapour . . .

Like Earth's storms . . .

. . . yes, exactly. And cooling it again with the turbines. You are breathing that exhaust.

I thought our air was nicer. More tropical.

You are right. And now we are heating the ship. Using only the jet engine.

●

Juno's preggers.

What? You're not kidding me, Ahiga?

No, Seb. She came into her first heat during the busy time.

You mean when we were building the shield and getting ready for the first burn?

Yes.

So that was . . .

Just over a month ago.

Are you sure?

Uh huh. She lost her appetite for a couple of weeks. And she was real affectionate.

So . . . I don't even know . . .

Seven weeks.

Wow! Shit! How far along is she, do you know?

Four weeks and two days. Turk didn't waste any time.

Sebastien's laughter takes him by surprise. It takes him over. It's not funny, it's delightful. There are tears in his eyes. Embarrassed, he looks at Ahiga.

The Navajo blood keeps Ahiga's face impassive, but a happy amusement is visible at the corners of his mouth.

Wow! This is great, Ahiga. Puppies in space! In about . . . what?

Twenty days. Give or take.

Holy shit!

Sebastien is having one of those moments where, distracted, a crew member floats free without realizing it. They have taken to calling it spacing out. Sebastien, in a slow drift and two-axis spin, bumps into a handhold.

Shit!

Ahiga looks at Sebastien with that expression he gets when the dogs do something silly. Seb twists around again so he can see Ahiga.

So – Ahiga. Have you told Ben?

Not yet. I was thinking we could do that together.

●

Ben, I think I may be going nuts.

Ben looks up from his work, surprised. It is not something Eric would ever say. Then again, Eric is Mr. Risk Assessment. And he's a pilot, so his own systems are part of that risk assessment.

What's happening, Eric? Ben gestures to a space beside his. Come on in!

Eric eyes the route for a second. Then he pushes off, way too fast. He hits a handhold behind Ben's head with his right hand and does a high-performance shock absorber stop with his right arm. Momentum killed, he twists right ninety degrees and pushes gently. Backwards, he floats slowly past Ben's left ear into the indicated space. The landing is accurate, soft, and comfortable.

It's Dad.

You've heard from Andrew?

Not exactly. But the old goat is going to be a father. To

someone younger than my son.

Ohh. Ben looks up and catches Eric's manic gaze. You ... you know ... that.

Yeah.

You're not nuts, Eric.

Yeah? Why not?

Because ... because you're not the only one.

Wait – because I think so, it may be true? Is that what you mean?

Ben nods.

I'm not alone. So who else, if I may ask?

Me.

You? Ben?

Yes. And Rachel. We both know something from our loved ones on the Ark. And we didn't have to tell each other.

Eric stares at Ben. You could say he was sitting, but he is just comfortably wedged into his cushioned landing place.

Loved ones. At a distance.

Yes. Ben smiles. Do you know who ...

... is the lucky Mom?

Yes.

Niloo. No doubt.

That makes sense!

Eric sees Ben's mischievous smile. Ben watches Eric's controlled composure erode. There is relief. Maybe he is not nuts. Maybe this is normal. There is a lot of new stuff out here. Accept it. Think about it. Learn about it. Use it.

Do you think it could be something like . . . like entanglement? In quantum physics? Knowledge at a distance?

Yes, I have had that thought, Eric. I want to bring that up with Naveed. See if he thinks we're crazy. Oh, by the way – did you know we're going to have a mom on board?

You're kidding. Rachel?

Ben laughs. No, Juno. We're going to have puppies on board. Next week.

•

So – you remember our path out here was a spiral . . .

If you say so, Naveed. Mostly I remember that terrifying low pass over Earth.

Yes, Ben. We used our Earth for a good deal of the required delta-V. But remember Mars?

Yeah. We buzzed Mars too, says Eric.

Don't remember. Maybe I was asleep.

Anyway, says Naveed, it's a spiral going home as well. Since we're all in orbit around Sun, our first burn gives us a bit of retrograde velocity. That allows Sun to attract us, to accelerate us toward her. Here – wait – let's look at it on the Solar System Sim.

Right, says Eric. Hang on, I'll back-time to first burn . . .

See, says Naveed, this is us. It's like we're backing away from Ceres. And as we back, we start to fall toward Sun.

And I thought buzzing Earth was bad, says Ben. This is really scary. Sun's gravity . . .

True, says Eric. If we wanted to – say, leave the Solar System – we wouldn't have to burn all that much fuel. Set it up so we go blisteringly close to Sun. Then we'd be pulling enormous G's for days. With luck . . .

Of course we wouldn't do that, Ben, says Naveed. Too hot. Too much G. But what Eric says is true. We could – in theory – get close to Sun escape velocity.

OK. And leave the Solar System. For God knows where.

Yup. It is the Eric-Naveed team speaking again as a choir.

Head for the next star, maybe, continues Ben. But not this time?

No, Ben. Look at the Sim. See how we're approaching Mars? Or rather, how Mars is catching up to us?

Don't worry, says Eric. It's not going to hit us. Watch.

This is about two months from now, says Naveed.

Indeed, thinks Ben as he watches the near miss. Scary as hell, but we pass just behind Mars in its orbit.

I don't want to watch, he says aloud.

Naveed chuckles. We are watching the ship's trajectory closely. But look – he points at the trace – do you see the plan?

Ben watches as it unfolds. Mars' gravity is briefly a large factor. Applying a force. Bending the ship's path.

It's analogous to an airplane, says Eric. Sort of. Trading potential and kinetic energy. Except there's no drag. Or lift. Except Mars' gravity.

Now Ben can't help watching. The ship's trajectory flares outwards, its spiral, its orbit, becoming less of an ellipse. Now they won't go that close to Sun . . .

Eric must have sped up the Sim. Ben can see Earth days spinning by in the counter. He can see Earth herself, way over there, hurtling around her orbit. Earth is going to catch them too, he sees. That's how this coming home is going to work. He shudders.

•

Ferdi, j'ai peur.

Pourquoi donc?

Omar has had so many reasons to been afraid, thinks Ferdinand.

I'm afraid for all of us, says Omar.

But why?

When we do the Mars and Earth flybys. With this enormous chunk of ice.

And?

Doesn't the gravity force act on the centre of mass?

Um ...

And wouldn't there be a moment on our attachment to it, trying to rip us apart? I'm not sure, but ...

This is a new Omar, thinks Ferdinand. He has emerged. He is thinking about the crew.

That's a good point, Omar. I'm not sure either. Let's talk about it with Eric and Naveed. And Gopi.

•

Hey Omar – would you have some time to help Ahiga? He's swamped.

Sure, Seb. Didn't know he was on a project. What is it?

Puppies.

Puppies? Omar's eyes are wide. Yes – I remember. Juno is ...

... was. Since yesterday there is a litter of five.

Oh, my ... my ...

Puppies in space.

•

It's not the same poopenplatz. The patch of timothy is still there, but at the opposite end from the platz a nest has been rigged. Cushions, rolled blankets, and netting are fastened with twine. Juno rules its centre like a sun. The trajectories of the five planets could scarcely be called orbits. They are chaos, uncontainable by the very weak gravity of the spinning ship.

Or of Mom Sun.

The instinct of newborn pups is to form a single, squirming mass. With her nose, Mom gently separates the mass into two wiggling nursing lines. But here, on board the belt ship, the conceit of Mom as Sun seems to be breaking down. Gravity and orbit give way to fusion and element formation, driven by the weak force and beta decay. Pups, like electrons and neutrinos, randomly escape the nest and drift out into the universe of the ship.

Copper Juno and brindle Turk have a fine-looking litter. Naveed, pinch-hitting for Ahiga, reaches out and catches little Journey as she drifts out the opening in the netting. Her brindle would work well as camouflage in a thicket of copper plumbing. She nibbles Naveed's fingertips as he lovingly places her back near Juno.

Hi Naveed. I'm here to learn the drill.

Omar makes his way past the poopenplatz to where Naveed is stationed, near the opening in the net.

I'm also here to . . . I want to learn some physics. Last night I was suddenly worried about the ship. About the Mars and Earth flybys. About our attachment to that huge chunk of ice.

Look! Here comes Whiteout!

He is entirely white, except for a copper patch around his left eye. He looks pleased with himself.

I think I'll let him explore for a minute, says Naveed. He's having such a good time.

The pup drifts through the opening and away toward the platz. He twists his body so he is looking back towards Omar and Naveed. He stretches, paws extended ahead and behind.

He's learning attitude control, says Naveed. I don't think he has trajectory down yet.

Whiteout is on course for the platz, or nearly so, going backwards in a slow roll. His back, then his side and then paws brush the timothy, killing his momentum. As he pushes up to a sitting position with his front legs, he takes a little widdle before drifting away. The universe is unfolding as it should.

OK, tyke. Good boy! says Naveed as he catches him. Good first solo!

He hands Whiteout to Omar.

Their puppy teeth are sharp, but they just nibble, he says.

Omar holds the little ball of fur. The pup's living force is immediately apparent, merging with his own. He feels his reaction as a dipole would in a magnetic field. Or like one mass influences another by bending spacetime.

There is a warmth. He loves this pup. He does as he saw Naveed do as he entered the chamber. He lets Whiteout nibble his finger. He strokes him. He gently places him back by Juno.

●

For now all five pups are nursing.

So, Omar, says Naveed. About our attachment. You are right to worry, of course. I have been learning some physics myself, in the last week or so. The fact is, we are an experiment. We are doing something that has never been done before. We don't know anything for sure.

Naveed pauses, shakes his head. Not for sure.

Omar can see Naveed's thoughts going inward. He glances at Juno and the pups. All is as it was, but he had better keep an eye out. He sees that responsibility for the pups has already been passed to him.

And it's not just us, continues Naveed. It is the Ark, as well. Naveed looks out for a second. Are the pups . . .

Got it, says Omar. I'll catch.

OK . . . thanks . . . You see, we both have spin. There's more . . . more than I was aware of. More that has already been done. From Spacelab, way back then; and more recently from Gravity Probe B, a polar orbit physics experiment with unbelievably accurate gyroscopes . . .

And?

. . . and a lot of what I thought would work on the Ark . . . won't.

Hang on . . .

Omar is watching the nest. A miniature Juno is floating toward the opening.

That's Justice, says Naveed. The other female.

She is the spitting image of her mom, down to the white tip of her copper tail. She looks modest but purposeful as she drifts. Omar longs to hold her, but he waits, as Naveed waited with Whiteout.

Good trajectory, says Naveed.

They watch as Justice drifts, not toward the platz, but almost away from there and toward Naveed, who pushes gently away so as to prolong her flight.

That's good, Honey, says Naveed. Keep it coming. I'm here.

Omar glances back at the nest. The three males are in a tussle. A miniature Turk – perfect camouflage brindle – emerges on course for the opening.

That's Typhoon, says Naveed. At least that's what Ahiga has been calling him. He's been having some trouble naming the males.

Naveed has caught Justice and his stroking her fur. Nice flight, Sweetiepie.

Typhoon's velocity surprises Omar. He has to steady himself with one hand and reach out to catch him with the other. The close body once again kindles a powerful warmth.

Reluctantly, Naveed and Omar return their charges to Mom.

So, spin, says Omar. Something won't work on the Ark.

Naveed sighs. Yeah. I planned the 2 RPM spin around the hub. No problem there, or not much. But the diurnal rotation of the axis, for day and night . . . I don't know what I was thinking. It has been bothering me since we hooked up to this block of ice.

How?

It came over me slowly. You idiot! This is a gigantic gyroscope! It will have a huge resistance to a change in its axis of rotation. That's for one. And what came over me was the suspicion that even if we did succeed in inducing that diurnal rotation – and sure, the two rotations could be summed and considered as a single rotation about a new axis – but still, I had the suspicion it would decay to our original gravity rotation, around the hub. Preservation of angular momentum, or something.

Omar glances at the pups. Most of them are asleep, taking that puppy-nap that begins in an instant.

So – only one axis of rotation is possible? Or practical?

Yes. I read up on it. The Ark will wind up spinning around its principal axis of maximum inertia. In other words, around its hub.

And if you – say, using thrusters – get that axis spinning, so the hub is changing alignment . . .

That's called Polhode motion, with the axis describing a circle or an ellipse.

It will degrade.

Yes.

The two humans turn and consider the canines. They are asleep in what would be a heap if there were more gravity. As it is, it is some sort of mutual embrace.

A head pokes out. Omar thinks at first it is Journey. But the rest of the pup, as it breaks free from the heap, is not Journey. The copper brindle is broken by patches of white, more and more of them – and bigger – as you move aft. The tail is white with a copper tip. He is a funny-looking thing.

Naveed laughs. That's Coriolis, he says. At least, that's what I call him. I don't know if Ahiga is going to go for it.

Coriolis, like the force?

Yes, like the force that is not a force. At least, the first such force I encountered. There are going to be more. Like gravity.

Coriolis is on track for the opening. Omar shifts position for the catch. The pup sticks out a front paw, catching the edge of the net, then retracts the paw. He winds up in a slow backward tumble, on course for the platz.

This is going to be interesting, says Naveed.

Omar has pushed off and is following Coriolis, just in case.

Stretch out! counsels Naveed. Slow that rotation!

Coriolis does. As he passes inverted, relative to the humans, he sticks his paws out fore and aft.

Attaboy! says Naveed.

The rotation continues, but more slowly. A half-rotation later, nearly upright and head-first, Coriolis has time to draw in his hind feet and prepare for the landing, which is soft, uneventful, and on the grass. He takes a leak and looks up at the humans. It is a how'm I doin'? look. He pushes off toward Naveed.

That's my boy, says Naveed, catching him. Meet my friend Omar.

Omar accepts the funny-looking fur-ball and cradles him in his hands. Wow, he says.

Yeah, this one is something else, says Naveed.

●

It was hard to put Coriolis back. Omar wanted to keep him. Even now, he imagines the pup on his shoulder, nuzzling his ear, maybe giving it a little lick.

So, Naveed. What about our great block of ice?

Yes. Our experiment. In which we are part of the apparatus.

Omar lets the observation sink in. He can still imagine Coriolis on his shoulder.

We are all part of the apparatus, he says.

But we're not along for the ride, says Naveed. Remember – you designed the steam thrusters we added to the block. And the attachments for the thrusters we cast into the edges.

Omar nods, but he is watching the netting. Coriolis has appeared at the opening. He pushes off, gently, toward Omar.

And how we used them to align carefully for the first burn,

continues Naveed. And then to spin us for stability.

The pup is on course for Omar's right ear, but he hooks a front claw in the shoulder of Omar's jersey. The landing is not super-pretty, but neither participant seems to mind. The pup has a new friend.

Omar's new friend clings to the fabric on his shoulder and licks his ear, even giving it an occasional nibble. Omar realizes he is crying. He realizes that Naveed can see. Yes, he says.

And so far so good, says Naveed. Kindly and delicately, he engages Omar's gaze. We are on plan. But you're right. The Mars flyby is something new. New and untested.

And we're going to test it, says Omar.

Yes.

Naveed, Omar can tell, is moving back and forth, occupying both physical and emotional realities.

Yes, continues Naveed. But not without precautions. First, we're going to align, and stay aligned, with the Mars G vector during the flyby.

So it will be like the burn.

Yes, except the force – the thrust – will not be local, like it was in our rocket motors. And second, perhaps you and Gopi can put strain gauges on our attachments. So when we analyze all our data, we will have a science experiment.

Sure, we can do that. Omar has the pup in his arms and is stroking his fur.

And for what it's worth, says Naveed, I am pretty confident, at least in the Newtonian physics of it. I think there will be no strain, regardless of alignment. If you analyze our vessel as separate pieces, and consider them equidistant from Mars . . .

. . . in Newton's gravity equation.

Yes. You can show that the accelerations on all pieces of us are the same. So no moment.

•

Yes – I have talked it over with Omar. And with Eric and Gopi. We are confident in the Mars flyby. At least with the Newtonian physics of it.

So, says Ben. We are part of an experiment. And you say we will survive. That's good enough for me. But . . . you said at least with the Newtonian physics . . .

Yes, says Naveed. Newton is all we need for this maneuver. But now that we have the strain gauges wired, Eric and I decided to gather all the data we can. To look for relativistic effects.

Oh? says Ben. I'm curious – could you give me an example?

Sure. Frame dragging. While our path is being influenced by Mars, there will be other – very small – effects. And since the ship and its big block of ice are spinning, we are a huge gyroscope. Eric thinks we might just be able to detect some frame-dragging. That's when a relatively large body – like Mars – distorts spacetime enough to change our own inertial frame of reference.

Whew, says Ben. OK.

Ben is rubbing his fingertips together, an uncharacteristic fidget.

Since you're here, Naveed, I want to ask you something. I'm not sure if it's physics. Or what the heck it is.

I'll try, says Naveed.

Yeah. How do I start. Straight in, I guess.

Ben enfolds his fingers to stop the fidget.

A few of us have found that we know things. About loved

ones. Loved ones on the Ark.

Ben waits. Details can come later. He watches Naveed's reaction. It makes Ben think of a Buddha statue.

You said a few of us.

Yes.

You know, I have been studying so hard this last few weeks, learning so much, changing my mind so much . . .

Ben, too, emulates Buddha, listening.

. . . that, well, I didn't realize what I know until you asked me.

They sit, if it can be called that in minimal G. Ben tucks his legs into the Lotus pose, feet near opposite knees. He doesn't do the palms-up thing, but it is close.

Naveed smiles. Ameerah is near term. It is Isaac's child.

They sit. It is not enlightenment, but it is something. They are getting there.

You and Ameerah are close.

The contemplation clock ticks. We are on parallel tracks, thinks Ben.

I don't think there's even a word for it, says Naveed. We're not lovers.

Like Colin and me, says Ben.

The silent, parallel contemplation continues. Naveed nods. It is a slow and small nod, the ups equal to the downs. As if he were trying not to disturb his physical equilibrium.

You know something about Colin, he finally says.

Yes.

Ben has his eyes closed, a risky behaviour in low G when

unattached. Perhaps he, like Naveed, is calibrating his tranquility by his physical stillness.

Colin and I are halves of a whole, he says. Complementary pieces of a system.

Naveed watches Ben's very slow drift. Or is it his own? The ship is out of focus, and his perception is ignoring his peripheral vision.

Yes, he says. The system is not for procreation.

Naveed realizes he can't be really sure about anything. Drifting free, but almost still, he observes the eyes-closed, meditating Ben.

Not for sex, says Naveed. But for love.

Yes. For love.

Ben disentangles his feet. Slowly. He almost succeeds in holding attitude, hands free. In slo-mo, he reaches for a hand-hold.

Tell me, Naveed. Could this have anything to do with entanglement?

•

Bodies, thinks Naveed.

It is a new thought. As if they hadn't been here all along, he thinks.

Bodies are mass.

He is alone on pup duty. The five are asleep, one mass close to Juno. He imagines them as masses in space – the pups so close and still that they cohere, Mom Sun so close they orbit her.

I am not blind to beauty, he thinks. It just isn't what I have been thinking about. Ameerah, short and round. Now I imagine, rounder still. She has always known she is not like Niloo, a man magnet. Youssef was sweet on Ameerah, but he got distracted.

It has an inevitability, he thinks.

Two heads pop out. Puppies wake as fast as they drop off to sleep. Juno nuzzles the heads toward her teats.

I love her. I always have, but my head has been busy. Now she is in the covenant, because she knows what her purpose is. Probably better than any of us.

Bodies, though. They have a certain inevitability. When they are close something happens. They attract, although for one reason or another we often deny it.

Justice, the mini-Juno, floats out of the opening. Her aim is good, even though Naveed is some distance athwart-ship. He is ready to catch her, but her progress is languid enough that he waits. She twists paws-first and cushions her landing on his chest, where she tries to hold on. Naveed cradles her in his arms.

Nice one, sweetie-pie. You're getting good.

Unconsciously Naveed perches the pup on his shoulder, as he saw Omar do with Coriolis. Like him, she hangs on. Like him, she licks and nibbles his ear.

Sorry I'm late. Got drawn in. Trying to quantify Mars frame-dragging.

Eric stops at the portal, observing Naveed.

Hey, that's cute. How's he stay there? Claws?

She, says Naveed. This is Justice.

Oh. Eric drifts slowly along the chamber, doing a slow roll.

Does that hurt?

No. Her little claws are just grabbing fabric.

No, I mean your ear. Doesn't that hurt?

Naveed laughs. Not hardly. So. About frame-dragging . . .

Yeah. No. No chance.

How big is it?

Tiny. The Gravity Probe B experiment found 39 milliarc-seconds. *Per year.* That's in Earth orbit.

Per year. OK. So for us …

Yeah. So Mars to Earth mass is 1 to 10. We'll be in a Mars-influenced curve for what – 3 1/2 hours? That works out to a factor of about 3.5×10^{-4} relative to an Earth year. That's if we were in orbit, which we won't be. With Mars mass that's 10^{-5}.

So what does that work out to in …

Units that mean something to us? 39 milliarc-seconds is just under 10^{-9} radians. With our factors thrown in that's on the order of 10^{-14} radians.

OK, says Naveed. No way we could align on a distant star and measure to that accuracy. Gravity Probe B measured the precession of a gyroscope in the gravitational field of a rotating body, right?

Yeah.

OK, so we won't hold our breath.

No. Eric looks around. So, what do we do – catch them as they drift out of the net area?

Yup. Watch.

The mass that is the puppy blob is squirming, indicating the imminent expulsion of a smaller mass. A head appears. Journey, thinks Naveed. No – wait! You're not going to get me this time! It's Coriolis!

The fission is complete. The small mass, eponymous with the force that isn't a force, emerges on course for the opening.

Who's this? asks Eric.

It's Coriolis, says Naveed as he tracks the pup's flight.

Who named him? asks Eric.

Naveed laughs. I did.

I can't forget my little Justice, thinks Naveed, as the little claws cling tighter to his tunic.

Why? asks Eric.

I shouldn't have worried, thinks Naveed, as Coriolis makes a pretty good landing on his other shoulder.

You named him – it's a him, right? You named him after a force.

Yup, he's a him.

There is a pup nibbling on each of Naveed's ears. He laughs. Oh that tickles, he says. He reaches up and strokes the pups. Why? I don't know why.

He makes his way back to the opening and arranges the pups around Juno.

Eric, continues Naveed, do you remember how we scared Ben with the Sun sling maneuver?

Yeah. To escape the Solar System. So that's what I do? Catch a pup and then put him back?

Yup, that's it. 'Course you can cuddle him a bit, if the traffic isn't too heavy. That was the first time I had two at once . . .

So we decided not to, right? Leave the Solar System? Way too hot. Too much G. Besides we don't want to go that far just yet.

Eric, says Naveed. That's the thing. There may not be any G at all.

No G?

I know it seems weird. But think of orbit. Or now. We're on a curved path.

Yeah. No G.

But our motion is Newtonian.

Yeah.

Newtonian in curved space.

Holy shit! Of course!

The pups are learning, too, doing what they have to do – cohere, venture forth, learn their surroundings, then cohere again. Here, they know they can fly, but they don't know why. Eric, slightly nervous about this new task, is staring at the furry mass. Once again a smaller mass is ejected. Naveed has moved to one side to allow Eric try his hand at puppy-catching.

Who's this? asks Eric.

This is Whiteout, says Naveed.

I like that name. Is he a pilot?

Yup.

The pup's brown eyes – one in a copper patch, the other in the white of the rest of his body – fix on Eric. With a front paw, he catches the edge of the netting and pushes off obliquely. He winds up in a forward somersault and a slow roll to the right. He draws in his paws and tucks himself into a ball. The rotation speed about both axes doubles. He is headed straight for Eric's chest.

He was already good at attitude control, says Naveed. Looks like he's getting trajectory down, too.

At the last second the pup pops out of his ball shape, extending paws fore and aft. The rotation slows enough so he can plant his hind feet on Eric's shirt.

Holy shit, says Eric. He's good stick! You're good stick, pup!

Whiteout's front paws land softly, like a nosewheel. He looks up proudly at Eric.

And you know it, don't you? Eric strokes the pup's fur. You know it!

•

I'm sorry, Ben, says Naveed. I don't have an answer. Just a lot of thoughts floating around.

Naveed takes a breath. The chamber is all music. Rachel's violin and bow are held to the wall in improvised clips. Next to the keyboard is a screen with a partially-completed Sibelius score. Ben and Rachel have been working on something.

It's like music, continues Naveed. Then stops, suddenly struck by Rachel's beauty. Rachel, how do you do it? The Chaconne. How do you bring it to life? Make it so wonderful?

Hah! It is laughter, smile, exclamation. Rachel focusses her brown eyes on him.

It *is* wonderful. Something I love. I guess I . . . when it works well, it's because I'm listening. Listening with, I don't know . . . It feels like a furious intensity.

Maybe it is beyond meaning.

Yes, Naveed! You're right. I'm not thinking about meaning.

I'm thinking about your floating thoughts, says Ben. Could you share them? Rachel and I could listen. Like music. Maybe not for meaning.

I didn't realize I knew about Ameerah, says Naveed. Because my head was full of physics. And my feeling is that to survive we need that knowledge. All the knowledge of mankind.

Hold it cheap those who have never hung there, says Ben.

Just came into my head. It's a poem.

Hopkins, says Rachel.

Yes.

Naveed looks back and forth between them. The man with a depth none of them had suspected. The beautiful woman. The new couple.

Not just the knowledge, he continues. Also the timeline and evolution of that knowledge. I have been reading the Feynman *Lectures on Physics*. From the 1960's. Gravity Probe B wasn't born yet. Then in 2011 it was there. Two more of Einstein's predictions validated. Four years later the LIGO detected gravity waves. Gravity waves! Compression and rarefaction, just like sound. And audio frequency, to boot! Music!

That progression . . . says Rachel.

Naveed nods.

. . . makes us hopeful, says Ben. Even though what is truth seems to be evolving.

Yes, yes. That makes it hard, of course. People expect truth to be eternal. Fixed.

But not always, says Rachel. True?

More important, says Naveed, is that truth is what we share. You might say that truth and love are the only things that we truly share.

Sharing is the purpose of truth? asks Ben.

Yes, I think so. It is what connects us. Certainly science and math lead me to that conclusion.

I'm thinking of our Earth, says Ben. Nations, cities, neighbourhoods, even families. Split apart into millions of separate . . . truths? Maybe. By social media slicing and dicing us. Serving us up as certainties. For the profit of a very few.

Maybe sharing math and science are a bit like performing music, says Rachel. We agree that the Chaconne is wonderful, even if we don't know quite how it works.

Rachel plucks her violin and bow from the wall. Bows up and down from her A string. Tweaks the tuning of the E string. Launches, without a word, into the Chaconne. Eyes closed, shoes stuck to the floor, she plays. Very low gravity – even non-existent gravity – have become a norm for her. She can move, conducting with her body, and become a servant of the music, sharing a truth that no one understands.

It is thirteen and a half minutes of wordless wonder. The men are transfixed. As the final cadence dies away, they bow their heads. There are tears running down their cheeks.

Oh, my little Justice, says Naveed.

That's one of the pups, isn't it? says Rachel.

Yes, Rachel. She makes me cry, too.

Ben and Rachel make eye contact. Ben wipes a tear from his cheek. They wait.

Bodies, says Naveed. I have been thinking about bodies. For the first time, watching the pups. How could we re-phrase that saying? Some call it *Einstein Lite*.

He stops, perhaps embarrassed to be speaking of bodies.

Ben prompts. Something about mass and space?

Naveed pushes on, red-faced or not. It is perhaps a partial reaching toward our question, he says. Yes. Mass and space and maybe bodies, too, Ben.

Oh good! I hope so, Naveed. Our entanglement question. But first – tell me about *Einstein Lite*.

Yes. Well, Newtonian space turns out to be a special case – flat space, but where a mysterious so-called force called gravity operates. Einstein saw that gravity is not exactly a force. Instead, you could see it as Newtonian movement, but in a spacetime that is curved. Like the planets moving around Sun. Spacetime, he said, is curved, pushed, pulled, stretched and warped. By mass. Stuff. Even bodies.

And the famous saying?

Matter tells spacetime how to curve, and curved spacetime tells matter how to move.

And the pups, says Ben. Bodies. They are the mass? We are the masses?

We are certainly masses, says Naveed. And we influence each other. And the closer we get, the more the influence. Perhaps it is even like Newton's equation for gravity.

Proportional to the product of the two masses? Divided by the square of the distance separating them?

Precisely, says Naveed.

What about divide by zero? asks Ben.

Naveed colours. Ah, yes, he says. Zero. Well, perhaps the influence tends to infinity as a limit, if such a thing makes sense.

It does. Of course it does, says Rachel. That is a beautiful thought.

Naveed and Ben wait, contemplating completions of the beautiful thought.

Could I try to put it in terms of *Einstein Lite*? asks Rachel.

Oh yes, please, says the male chorus.

Bodies tell truth and love how to curve. How to stretch and warp, says Rachel. And truth and love, because they are shared, tell bodies how to move.

The male chorus nods in sync. Oh yes, I think so, it says.

And *hold it cheap*, continues Rachel. Hopkins was speaking of despair. Of cliffs of the mind: *Hold them cheap/May who ne'er hung there*. There is a respect. A great respect. I think that's why the line came to Ben.

She looks up. No, I *know* why. It is we who are hanging there. We who have our asses out . . . on the tightrope.

Naveed can feel embarrassment creeping into his cheeks again.

Naveed, Rachel continues, you said that to survive we need all the knowledge of mankind.

Yes, and then some, says the male chorus.

Perhaps our survival is hanging by a thread, says Rachel. But it is a thread made strong by all the truths mankind has shared. Throughout all generations. And by love.

And by love, echoes the male chorus. Throughout all generations.

Magnificat anima mea Dominum, Rachel smiles. *Ecce enim ex hoc beatam me dicent . . .*

. . . *omnes generationes*, concludes the male chorus.

> ~ *My soul doth magnify the Lord . . .*
> . . . *For behold, from henceforth: all generations shall call me blessed.* ~

●

Home

Part VI

VI

Home

Are God and Nature then at strife,
That Nature lends such evil dreams?
So careful of the type she seems,
So careless of the single life;

. . .

'So careful of the type?' but no.
From scarped cliff and quarried stone
She cries, 'A thousand types are gone:
I care for nothing, all shall go.'

. . .

Man, her last work, who seem'd so fair,
Such splendid purpose in his eyes,

. . .

Who trusted God was love indeed
And love Creation's final law –
Tho' Nature, red in tooth and claw
With ravine, shriek'd against his creed –

. . .

from In Memoriam

~ Alfred, Lord Tennyson ~

I don't know. Dad was cryptic.

Ben waits. Eric shows no sign he will speculate further.

OK, says Ben. It seemed to me like the Earth maneuver went as planned. Still scary as hell.

Well, pretty close, says Naveed. But remember the burn we did a couple of days before?

Yes, says Ben. A minor correction?

Actually, our trajectory was on target, says Eric.

Why, then? thinks Ben. I know we changed course. He waits, looks at Naveed, who shakes his head in that Persian way.

He's no help, thinks Ben. I know the Ark has left Moon orbit and we're following. But Eric is more that usually unforthcoming. What's eating him?

He looks back at Eric. So?

It was just after I heard from Dad, says Eric.

Ah, that's a clue, thinks Ben. OK, he says. Do you guys want to show me on the Sim?

That seems to do the trick. Ben watches as Eric backs up the Sim to before the correction burn.

Naveed narrates. So Ark leaves Moon orbit. Times its burn so it will wind up in Earth orbit, but just outside Moon's. Same direction but slower, so retrograde to Moon. From Earth, Ark is a small star, falling behind Moon, then overtaken and eclipsed a year or so later.

Ben nods.

So we don't want Moon orbit any more. We want Earth orbit, just like Ark, but slower, with Ark catching up to us.

Ben watches as Eric slows the Sim. Now it's not days, but hours slipping by. The belt ship has curved around Earth as it did around Mars, its trajectory bending away from Sun into an orbit similar to Earth's. Eric zooms in and turns on Traj Hist, where each body leaves a slowly vanishing line in space.

They are approaching now. Eric switches to real time and turns on Traj Proj.

Ben can see how it will work. There will be another burn, he says. To let us approach Ark. Or to let the Ark approach us.

Yes, says Naveed. Tomorrow.

Funny how this is not so scary, thinks Ben. Maybe because Earth is behind us, falling away. But I'm still in the dark. We were going to join Ark in Moon orbit and maneuver from there. Why has Ark cut loose? Left Moon?

Too much company, says Eric, answering the question Ben hasn't asked. Remember Dad's Potemkin stuff? Nation states proclaiming our works as theirs?

That's before I came aboard, says Ben. But sure. It's legend.

Well, since we left, others have been catching up. First India's lander went splat. Then Israel's. But then India stuck one. Others are following.

Moon orbit is going to be busy, says Naveed.

So . . . Noah . . . starts Ben.

Huh, says Eric. I think it's Dad. Or his idea. I think they've mined enough mass by now. I think with our water Dad thinks we're good for some years. I think he wants to back off. Avoid contact.

Ben looks at the two men. Then at the Sim trace, now painting them in real time. Then back at Eric. He didn't actually say that, says Ben.

No.

But you know.

Eric sighs, his frustration visible.

Yes, he says.

•

I have never felt better, thought Ameerah. Here I am, an ample baby at each ample breast. Not that I'm immodest. They *are* big. Both the babies and the breasts. And I was pretty darn big too, before they came.

Dear Latifah. What a help and companion she has been! Especially since that day she said, Honey, you got two in there! Thanks to Tifah I was never afraid. Those last months she coached me every day in the Lamaze techniques. Slow deep breathing. Shallow, fast, panting breathing.

That first week she said, Ameerah, I want to get Dad in here. He be a part of this too. It was kind of funny watching Isaac breathing with me, like it was the boy who would be having contractions. She said to me that week, Honey, I think we're going to get the boys to name the babies. You down with that?

I was surprised, I have to admit. But in a day or two I saw the wisdom of it. It is one thing to have a covenant, and another thing entirely to have a social structure working to the same end.

And when we told Isaac there were two – that was priceless. I watched the emotions roll through him, his transparent features readable like a book.

He took my hand and looked at me with those blue eyes. Did the innocent boy shuffle off his youth in an instant? No. But I could see something taking root. I could see myself in his eyes, his concern for me. For me and the babies. From that moment it seemed he never left me.

He did, of course. We ate and slept and went through the normal rhythm of the days. We rehearsed with Latifah until each stage of labour was as familiar as getting dressed. But when my contractions started Isaac was there in a minute and never left my side. It was Tifah who said, you two doin' fine, I gonna go and get me a bite. She went for several over those eighteen hours.

Isaac just went to pee when I was between contractions.

And it was Isaac who said to Latifah when she came back, I think we're in transition. D'you wanna check?

Well, she did, and I was ten centimetres with a lip.

Almost there, honey, she said. She put her hands under my big belly. First one's good, she said. In position.

Then my waters broke with a rush. Good thing we're on the 0.1 G level. We were able to sop up the fluid. For a second I imagined myself in zero G, my fluid floating around me in little droplets. Me, embarrassed, trying to chase them.

But no, we're here and we all weigh one tenth of our Earth weight, which is fine with me. My arms are tired enough holding these two big boys to my breasts. Imagine if they weighed ten times as much!

I remember my numb relief as the first one came into this world. This world!

Yes, right here. Where I chose to be. Where I'm doing exactly what I chose to do. And somehow a miracle is happening. The satisfaction of the baby's movement somehow makes the pain – not go away, but go somewhere else. Somewhere more remote.

Next push and the baby's out, says Latifah. She has both hands down there, holding – the baby's head, I guess.

That's right, that's it, good. Good!

Latifah held him up. Look at this! A fine big boy!

He was pink to the point of red with circulation. The picture of health. With the cord dangling off him. Latifah was reaching for a clamp. He was crying – breathing, all on his own.

What you gonna call him?

She had discussed this moment with Isaac, of course. Now she was triumphant, looking at him and smiling.

Eric, says Isaac.

After your Daddy!

Um, yeah.

Latifah turns Eric around, inspecting him from head to toe. You OK, boy, she says. We give you a minute on your cord even though you breathin' good. Then we gonna wrap you and lay you down for a bit. You got a sib comin'.

There we go. All right! Now Isaac, give me a hand here. Your next person needs a little straightening out. See where my hand is? Push here, like this. Gentle, but firm. That's his butt.

I couldn't help it. You think it's another boy? I asked.

Tifah laughed. I don't know, Honey. I'm just mouthin'. That's it, Isaac. Good. His head's engaging. But he a bit twisted. That butt's gotta go down.

Isaac pointed with his free hand. Like this?

Yeah. We want to turn him about a quarter-turn so he face up. Makes it all work better. Now don't push yet, Honey. Lemme hear that panting.

Isaac, trained like a dog, started panting before I did. I almost laughed. That was good, because what I did was relax and let their hands work. I felt the baby move – twist in my womb.

Hang on a minute, Honey. Gotta check for engagement.

She was so sure in her movement. So calm. So definite. Sure – I was the one giving birth. But it was my body and Latifah and Isaac doing the work, it seemed to me. I was almost a spectator.

Head's engaged, said Tifah. Just right. This be a dark-haired boy! OK, Honey. What do pilots say? You're cleared to push at your discretion.

I guess I did – or my body did. By this time she had handed light-haired Eric to Isaac, who was watching the second birth with Eric clutched to his chest.

They were watching. I was pushing. It was not intellectual. My body seemed to know what it was doing.

Isaac was holding Eric. Latifah was holding my hand, talking to the baby. To the baby we were about to meet.

And then she wasn't holding my hand. She was catching the baby.

Oh, you a beautiful dark-haired boy, she said. Like your Daddy.

She held him up. Gave him one just-right slap on the back, and he cried.

That's right, boy, she said. You show them how it's done. She held him up for us to see.

He *is* beautiful, like his Daddy. Pale skin. Long and lean. Dark hair and blue eyes.

They fraternal. Not at all alike, says Latifah. She looks around for Isaac. Gives her head a toss. So what you gonna call this one? This lovely boy?

Jacob, says Isaac.

All right all right! Jacob and Eric!

Latifah takes a step toward Isaac. She wraps Jacob in a blanket and motions for Isaac to take him. He doesn't hesitate. In his arms the babies are aligned, side by side, on display.

I bet they hungry, says Latifah. I know they gone be fine, 'cause you been leakin' colostrum these last few days, and that's all they need right now.

She motions to Isaac, who steps closer.

Left side, left breast, says Latifah, as she takes Eric and offers him to me. I am uncovering my left breast before I realize what I am doing.

Right now it just be a teaspoon or two, says Latifah. But that's OK, 'cause that be the size of his stomach.

Isaac's eyes are wide. I realize both Latifah and I are laughing. Whether it is relief or the tickle of Eric's little mouth on my nipple, it just seems to have happened. I am flooded with gratitude.

Isaac is holding Jacob with both hands, preparing to hand him to Latifah.

So the story be, says Latifah, just a teaspoon be fine, but a teaspoon often. They be awake, put them to the breast.

I was already uncovering my right breast. Sure enough, there was a wet spot on the gown.

See? says Latifah. She nods at Isaac. You got him, Papa. You bring him to Mamma. She looks me in the eye. And Mamma, don't you worry. See, there's more to the story. Today it's teaspoons every two hours. Tomorrow a little more. 'Cause every time they nurse your body respond. Your lactation progress. Next day some milk in the colostrum. Next day more.

Isaac is settling Jacob into my right arm, helping him line up comfortably with my breast. He is speechless with wonder.

. . .

It is four days later. Latifah is here for her morning visit, checking the twins and weighing them, talking to me and I know observing my mood. But I'm feeling fine.

They down about five percent, she says. But that be right on schedule. And the story say that next week they start to gain weight. So let's see – how you doin'?

Tifah walks over and uncovers one of my breasts. She pokes it with an expert finger. Four fine jets of milk squirt almost a metre into the air, and keep squirting for several seconds after she takes her finger away.

Oh yeah, Honey, she says. You doin' fine.

•

After the austerity of the belt ship, the Ark takes Naveed by surprise. It is smell, more than anything, he thinks. True, the Belt Ship air was more moist and comfortable after we got the Carnot cycle turbines spinning. But this – it is from my youth in Iran. The country. Loam, leaves, and rain. The simultaneous scent of rot and life. Compost and bloom.

He has been descending level by level from the hub, trying to acclimatize to more G than he has felt in a long time. Well, with the possible exception of a few minutes-long burns, and those only before they took on the ice block. Now at the 0.8 G level he is about to descend into the outer ring, into what he visualized and then designed back then as *parks*.

Naveed steps through a doorway and onto a balcony and is instantly in tears. Good thing I'm doing this tour alone, he thinks. There is a warm, gentle breeze on his face. This is late spring or early summer, after the suggestions of September he had been getting closer to the hub. A small bird flies by him and lands in a treetop about one level below him. He looks up. There must be at least a couple of levels above him, giving the trees room to grow, but he can't continue looking up because of the glare.

Another bird flies by and alights in the same tree. One of them starts to sing. Naveed recognizes it as a thrush, a bird he knows well from his adopted Canada. Starting in May, he would learn their tunes. Different tunes every year, and a different tune for each individual bird. Every year two, three, or four birds hung around his home. He knew their songs – motifs, really – and would whistle them back to the bird. He had no idea what the birds thought of his imitation.

Naveed wipes a tear from his cheek and listens. The first notes – *sol mi do sol* – make a major 6/3 chord, the *do* being on top. The bird then adds *mi mi mi mi*. How close, he thinks. How close to the very first Canadian thrush he heard. How long ago was that? Ten years?

Naveed whistles his imitation. The bird answers. Is he trying to find a mate? Am I messing that up? thinks Naveed. Maybe I better not.

Ameerah is in his head. Visiting her is next on his list, but she's here now, in this summer breeze.

•

Ahiga, Turk, and Juno are supervising the pups. They have made it down to the 0.3 G level in their training.

Ahiga and Turk seem to be communicating, more than supervising. Turk is pant-talking, demanding Ahiga's attention. Ahiga breathes and emits the occasional click or growl. Neither of them notices when Whiteout jumps up, does a somersault and full roll, then sticks a four-paw landing. As he lifts his head, he sees Eric in the doorway. With a confident smile, he jumps again. Eric braces for the catch. The top of the pup's 0.3 G parabola is magically a couple of centimetres from Eric's chest. Eric just has to close his arms.

Man, Ace. You're getting big, says Eric. And you're not having a real hard time with G, are you?

He strokes the wiggling dog as best he can. Whiteout's soft muzzle is pressed against Eric's face.

You're getting to be a real muscle-y guy! Before long I won't be able to lift you anymore. Even in 0.5 G!

•

It's all right, thought Rachel, steeling herself. Just do it.

She works her way down to the 0.5 G level, where many of her friends seem to have taken root. She has been home less than a day, and comprehending the changes since they left on the belt mission is just as difficult as re-adapting to G. Her feet hurt and her arms feel heavy at her side. She plants her palms on her hips for support.

Latifah should be in this quadrant, thinks Rachel. Unless she's got a class or a delivery somewhere. I suppose I could ask someone ...

Sweetie! It's you!

Rachel looks around. Tifah has a huge smile. She also has a huge belly. Oh I'm so happy to see you, says Rachel. Oh I'm so happy it's true!

Latifah enfolds her in an embrace – not a trivial task with the size of that abdomen. Rachel feels her doubt and fear melting away.

Oh welcome home, Sweetie! You look as delicious as ever, says Latifah. Are you in love?

Rachel colours, speechless. She gives way to Latifah's embrace, her knees weak.

Let's sit, Honey, says Latifah. Let's sit and chat awhile.

●

Naveed has brought friends to the reunion.

I thought you should meet the females, he says. If I'm going to meet the males.

He has one pup under each arm, a feat still barely possible on the 0.1 G level.

Yesss, says Ameerah. They're ... beautiful!

Beautiful is a full four syllables of music. She opens her arms to display the babies.

Yes, says Naveed. They are beautiful. Could you introduce me?

Eric, says Ameerah, nodding at her left armload. She smiles at Naveed and the pups before displaying the baby in her right arm. And Jacob.

Wow, says Naveed. Well, here's Journey.

Journey squirms as Naveed twists to present her.

Oohh! sings Ameerah. What do you call her coat? Is there a word?

Copper brindle, says Naveed. She's a perfect mix of her mom and dad.

Oohh, yesss! With difficulty, Ameerah manages to tear her gaze away and do the polite thing. And this person?

That's my little Justice, says Naveed.

Justice is wiggling in his arm, trying to get her face closer to his.

I can see that, says Ameerah. Looks like you're made for each other.

Naveed blushes. And you? Are you OK?

●

OK, Dad. How far along is she?

Andrew opens his mouth and inhales. But he doesn't get any further. He stares at his son as if dawn were breaking. A blush of red blooms on his neck, below his ears. It is most unlike Andrew to be struck dumb.

I don't mean to . . . I'm happy, Dad. I'm happy for you.

Gazing at his son, also a father, he begins to recognize what is passing between them. Not just a father, but a grandfather twice over, he realizes, as if for the first time.

It is the first time, he thinks. Sure, he knew Ameerah had given birth to twin boys. Sure, he knew who the father was. But until Eric was standing before him, the knowledge hadn't – what, clicked into place?

I love you, Dad. I'm really happy to see you.

Andrew opens his arms. That he is doing so seems impossible, because his thoughts are not involved. His thoughts – what he is living – are a dream-like rush of a thousand landings. It is that instant when time stops. That moment the flare begins and there is no there but here. The here a set of asymptotic curves in three dimensions – no, four – all moving toward the touch of that first wheel or landing pad.

Now with his son in his arms, it is like the rollout. Or, latterly, the engine shutdown. You can still screw up, big-time, because you're still in the thick of it and your concentration isn't anywhere near what it was a moment ago. You are still rolling down the runway at expensive speed. Or the struts are still compressing under the local G – balance still a goal, not a fact.

Now with his son in his arms he knows. He knows that Eric knows and has known. There is nothing for him to say.

Don't screw this up, is what he is thinking. You've stuck thousands of landings. You've screwed up three marriages, at last count.

The genealogy is lined up before him. A begat B begat C. This son of his is a grandfather. He himself is, right now, a great-grandfather. And he, Andrew, is not yet done being a father. Gently, holding Eric by the shoulders, he pushes him out to arm's length so he can look at him, blue eyes into blue eyes. No, there is no need for him to say a word.

Dad, says Eric, there's someone I'd like you to meet.

Magically, Whiteout has replaced Eric in Andrew's arms.

This guy is good stick, Dad, says Eric. You won't believe it!

•

Thanks. Yes. Fingers crossed.

Colin puts down his chef's knife. Puts his fingertips down on his cutting board, as if he were preparing pizza dough.

He laughs. Touch wood.

Ben laughs, too. It has been a while since he has been swept up in his friend's presence. So, ah, is there a due date?

Don't know for sure. But Tifah says within a month. And from the way she looks, that's no lie.

That's wonderful, Colin. Ben drifts slowly around the prep table. So you're cooking for the whole ship?

Heavens, no. I have a lot of help. It's all organized in chains now. Dominic's bread, for example, starting with Alex and Nurul. They develop the wheat strains. Then you grow the wheat – farming. Then harvest, milling . . . hey, speaking of bread, you gonna do beer?

Sure, if we agree. That we want it and we can handle it. As a society. Ben is still circling the table, with no apparent purpose. He is eyeing the vegetables Colin is preparing, beer having been sidelined for the moment.

Can I help?

Colin laughs, moving his chef's knife off the cutting block and placing it neatly at the side. I get the feeling, he says, I better not try doing two things at once here. His fingers are back on the block in the pizza dough position, except the thumbs are on the near edge. He tries the direct approach. You knew stuff about other people?

If Ben is surprised, it doesn't show.

No. It's not that. Many of us on the belt ship knew things

about people on the Ark. People we're close to.

Wait a sec. Colin abandons his knife and cutting board and starts his own tour of the table. He stops, holding the edge of the table, and closes his eyes. You want to follow all this up. You have a feeling about connection and love. How it's going to help us.

Yes.

And there's more. Something more immediate. He opens his eyes and catches Ben's light nod. You want to know if Noah knew.

Colin pauses again, keeping to a musical rhythm – a repetitive motif beginning on the upbeat after a bar of silence.

You want to know if Noah knew.

If Noah knew that Art had died.

If Noah knew that Omar was redeemed.

•

So you did a frame-dragging experiment? Wesley sounds excited. With the ice block?

Naveed sighs. Actually, no. We would have loved to, but Eric did the math. It was . . . I forget, but it was many powers of ten below what we could detect.

Oh. Yeah. That makes sense.

They are strolling along paths in the outer ring, wending their way among crops and mini-forests. It is ambrosial, and bucolic but without the sheep. Naveed, though, is trudging more than strolling. One G is still a bit much.

But I like the way you said the whole ship was an experimental apparatus, Wesley continues. With the ice block.

Yes. Omar was worried about the connecting trusses. So he

and Gopi rigged strain gauges. For our encounters with Mars and Earth gravity.

And? Wesley has that smile he gets when he is teaching.

Naveed has spotted a bench where three paths join. Mind if we sit for a minute?

Sure.

As they sit a bird flies by and lands in a tree. He sings. Naveed recognizes his thrush.

Mars was the rehearsal, he says. The test. Earth G would be ten times stronger. So Eric and I – we started the maneuver with the ship and the ice block aligned on the G vector.

So if there were a force, it would be compression. Or tension.

Right. No bending.

And? Wesley has the smile again. Naveed feels like a student.

No compression. No tension. So we . . .

You and Eric.

Yes. Well, Eric. He had designed an attitude system to keep us aligned. When we saw no strain on the gauges . . .

Uh huh.

Eric looked at me and said, One degree? and I nodded yes. He had designed a control for the allowable attitude error. To avoid needless thruster firing.

Uh huh, says Wesley.

So he let it go up to one degree.

Uh huh.

The two, then five. Nothing. I looked at Eric. It was a weird moment. He looked at me with a funny smile. We were being so careful. But there was nothing on the strain gauges. He tapped a few keys and brought up our G sensor. It is on the ship's axis, so the tiny G of our spin wouldn't show up. It read zero.

No strain, no G, he said.

No G, no strain, I replied.

We both laughed, but we both felt stupid, too.

You shouldn't, says Wesley. I admire you. You were doing an experiment. You were doing one of Einstein's thought experiments. Except, as you say, you were part of the apparatus.

The one about being in a free-falling container? Even now, months later, Naveed still feels sheepish.

That's the one, says Wesley.

We talked about it, Eric and I. We couldn't believe we . . . I don't know. That we had to test it.

Wesley's smile is more open, almost triumphant.

But you did test it! Good for you! And you thought about it. Good for you!

The thrush sings again, but he doesn't remove the colour from Naveed's neck. Perhaps encouraged by the thrush, Naveed presses on.

What we thought was, of course there's no G and no strain. Our course is a Newtonian straight line.

Yes, says Wesley.

This curve we are describing, in the simulator – heck, relative to the solar system – is a Newtonian straight line. But we timed it so it would pass near Mars. And then Earth. Because orbit is cyclical. Periodic.

Uh huh.

And because we went close, our path would go through a ripple in spacetime. A section that is curved. On a smaller scale than Sun's curve. It's no different, really, from being in orbit.

Wesley smiles broadly and claps Naveed on the shoulder.

Well done, you two, he says. That's a beautiful example of the advancement of science!

●

Yes, says Wesley. He knew. I think he knew immediately that something was wrong.

Did Noah talk to you about it? Ben is doing his best to be a support and not a threat. He can feel the unease rolling off Wesley in waves.

Not at first.

Ben waits. He can see Wesley forming the story, perhaps for the first time.

Yeah, says Wesley, after the silence. You see – I think Art was still alive. I mean, when Noah knew but didn't talk about it.

Ben concentrates on listening. On listening and on playing back what he can remember. On keeping the two synchronized.

By the time we talked, a few days had gone by. Noah was in a strange state. He still couldn't put much into words. *It's Art*, he would say. I would listen, as you are listening now. *It's Art. I don't know.* That's about all he could say.

In his head Ben is listening to Art in Stores F the day Rachel revived him. Art was about to tell the story of Omar. But just before, Ben remembers, it was the story of Art. He has not thought of this before, not remembered it until now. *It's like there is a window*, Art had said. *I can see clearly. But the window is going to close.*

How many stories am I hearing? thinks Ben. Art's. Omar's. Noah's. And Wesley's and mine.

I was worried, continues Wesley. So I stopped by to see Noah several times a day. I don't remember for how many days. Then one day . . .

Wesley closes his eyes and bows his head.

. . . one day it was different. He looked at me with big eyes and said, *It is done.* There were tears rolling down his cheeks. I just sat with him then, because I could feel it, too. You, Ben. You had a ceremony. You and Rachel.

●

Ben said we did well, thought Naveed. I have to remember that.

He has been spending most of his waking hours in the outer ring. Why, he is not sure. He is still working on it. He knows it is partly for Nature, if you can call it that. More accurately, you could say *other species*, or *life other than human.* Or maybe just *life.*

That's good, he thinks. I like that. *Life. Bodies. Place.* Because mass, energy, and curved space are not everything. There is more than just the Einstein stuff. But that stuff is the base. Under certain conditions, life can spring forth from that base.

I'm making no sense, thinks Naveed. I'm just an engineer. A dilettante in everything else. He sighs. Well, maybe a learner . . .

He has been mostly alone these last weeks, re-living the voyage of the Belt Ship. It is like a waking version of a bad dream. Failures and missteps from the past push their way into his consciousness, displacing his attempts to . . . what? Think? Think productively? Make something new?

The outbound trip swims into his head, making him dizzy. His favourite bench is just ahead. He walks the ten paces and sits, closing his eyes. The Belt Ship is whizzing by Earth, just missing her. Scary as hell. He and Eric had worked it out, using textbooks on Orbital Mechanics. Yes, and using his insights on periodicity – in this case the position of Mars in its orbit relative to Earth. And the Mars flyby had worked, too. After that they were in a transfer orbit in the plane of the ecliptic, the apogee somewhere in the Asteroid Belt. That much had worked.

But looking back, thought Naveed, were he and Eric the only ones who knew even that much? Captain Omar, engineer and pilot, but distracted by . . . it was as if he were split in two, two people who weren't speaking to each other. He didn't understand our navigation then, and he still doesn't. Somehow his split self slipped under Sebastien's radar. Easy to see now he was already smitten with Ferdinand. That slipped by Ahiga, too.

Or did it? Maybe we were all too taken with Ahiga's ability to talk to the dogs to realize he could feel us, too. All of us. We think of him as taciturn. Perhaps it is only that he has very little need to speak.

Ben, thought Naveed. He was on board because he wanted to come. Was he already in love with Rachel? But Sebastien was fascinated by Ben. By Ben and Colin. In the end it was Seb and Ahiga sensing Ben's big, calm presence. A wordless presence, like Turk. Ben was unaware of our close encounter with Mars. I guess I was asleep, he said. But no. Maybe he was, but that's not it. You *could* sleep through it. There was no G.

There was no G! Naveed is suddenly sweating. His fine, beaked nose is dripping, and it's not snot. His underarms are a swamp, drenching those parts of his shirt and launching odour particles like a dog in heat.

He looks around, embarrassed. He is alone. He *never* smells like this! He breathes out, trying to still the reaction. Ignorance!

But what he feels is shame. We were like – what is the saying? English, not Persian. Not French. *Babies in trees?*

He opens his eyes. He is still alone, surrounded by trees. There is a bird. He doesn't see the bird, but he hears its song. Two long notes. The second exactly one full tone lower than the first. The Black-Capped Chickadee.

He sighs again. Controlled breathing to control what he is having difficulty controlling. The bird helps.

Maybe it – the shame – has come because of Feynman. He has been reading the *Lectures on Physics* since they left Ceres orbit. A bit at a time. A very little bit at a time.

Feynman is a great teacher, thinks Naveed, but a brutal one. He doesn't tease open a student's understanding so something new can slip in.

No. He writes an equation on the board. This is Quantum Electrodynamics. Follow me in. If you can.

Naveed is breathing again. The chickadee sings his two-note song.

Yes – maybe that is where my shame comes from. I can't always follow him. It is a long and arduous journey.

Journey. We survived ours. I have to remember that. Journey is Ameerah's pup. They were instantly close. You could see it plain as day.

Naveed can feel his face and neck flush. Probably his swamps are burping different odour particles. Ameerah. I would do anything for a few minutes in her presence, he thinks. He shuts his eyes again and listens for the chickadee. He breathes slowly until the smell of the trees displaces his own smell.

I have to remember Ben says we did well. I have to remember Wesley said we did well.

But we lost Art. Art understood us. With all our weakness and folly. Art *did* love us all. He understood, better than any of us, what our mission is. Better even than Noah.

Ohhh! There are tears running down Naveed's cheeks. He laughs. My stupid body is producing all these liquids, he thinks. What's next? And what does all this have to do with knowledge? With reason? With moving ahead with what we have to do?

He breathes in the smell of the forest. Well, a woods, really. There isn't room for a forest on the Ark. Babes. *Babes in the woods.* That's what we are. All of us.

•

It is a party. No beer, or at least not yet, but the space has potential. It has grown out of Wesley's observation, at the covenant ceremony, that citizens of the Ark need a place to gather.

It is a church and a dive bar. Or neither. Or everything in between – theatre, restaurant, concert hall, pub.

Wesley reserved a full 0.1 radian arc on the 0.6 G level. The hall is 100 metres long, 62 metres wide, and 38 metres high, fulfilling the proportions of the Golden Ratio. As yet unfinished, the acoustic is still too echo-y. But that will change. Ideas will flow in as parties, concerts and ceremonies occupy its bare space. It will slowly morph into its potential and into its importance for the community.

Today is pilots' day. Andrew is preacher, concertmaster, bartender. Colin has prepared a vegetarian feast. Dominic is stacking ciabatta alongside the baguettes and round loaves. It is a mouth-watering sight.

The pilots are gathered, with their pups, on the raised apse/ choir/stage/bar. Andrew. Eric and Whiteout. Isaac. Ameerah and Journey and babies Eric and Jacob. Ferdinand. Omar and Coriolis. Youssef. Andrew has used the last hour to have a pilot briefing before the others arrive. He is in a good mood, even for Andrew. Problems, it seems, can be laughed away.

He's still a good Captain, thinks Ameerah. Funny – the pilot part of me has been on hold since I began to get big. But he has made me feel like a pilot again. And this group has been through a lot together, especially since Youssef and Isaac tipped over. The way Andrew got the operation – heck, got *us* – going again. Now our group has been years apart. So this is a reunion of sorts.

She looks around the huge room. The non-pilots are beginning to drift in. All are initially attracted to Colin and Dominic and their feast-spread table down in the centre. The pilots in their place of pride are, at least for the moment, ignored.

I know what Andrew is going to say, thinks Ameerah. He hinted as much to us. We knew already how father and son and grandson had put code and flying skills together in the landers. Now there's more. It is Andrew and Wesley who flew the Ark out of Moon orbit. Niloo who joined them to engineer the attitude and flight controls. So piloting and engineering and physics have all come together.

And I hear from Wesley that Eric and Naveed made a pretty good team while they were away. That Naveed is into physics and Eric into math. I'm so glad they're back safe. I didn't realize until I saw Naveed . . .

Andrew is waving . . . oh, it's Niloo. Look at her! She is getting big! Oh – and Rachel and Ben heading for Colin. She's got her violin case!

Ameerah.

It is Isaac, opening his arms. I'll take them, Ameerah. Go get something to eat.

He hugs her, in preparation for the transfer. They've fed. You haven't.

Journey . . .

Take her. I see her sister coming in.

Isaac has New Eric cuddled in his left arm. Ameerah uses both of hers to transfer Jacob. She looks out over the gathering crowd. Sure enough – there's little Justice, not so little anymore, trying to get Naveed's attention. She wants him to pick her up, but he is holding his violin case. He looks perplexed.

Niloofar gets to him before Ameerah does. By the time she gets close Niloo is jabbering away and Naveed is looking increasingly confused. It takes Ameerah a minute to realize, from the music of it, that Niloo is speaking Farsi.

Naveed responds with monosyllables, and with nods which could be yes or no or both.

Niloo is obviously in one of her moods. Ameerah can't recall seeing her like this since before they left Earth. Ameerah does not know a word of Persian, but – two or three times so far – she thinks she has caught the word *Wesley*.

Justice has wiggled away from the distracted Naveed, delighted to smell her sister. Ameerah can smell the food, but she is on her knees, each of her hands connecting with a pup. She is aware that Ben and Rachel have joined Colin and Dominic at the food table.

I have dreamt, too . . .

Perhaps distracted by the group at the table, Naveed has switched to English. But in Persian or English, Niloofar is still pissed.

Not dreamt, Naveed. I *heard* him prattling away about Constantine. The establishment of Christianity in the Fourth Century. Nicene Creed. Blah, blah. I don't like being *invaded*, Naveed. Nobody – *nobody*, Naveed, does that to me! Whatever system he has set up to pipe that shit into my ears . . .

Naveed offers a distraction. Niloo. Did you know today is Easter?

The Persians have drifted so close to the table that Ben, hearing English, cannot help getting caught in the conversation.

Last night was Vigil, continues Naveed. We were here, in this room, playing Bach. We are planning more for today.

Yes – a bit more upbeat today, says Rachel, giving Niloo one of her beautiful smiles.

Struggling to her feet, Ameerah tries to make sense of this scene. Invasion. Constantine. Easter. Wesley?

Rachel. It has been years since she last saw her. She knows Rachel and Latifah are close. "... *a bit more upbeat today* ..." That voice gives her goose bumps.

Dreams. Naveed spoke of dreams, thought Ameerah. Who have I dreamed of? Who might have dreamed of me?

You know, says Ben, I dreamt of Constantine last night.

What! Niloofar spits the word more than says it.

It is strange, thinks Ameerah. Niloo is at her most beautiful when she is angry. And Rachel ...

She sneaks a glance in Rachel's direction. Rachel's beauty is shyly hidden. When she smiles, it bursts forth like Sun coming from behind the clouds. Ameerah looks away, embarrassed by the sudden tightness in her chest.

Yes, says Ben. Not surprising, really. I spent some time yesterday talking with Wesley about Constantine.

Niloofar fixes Ben with a withering stare.

He is quite ... well, het up by him. And I admit, the human conundrum presented by the man is ...

What did he say about Constantine? asks Colin.

Well, says Ben, he was the first Roman Emperor to convert to Christianity. He set up the Council of Nicaea, from which emerged the Nicene Creed, used to this day as the Credo during the celebration of Mass.

Sounds OK so far, says Colin.

That was in 325. The next year he had his oldest son executed. His wife was next, a month or so later.

Oh, says Colin.

Yes, says Niloofar. Crispus and Fausta. And why? Why, do you think?

Oh, my, thinks Ameerah. You think you know people. She knows their names! Ben looks like he has been hit with a club!

Why. That is a good question, Niloo, says Ben. And I have another. How do you know this – this stuff piped into your ears – comes from Wesley?

It's *his voice*, Ben. I'm not stupid!

And what about . . . what about when Persia invaded Armenia. I think that was in 336?

That was Prince Narseh. I know Armenia was Christian. But we didn't *invade*. Narseh didn't persecute Christians. We were just protecting our western flank. But look at Constantine! He was mounting a crusade against Persia. A *cru-sade!*

True, true, says Ben. But then he got sick and died.

This was supposed to be a party, thinks Ameerah. Now all the air is gone from the room. But the pups don't care. They are rolling around together, playing bitey games. They don't care about Constantine.

But Crispus and Fausta, Niloo, says Ben. I'm curious. Why?

He was boffing her, you fool, says Niloo. What emperor is going to allow that?

Oh my, thinks Ameerah. Now the air is really gone. But the

pups. They are bodies attracting. They are dragging Naveed and me with them. And here is Andrew, filling the place beside Niloo where Naveed was a minute ago.

Andrew's smile seems to have a calming effect on Niloo. There is more movement, of people and dogs, opening up a corridor.

And here is the man himself, says Ben.

Indeed, Wesley is making his way toward the table.

Wesley! We have been talking about you, says Ben. Or about Constantine. But never mind. I think the time has come to talk about our present . . . our present question.

Ben greets Wesley, two arms on two arms. Wesley looks Ben in the eye. Wesley's nod of assent is barely perceptible.

So, everyone. Ben opens his arms to the crowd. Here it is. We have mass and water and life. We are doing well. We will celebrate. But now we have to talk about another thing that is happening.

Ben looks around at the assembled citizens of the Ark. They have formed a circle around the table The pilots have come down from their stage.

We — some of us, or perhaps most of us — have experienced something new and strange.

•

I shouldn't worry, thought Naveed. There are so many things this could be about. Wesley said, Meet me at our bench, so here I am.

It is easier here to be still.

Still, it is not the silence of a starry Persian night in his youth. There is a distant whoosh of moving air, but come to think of it, there is no breeze today.

I will have to ask Wesley, he thinks. If I can remember.

In the distance, a thrush sings:

sol sol sol sol mi do

A 6/4 chord. A short burst of percussion on *sol* to finish.

Not my original thrush, thinks Naveed. A new person.

He is suddenly back in the big room two days ago, one of the elements in the horseshoe around Ben. Once again, he is part of an experimental apparatus. We were an amoeba, he thinks. One body changing shape. It is not clear how. But as our shape changed it became readable. There was information there. Like a string of ones and zeros becoming hexadecimal notation. Then ASCII tables and printed letters, words, paragraphs.

Maybe the information was there all along, thinks Naveed. But the horseshoe, for the time Ben was speaking, had structure. It was as if we solidified, our water becoming a crystalline lattice of ice, held together by weak hydrogen bonds . . .

Sorry to startle you. May I?

Of course.

Wesley did startle me, he thinks. I was somewhere else.

Wesley sits as Naveed shifts slightly and gestures to a spot beside him on the bench. The new thrush sings into the ensuing silence. Possible topics begin to sift back into Naveed's thoughts.

Action at a distance? Naveed realizes his thoughts may have leaked out.

Wesley laughs. Thoughts at a distance? Or the force that isn't a force? He smiles. I like those thoughts. We'll talk more about them. But no.

Wesley adjusts his butt slightly and crosses a leg, preparing for exposition.

You probably know through Eric that Andrew was

preparing for a while to fly us out of Moon orbit . . .

Naveed, as he nods, is thinking he has to remember to ask Wesley why there is no breeze here today.

. . . and of course you know he did, just before you got back. He shakes his head. Of course you do. Get your act together, Wesley.

The thrush sings, allowing Wesley time to regroup.

Did you know there's a global pandemic on Earth?

Naveed shakes his head. No words come.

Of course. It's not like we're watching TV up here.

The thrush adds two percussion bursts this time.

It's nasty, Wesley goes on. It's everywhere. Over two million people infected. Almost ten percent of that number dead. And it's sneaky. If you catch it, you are asymptomatic for a week and yet throwing off virus at a great rate, infecting others.

Naveed works hard, trying to catch up, to stay abreast of the implications. So there's very little information . . .

Exactly. So the spread expands exponentially. The only thing that works so far is self-isolation. They're calling it *Social Distancing*.

So for us . . .

So far so good, says Wesley. No one has come on board since the end of the year. And as far as we can see no one has the virus. But just now I briefed Rachel on it and got her access to the information. She is going to work with Nurul to devise some testing.

Is that why . . .

There's more. Moses is not on board.

But we have left Moon orbit . . .

Yes. Before you got back Andrew knew Eric knew enough to follow. This Earth orbit we're in – he set it up so you wouldn't have a large delta-V to follow and intercept.

Yes. He did well. It wasn't a long burn.

And there's still more. Andrew and Niloofar follow all Moon traffic, of course. But they look at Earth orbit, too, out to geosync diameter.

Oh, and . . .

West Point graduated its first Space Force class. The military has its first warrior satellite up. So do Russia and China. So far it's mostly just jamming, but . . .

Naveed sighs. He slumps slightly and closes his eyes, trying to follow multiple implications to their possible outcomes.

Makes sense, he says. We cut ourselves loose.

Yes.

We can, so we do.

Yes.

There is a breeze starting up. More birds sing.

What about Moses? asks Naveed.

That's what was holding Noah back, says Wesley. But Moses has been busy down there.

Doing what? asks Naveed.

Wesley smiles, shakes his head.

Making money off the pandemic. Lots of money.

●

I must admit, thought Ameerah, that since the party the number of bonds between and among us has overwhelmed me. It was the way we sorted ourselves into that horseshoe shape in front of Ben. Of course the pups had something to do with it, too. I remember Coriolis herding Ferdinand toward Omar. And Ahiga, who might have surveyed from the sidelines with Turk and Juno. But Typhoon kept herding them all closer to his brothers and sisters.

What about Whiteout? What was he doing? Was it about pups or people?

It didn't seem to matter to Whiteout. After his pushing and nudging and encouraging we were – Eric and Isaac, me and Naveed, and even Youssef – close to Niloo, who, like Youssef, has not been predisposed to love dogs.

But it was not just us. It was everywhere in that horseshoe in front of Ben. I could see the bonds – beautiful lines of light that twisted slightly as persons shifted their weight to the other foot or feet. Lines at all angles, intersecting in different planes as I moved my head. It was lovely.

How real was it? I am still struggling with that, but in the beauty of the moment I decided to enjoy it. I think it was then that the bond lines took on the colours of the rainbow. The saturation and the intensity of the colours was not steady, but pulsed like the beating of a heart.

The colours ranged from the reddest red through the rainbow to blue and on into white. I think my emotion must have dulled my observation, because I can't remember much about what colour was connected to whom, but I do know that the dogs, and in particular the pups, were anchors only for lines of the purest white.

It was a dream, but a dream that will stay with me. We were not individuals, but a moving, living structure. A structure which was and is itself a being.

As for the lines I myself anchored, I will not speak of them now except to say they were many, many more than I imagined, and of every hue.

●

The same birds sing. The same bench bears the one-G weight of two men. One is in his prime, routinely troubled by pangs of anxiety. It seems the more he learns the less he knows. Will this ordinary intellect of his be up to the task?

The other is in the first flush of old age, where aches, pains, and stiffness are the norm and imperatives have multiplied. But with these has also arisen a blessed peace. Time remaining forces a triage. He will do one thing at a time. It will be enough.

It has been some time since we sat down, thinks Naveed. Perhaps I should . . .

He doesn't. He knows, somehow, that this silence is important. The anxiety has left him. Wesley has a lot to tell me. And more to teach me.

Naveed, do you ever wake up knowing things you didn't when you went to sleep?

Yes, I think so . . .

It happened to me today. I believe that is what sleep is for. At the end of the day we become saturated with new information. New learning. We have no place to put it. So overnight, without the burden of consciousness, our brains – our being, more like – can accept it. Acknowledge. Arrange. All this new stuff. Can make meaning. So we can know what we must do.

Naveed understands. He understands, at least, that he doesn't have to speak.

Where do I start? Why we're here in the first place. It is because we are aware that Earth is in peril. What came to me this morning is that the Pandemic is Earth fighting back. On every front the effects are bad for Humanity but good for Earth. The economy is on hold. Travel of all kinds is five percent of what it was. There is a glut of oil. On the futures market the price per barrel is below zero. Crops are being plowed back into the ground. Slaughterhouses and meat packing plants are exacerbating the spread of the virus. And people are dying.

And we are cut loose.

Naveed isn't sure where this thought came from, but he did say it.

Yes, Naveed. The Pandemic has forced our hand. There are so many things . . . one at a time, Wesley . . .

Naveed sneaks a peripheral vision peek at the glare. What would be Sun, on Earth.

Mirrors, says Wesley. Well, you know we're spinning on one axis only.

Did you try . . .

The vertical axis spin? For day and night? Yes, but very briefly . . .

Wesley falls silent. Shifts on the bench. He looks uncomfortable, thinks Naveed.

Sorry. I didn't mean to . . .

Wesley holds up a hand.

No, it's fine. I have some articles for you. For us. And some amazing videos. All in the New Net Archives. But the bottom line is we want what we have now. A flat spin. About the Ark's axis.

Naveed lets silence be silence.

It's a good thing we are a disc. A flywheel. A bicycle wheel. Two of the axes are identical.

Naveed can't help it. Why?

We'll take this up tomorrow. But in brief – it's about energy and momentum. And stability. Or lack thereof. You'll see how a T-handle shape can go unstable for a time. Go through what they call the separatrix. Flip end-for-end.

Wesley takes a breath.

As you rightly say, Naveed, we're part of the experiment. We don't want to be inside a T-handle shape that flips.

Naveed's stomach drops. How close were we to being a T-handle, he thinks. The Belt Ship and the ice block. He feels ill and slightly dizzy.

How lucky we were.

Wesley lets the thought dangle between them. Waits for the gentle breeze to move time and let emotion morph. For peace to return.

Part of the experiment, he finally says. He smiles, turns to Naveed. We're still here, he says. And we're still part of the experiment.

Naveed lets out a long breath. Waits for the next one.

Yes, he says.

●

I was surprised, Niloo, says Ameerah. Crispus and Fausta. Prince Narseh.

Can I hold one of them? I want to know what I'm getting into.

I don't know what makes me say these things, thinks Ameerah, as she hands Eric off to Niloofar.

This is Eric. Same name as his granddaddy, your adopted son. So this one is your adopted great-grandson.

Maybe I just want to see her looking beautiful, thinks Ameerah. Niloo purses her lips and colour rises to her cheeks. She is pissed. But she doesn't drop Eric.

OK, Ameerah. Wow. He's a big boy.

She rocks him gently. Is this OK?

That's perfect.

Prince Narseh I knew from school. From history. Can I sit here with him? He's heavy.

Of course.

As for Crispus and Fausta . . .

Ameerah watches a line of light trying to dance between Niloo and the baby.

. . . I don't have a clue where that came from. Or didn't.

You thought Wesley . . .

The line of light doesn't make her less lovely.

I thought Wesley. I was convinced, when I woke up.

Niloo is looking at Eric's face as she rocks him.

But later I thought, maybe it was a dream. Except I have never had a dream that real. Do you know what I mean?

Yes, Niloo.

She is losing that porcelain edge, but she is still beautiful.

I thought, well, duh, Niloofar, you have been working closely with him for a month. Maybe he mentioned Crispus and Fausta.

She is still looking at the baby's face. Ameerah can see a dim but definite line of greenish light between them.

Or maybe he didn't. But Constantine was so present, Ameerah!

She changes Eric to her other arm and rocks him some more.

I shouldn't have been so angry, Ameerah. Wesley is a good man.

Yes, Niloo.

Maybe I was dreaming. Or maybe . . . maybe I just knew.

Yes, Niloo.

•

Well you see water was pitting the turbine blades.

You mean they were about to fail? asks Naveed.

Well we are here, says Gopinath. And in the end you know everything must fail.

Gopi's physical presence does not dull the barb of the Karmic Wheel. Rather he is offering up inevitability as a gift, glowing in his cupped hands. He has been explaining the post mortem, as he calls it, of Belt Ship systems – in this case the Carnot Cycle turbines.

Oh, if we had known more we could have done more, he continues. His tall, dark elegance, his wide, white-toothed smile, and his bubbling optimism work like a tonic on Naveed, easing his anxiety.

We are knowing about the pitting of blades for over a century, Gopi says. They were having change of state in early steam turbines. In the books they are calling it phase change, even though there is no phase I can see and it is still water. Gopi laughs.

Naveed laughs, too. It has only been a week but already he has forgotten how much he enjoys this man's presence.

And two centuries ago James Watt understood this latent heat of so-called phase change. Or at least he was knowing about it.

Of course – James Watt, says Naveed. Why didn't we go back and read more . . .

You know it is OK, Naveed, says Gopi. We were making latent heat do some work. At least for a while. For long enough. And now we are back.

Naveed smiles and nods. We can do more now, he thinks.

You know I was late on Easter, says Gopi. I just heard Ben speaking. But I saw you and Rachel had your violins. Were you going to play?

Yes we were but . . .

I was so sorry not to hear. Will you play again soon?

I think so. Wesley and Ben were talking about doing a late Easter. Even Noah might come.

●

Thank you, Niloo. But no apology required. I wasn't offended. Heck, I wasn't even there.

But I shot my mouth off . . .

Yeah – I hear things. But I think in the room that day there was more surprise than anything else. And by the way, you brought up a valid point.

Prince Narseh?

Wesley fixes Niloofar with a look. No, Niloo. Crispus and Fausta.

I don't know where I got that. Did I make it up?

No, I don't think so, Niloo. Constantine had a terrible temper. Crispus was brilliant and handsome and – um, potent. As far as we can tell doing the arithmetic, he was married and had a son at seventeen. It is likely that he took a concubine at twenty-one and greatly annoyed his father. Fausta of course was Constantine's second wife and not Crispus' mother. And Fausta and Crispus were only a decade apart in age.

So it was possible.

Sure.

But.

But?

I can see it in your face, Wesley. Sure, but . . .

There is the story that Fausta was jealous of Crispus. Of his success. And she accused him of attempting to seduce her.

Or maybe he succeeded.

Wesley laughs. Could be, could be. Later scholars certainly think so.

But.

There is another woman in the tale.

His ex?

Wesley has a faraway look. He is smiling. No, his mom. Constantine's mom, Helena. Crispus was her favourite grandson.

So – she's jealous, too . . .

Perhaps. And there's the question of why Constantine . . .

. . . would off his own wife so quickly?

Yeah. Those later scholars are convinced Helena whispered dirt into her son's ears. Took advantage of his famous temper.

Hell hath no fury like a woman scorned. Niloo pauses, looks up at Wesley. Is that Shakespeare?

Wesley laughs. No, but close. It's a century later. William Congreve. But it's apropos.

Niloofar's eyebrows crowd closer together. You mean very like me?

No. Apropos means pertinent. Or germane to the story.

Oh, *munasib*, Niloo mutters to herself. Her eyebrows regain their normal separation. But maybe it is like me. I make things up.

I'm sure you do, Niloo. But this? Not necessarily. I have had the tale very much in my head this last week. Maybe some of it leaked across.

Niloofar's brows rise and her eyes open wide. She and he are a generation apart. But even so, Wesley feels a tightness in his chest. Daughters, he thinks. She and dear Ameerah.

I'm beginning to think that's true, says Niloo. That there's a leak.

●

Go, Ameerah. I can take the twins for an hour. You just fed them. They'll be all right.

After they feed . . . their diapers . . .

That's something I can do, says Isaac. Go. You haven't seen the farms.

What is the G?. . . I don't knooowooh . . .

Isaac laughs. The farms are at about – what? 0.75 G? Naveed will help you if you need it. You're a tough woman.

I was hoping we could look at some of the staples, says Naveed. You know – beans, corn, wheat . . .

The long stalks are waving gently in the breeze.

I know these, says Ameerah. Corn! They're beautiful!

Beautiful is four distinct musical notes, like bird song. Naveed is reminded of his thrush. Thrushes, he thinks, if that's the plural.

The glare from above is warm on his neck and arms. The air has a delicious feel to it, as if photosynthesis were something you could bathe in.

Happiness, thinks Naveed. I talked to Nurul, he says. She's going to meet us here. Probably in the beans.

Oooh yesss. You know, I haven't seen her since before you got back!

They continue down the rows. Some of the plants, reaching for the light, are higher than their heads. Ameerah is moving briskly, the burdens of gravity seemingly forgotten. She opens her arms as if to receive the twins. She sweeps the space and gathers it in to her breast. Her eyes dart from stalk to leaf to ear.

It's life, Naveed! There are lights! Everywhere! Can you see the lines of light, Naveed?

He can see green glints from the glare, but no lines. He doesn't have to. He can feel what she's talking about.

Yes, Ameerah. Life. I can feel it.

Their view opens out. The corn is lower, presumably a later planting. Naveed's thoughts drift back to engineering. Or to engineering/horticulture. Is there no inter-planting in this compartment? I remember hearing they are doing it somewhere. Perhaps tailoring light and temperature cycles to see what works?

They step through the lock to the next compartment. A different feel. More moisture. New smells. Even a different light, although Naveed can't see why. There is the same diffuse glare from above. Are the glints from the plants different?

They step over for a closer look. The corn is high, but it looks different, somehow.

Oohhh! The lines, Naveed! Beautiful! They are darker. Intense green. Do you see them?

Naveed sees intense green, but it is not Ameerahs's lines of light. It is bean stalks, twining around the corn, climbing, seeking light.

Ameerah and Naveed stop, their feet blocked by huge, spiky leaves. A flash of orange underneath. Ameerah stoops and pulls back a leaf to see better.

Oooh, she says. A pumpkin! A baby pumpkin! She shakes her hand. And those leaves are prickly!

Naveed is looking at the next row. Corn. Climbing beans. Big, spiky leaves.

Squash! he says. He points. I think those are zucchini.

Ameerah! I am here!

Nurul has spotted them from a few rows away. She is on her knees, waving to them.

Naveed! Welcome home! Come over!

They make their way around row-ends and along to where Nurul is working on becoming part of the soil, her companion a backpack of electronics with wires and probes.

I am recording conversations, she says by way of explanation.

Conversations? asks Naveed.

It is what Alex is working on, says Nurul. Trees talk. So do plants, he believes. He wants to learn more.

Nurul is crouching among the spiky leaves, seemingly indifferent to their means of protection. Admittedly, she is wearing long sleeves. She is dwarfed by the towers of corn and beans.

Interplanting? asks Naveed.

Ahiga told us about this, says Nurul. It is called the *Three Sisters*. The plants co-operate. They are interdependent. And it is working beautifully!

Oh, says Naveed. Can you . . . I mean, how does it work?

The corn supports the beans, says Nurul. And the squash takes all the ground light, whatever filters through. Suppresses any other growth. Weeds.

And the beans? Are they like a parasite? Do they get a free ride?

Nurul laughs delightedly. No! She says. That's the best part. They are nitrogen fixers. They make the fertilizer, you might say.

Naveed digests this for a minute, thinking back to Earth and to factory farming.

No chemicals, he says. Just sharing. Co-operation.

Nurul gets up slowly. She smiles broadly, displaying her oneness with the earth. It is everywhere – hands, arms, face and neck.

Yes! she says.

Wooonderful! sings Ameerah.

Do you know how they communicate? asks Naveed.

Probably many ways, says Nurul. Here I am working on the electrical. Like our nerves, for example. Only slower. The roots intertwine. And fungi in the soil, over time, set up networks of tendrils – like our neurons. Kind of like an internet in the dirt.

Amazing! says Naveed. He gently touches a bean leaf.

Oh, you do that just like Alex, says Nurul. Alex thinks if we can decode what they say, we may be able to make things better for them sooner. So we don't go through generations to learn things.

A happy community, says Naveed.

Yeesss, says Ameerah. Nurul – are you?

Indeed, since she got to her feet, a discreet belly-bulge has been evident. Nurul reaches involuntarily for the bulge.

Have you talked to Latifah? Rachel? asks Ameerah.

I thought I would talk to you first, says Nurul.

•

They were obsessed with sin, says Ben. The Easter story brings us back into balance, in a way.

People and dogs are assembled once again in the big space. Colin has prepared another feast. Keyboard and violin cases are in evidence.

Wesley laughs. Ben is right about the Judaeo-Christians, he says.

Right from the beginning, Wesley, says Ben. The serpent. No?

Yes. Genesis 3, says Wesley. By the way, there is a wonderful new translation I have been reading. *The Five Books of Moses*, by Robert Alter. It re-creates the music of the ancient Hebrew. It is enough to tear me away from my beloved King James Version.

Eve is tempted, says Ben. She plucks the apple from the Tree of Life.

Wesley quotes:

> *And the woman saw that the tree was good for eating*
> *and that it was lust to the eyes and the tree was lovely*
> *to look at, and she took of the fruit and ate, and she also*
> *gave to her man, and he ate. And the eyes of the two were*

opened, and they knew they were naked, and they sewed fig leaves and made themselves loincloths.

Is that the new translation? asks Ben.

Looking very pleased, Wesley nods. Yes. I have completely fallen for it, as you can probably tell.

Ben is pleased to be the straight man in this duo presentation. He feeds Wesley's momentum as he continues the story of Adam and Eve. The consolation of knowledge. The sentences of labour pain, work, and death. The return to the soil from which they were made.

The pups have found each other and are doing their best, although they are way too big to re-create the squirming litter they were. From near the gaggle of pups, Gopinath's voice emerges.

Oh, I am learning so much! he says. Are your learnings saying that knowledge is sin?

The pups are in a tangle, nibbling and play-biting and wagging their tails. The tangle is large and energetic enough to be a hazard to the unwary. Nor are the pups silent. A chorus of expressive growls is punctuated by the occasional yip.

Wesley and Ben appear to have been struck dumb.

I see the violins, says Gopi. His smile floats above the crowd like oil on the waters. Will there be music?

I hope so. Wesley struggles to regain his composure, to put his thoughts back into some sort of order. We can safely put the question of knowledge and sin aside for now, and trust that there will be balance. Isn't it true, Gopi? The Karmic wheel of life?

Oh, yes! says Gopi. The great Krishna is a creator, but also is a destroyer.

So let's go to music, says Wesley. Ben?

Following Ben's cue, Rachel and Naveed drift toward their violin cases.

It is just a short piece, says Ben.

Just. Short piece, thinks Naveed. I am terrified.

They have been rehearsing for days. The piece calls for two viole d'amore, instruments with the range of a viola but with more strings, some of which, untouched, resonate sympathetically below the finger board. Some scores recommend substituting muted violas or violins. To do the lower voice, Rachel has re-tuned her G and D strings lower. She will be playing from a scordatura, a notation Ben resurrected from the 18th Century, where the fingering stays the same and different notes emerge. Well, almost the same, thinks Naveed. He shudders at the thought of what mind tricks Rachel will have to perform. That's why I'm doing the upper voice. I can keep standard tuning and standard fingering. Still, I have never played with a mute before …

Perhaps I have to do mind tricks too, thinks Naveed. I am not nearly the musicians they are. But I will do my best. The trick will be to stay in the music.

It is a piece from Bach's St. John Passion, says Ben. I will sing it in German, because the text and the notes cannot be separated. But I will tell you what it says. It describes Jesus, after he has been condemned and then whipped:

> *Ponder well how his back, bloodstained all over, is like the sky – where after the deluge from our flood of sins has abated, there appears the most beautiful rainbow, as a sign of God's mercy.*

The pups have quieted down. Naveed remembers what Ben and Rachel coached him to do. He looks up at the audience. Look up, they said. Acknowledge their presence, and feel how all will be joined, one body in the music.

A new arrival is taking up a position behind the pups. Noah! thinks Naveed. He looks older. Oh, my. Concentrate. We will be together in the music.

The heartbeat of the piece is that of a grazing elephant, or a god, or a tree. Its scope reveals our human patience to be that of a June Bug – ready to flit, between beats, off to the next thought.

So how does Bach grab us for long enough? thinks Naveed. How does he hold on to us so we can feel the pulse of a life larger than our own? He distracts us with something beautiful.

Naveed plays the beautiful figure, trying to listen, not think.

Rachel, her feet planted in 0.6 G, is conducting with her body. The metronome is her heart, but her heart is not quite metronomic. Her breathing, too, is connected to the music.

It is easy and natural to follow her.

Naveed is locked in sync with her, grateful he has the piece memorized.

At first it seems like something interesting has happened to Ben's voice. It is the third time that the middle syllable of the word *erwäge* is held on one note for an impossibly long time. It is on *sol*, like the first time it happened, but an octave lower. But as he holds the note there appears a lovely enhancement to the first harmonic. The vowel, though, is not ä, but ooo.

It is Turk, with his alto howl. He is in tune with Ben, on the octave. The effect is all the more magical because it doesn't seem possible that this note is being produced by someone with such a deep woof. The other musicians are working harder as they add the big dog to their number, but smiles are playing at the corners of their mouths.

The piece is over. Gopi's smile hovers above the heads of the crowd. His hands are joined in prayer before his face. Oh, yes! he exclaims. Thank you!

The species-diverse performance has left the rest of the audience nonplussed.

They're stunned, thinks Naveed. They're not going to applaud.

Oh, I hope there is more! exclaims Gopi. His head swivels, his smile scanning the crowd like a beacon. There must be more! He brings his hands together and claps rhythmically. Oh, Please! More!

Naveed, too, is scanning the crowd. Come on, he thinks. We weren't that bad!

I am searching for Noah, he realizes. Why?

Gopi's clapping is having an effect on the crowd. Or perhaps it is his stature and his smile. People shake their heads as if to throw off a spell. They look around, smile. Sporadic clapping begins in small pockets and spreads. The crowd is a crowd again, milling around, jostling, and touching, like an adult version of puppies in a basket.

Naveed's eye catches a still spot amid the moving bodies. It is near the back, intermittently obscured by arms, torsos, and wagging tails. Naveed stares, trying to integrate the millisecond snapshots he gets through the shutter of the crowd.

A man is sitting cross-legged on the ground. His elbows are on his knees, his fingertips supporting his forehead. Is he meditating?

The applause, which had been enthusiastic after a shy start, is tapering off. Wesley has appeared beside Gopinath. He claps the latter on the shoulder.

I should say so, Gopi! I hope there is more. I think our balance is being found with music. Further words unnecessary. What do you think?

Oh yes, says Gopi. Yes!

Ben looks at Rachel and raises his eyebrows.

Rachel's face reddens slightly, but she nods.

Rachel will sing this aria, Ben says. It's not from the St. John Passion, but it is Bach, from a cantata known as The Ascension Oratorio.

•

He speaks German, you know. Fluently.

I didn't know, says Ben. I thought he was South African.

Yes, says Wesley. First language Afrikaans. Second English.

And?

The family was in Germany for four years. Noah was a pre-teen. Most of his early schooling was in German.

Oh.

They sit. Birds sing. It is the bench where Wesley meets Naveed. Where Wesley meets anybody, nowadays. Where Wesley goes to think.

So. When we did the Bach . . .

Yes. He was sitting, already in tears after you sang *Erwäge*. Then Rachel sang the *Bleibe Doch*.

Ben thinks back:

> **Bliebe doch, mein liebstes leben**
> **Ah, leave me not, my dearest . . .**

Art?

Yes, says Wesley.

A thrush swoops in and lands on Wesley's right knee. Ben tries not to move or breathe. He is to Wesley's left on the bench. He has never seen a bird this close before. The thrush lifts his head and sings a motif in triple time:

re re re mi__do

He casts a bird-eye at Wesley, does a tail-wiggle, and flaps away.

That was not his first visit, says Ben.

No.

I'm honoured your friend would visit with me sitting here.

Ben waits, then tries an opener. I knew Art and Noah were close . . .

Yes.

Time passes. A breeze ruffles the leaves over their heads.

Yes. They were closer, even, than Noah . . .

Wesley shifts on the bench, crossing his legs below the knee. He has his eyes closed, Ben notices.

Noah's liaisons were all beautiful women.

They're not here, says Ben, instantly regretting it.

It doesn't give Wesley pause. Nor are the kids, he says. The women were models. Actors. He takes a breath. Are models and actors. Still, as far as I know.

Wesley's eyes are closed again. You knew I asked Rachel to go see him?

Yes.

He hasn't eaten for two days. Each time I see him I persuade him to drink a glass of water.

Erwäge, thinks Ben. Ponder. Consider.

He has no one.

That's right, Ben. He has no one.

Erwäge. But that makes no sense, thinks Ben. He has us.

Sebastien recruited many of us, but he was working for Noah. And it was Noah – Noah's character – that built those businesses, raised that capital, and developed space vehicles that outdid NASA.

Wait, *Erwäge*. Ponder further, thinks Ben. Take Naveed. Who does he talk about when he talks about joining? He was summoned by Noah, but interviewed by Noah and Art. Who tipped the scales for him? And for that matter, who tipped the scales for me, back on the Belt Ship?

We are here because of Art, he says aloud.

We are here because Art loved us, says Wesley. He persuaded Noah to love us. And it is not that he no longer does. We are his people. All of them, it would seem.

A thrush sings. It is the same one – the triple-meter guy, Wesley's friend.

Ben continues his silent conversation with himself. *Erwäge*. Consider. Think about it, Ben. Why is Art's death – what? The end of the road for Noah? Was their love that powerful? Were they lovers? Is it that Noah has never loved anyone else?

The thrush lands again, this time on Wesley's left knee. Ben is mesmerized by the front-row seat.

> *re re re mi__do*

The thrush eyes Ben, who – very slowly and carefully – nods.

Maybe, says Wesley. Yes. No. Yes.

●

Thanks for letting me hold the twins, says Nurul. They're beautiful. But so big!

Her head dips a fraction as she looks down at her belly.

I'm a small woman. I'm scared.

Ameerah holds back, thinking about size.

Latifah jumps in. Don't worry, honey. God, Allah, Nature – has a way of making it all work. She laughs, patting her own enormous belly. I sure hope so, anyway! She scoops little Nurul into her arms. Your sisters gonna take care of you, Sweetie. Be. All. Right.

There are tears on Nurul's cheeks. Latifah's three-syllable command to the gods has released Nurul's natural fear. And Latifah's hug has let it roll harmlessly away.

Ameerah steps in and hugs her, too. Yes, Nurul. We're all going to take care of each other. This is something we share.

Latifah laughs heartily, holding on to her belly for dear life. Oh Honey I'm so glad to hear you say that, she finally says, still chuckling. So before the men get here . . .

Little Nurul watches, wide-eyed.

. . . I'm gonna try and recruit you, Ameerah. You delivered so beautifully, so naturally – you're half-way to being a midwife already. And with the timing – me any day, Rachel, in theory, in a few weeks, Niloofar, for all I know, in a tie with her – we're gonna need help.

Latifah raises her eyebrows. Whaddaya say?

Ooohh, sings Ameerah.

You smilin', Honey.

Yesss. I can sure try. Isaac can . . .

. . . take care of the boys. Like he doin' right now.

Yesss. Maybe all the sisters can study together.

I like that. Oh, I like that! We'll all study together. We call it a . . . a seminar. You know, like Aristotle, if the old Greek had been a woman.

Latifah's enthusiasm is infectious. She has the three of them laughing. If I had to guess, she says, Colin going to be taking care of our baby while you deliver Niloo and I do Rachel. Or vicey-vicey. Honeys, we in production!

●

I'd like to see what you think, says Wesley. I've just come from Noah. I feel like he's fading. But he told me about a dream.

There are other people around, but there aren't. At least no one that Noah is aware of, for the moment. He is standing, moving about the room, occupied with something. Suddenly a tall man materializes near him. Very near. He is not young, but his skin is smooth. Its colour is neither white nor black nor brown, but dusky with overtones of purple and green. He wraps his arms around Noah. They are both naked.

The sensation is not unwelcome. Noah even feels attraction to this man. But he also feels uneasy, and disengages himself. This man is not my friend. I don't know anything about him. It wouldn't be right to start something with him under the circumstances.

That's it? asks Ben.

Yes. You know how dreams are.

Wesley has been attending to some Inertial Reference Systems he has stationed near the axis of the Ark – to quantify wobble, as he puts it.

Ben floats closer. I had almost forgotten how much fun this is, he says.

Yeah, says Wesley. I get my fill tending to these IRS's and the observatories. You're welcome to come along any time.

Ben doesn't hear. The disorientation of zero G as up and down cease to have meaning has taken him back to his years on the Belt Ship. To the feeling of risk and being much closer to death. To Art.

There are tears in the air, floating in front of him, he realizes. His tears. Noah's dream, as narrated by Wesley, now inhabits him. A minute ago it was just someone else's interesting dream. Now it is as if it were his dream and he was just waking up.

But why the tears?

Emotion, as usual, has taken hold before reason has a chance to catch up. He sees that he shares much with Noah. He has shared a powerful love. They have not been lovers. But he, Ben, has loved others. Does love others.

Wesley has stopped tending to his devices. He floats, along with Ben and Ben's tears. Waits. He catches Ben's eye.

You wanted to know what I thought, says Ben.

Yes.

Ben briefly considers a Leonardo man, a somersault, or some other zero G move. A conversation punctuation, like lighting a cigarette in the old days. He doesn't.

Art, says Ben. He loved Art, but the purple guy isn't Art.

Yeah.

Wesley closes his tool sac and fixes it back on his belt, stowing the lanyard. Ben has a brief feeling of disjointedness watching the aging teacher and physicist working as a technician.

The literary mechanic speaks:

Yeah. Who, do you think?

Ben watches the space between them, seeing Bach and Handel, Luther and the ancient Hebrews of the five books of Moses.

It's that other guy, he says. The guy with the scythe. He has come for Noah.

●

Ameerah, thanks for taking such good care of Nurul.

Of courssse, Alex. It is my purpose, now. Before engineering. Even before piloting.

Alex laughs. Well, I'm grateful. We want children, but I confess I worry, too. Selfishly, I guess. I don't know what I'd do without her.

Sometimes I just say things, thinks Ameerah. Did she invite you to our seminars?

Uh, yes . . .

. . . And? Ameerah watches as concentric oblate spheroids of light dance around what must be Alex's very busy brain.

I will learn . . .

Of course, Alex.

. . . so I can be useful . . .

Yesss, Alex.

. . . could I ask you ? . . .

Of course, Alex.

You know how Nurul and I are working on communication – between and among plants.

They are in one of the larger bio labs. There is life everywhere. The photosynthesizing life is the most visible, but Ameerah is sure there is more. As dark matter in the universe signals its presence only by bending spacetime, this other life does . . . something. Ameerah is not sure how she knows.

Yes, Alex. There is so much life here!

Could you help us?

Meee? sings Ameerah.

I have been talking to Naveed, says Alex. About what we're doing here. He told me about what you can see. Light. Life. Love.

Ooohh. Red rushes to her cheeks.

I believe it, Ameerah. I do. You could be so much help to us.

Ameerah's beautiful voice fails to fill. She nods.

Of course I'll come to the seminars, says Alex. And I know I'm adding another task and trade to your quiver. But still, I . . .

They are my task and trade, says Ameerah. Light. Life. Love!

Sometimes I just say things, she thinks.

●

It is a reunion of sorts. Dogs and their people. Belters and Arkers, now reunited. And the new ones – pups and twins.

Noah has not left his quarters in weeks. Ahiga and Sebastien, perhaps in harmony with the dogs, are aware of it.

Wesley, Ben, and Andrew have arranged the day. There are rotating shifts . Everyone will have an opportunity to participate.

Except Noah. He doesn't want to attend, and he is too weak to move.

What do you think, Gopi? asks Sebastien. Ahiga says the dogs know about Noah.

Yes, says Ahiga. They are not concerned.

But I am, says Sebastien. I am not sure why. Maybe my job? What do you think, Gopi?

I think it is the Sallekhana, says Gopi.

Sorry, Gopi, says Sebastien. The what?

Is it a death ritual, Gopi? asks Wesley.

Yes.

But not Hindu?

No.

Is it from the Jains?

Yes. Not Krishna. Not Buddha. Their person is Mahavira. When I was a boy my friend was always talking of Mahavira.

So he and his family were Jains?

Yes.

Jacob and young Eric are fussing. The pups gather round and speak gently. Ameerah sits on the floor, and with the pups as shield, begins to nurse the twins.

You know, I think you're right, Gopi, says Wesley. The Jains were an influence on many of our prophets. Gandhi . . .

Oh, yes! says Gopi.

. . . and Mandela and Martin Luther King, says Wesley. What are the principles of Jainism, Gopi?

They are truth, non-violence, minimalism, and celibacy, says Gopi. I am trying for them myself, but maybe not always.

Minimalism? asks Sebastien.

Maybe eating and drinking? suggests Ben. Or not?

The Sallekhana, says Ahiga. It is the ultimate minimalization and purification.

It is not a question.

Wesley nods, almost imperceptibly.

Renunciation of food and water, says Ben.

Oh, yes, Ben, says Gopi. It is the way.

•

You mean as structure?

Naveed colours. He realizes his disbelief must be showing.

I know it sounds crazy, says Alex.

Naveed regroups. Puts his head in structures mode. Structures used to be wood or stone, he thinks. There was no metal or composite. There was glass, but . . .

I have loved trees since I was a boy, says Alex.

Naveed's thoughts shift again. He is a boy on his bicycle in the Persian hill country. Yes, he says.

A tree can live another hundred years after beetles and birds and fungi have hollowed out its centre, says Alex. If the cambium and bark are relatively intact, the structure can still be sound.

Naveed visualizes a huge metal tube, perhaps one of those stanchions holding banks of lights at a ballpark. Yes, he says. Of course. They need water, and air, and . . .

Alex nods. Solar energy. But they need more.

As diligently as he has been following Alex, Naveed is now at a loss.

More? He feels stupid.

Alex nods. They are very much like us, he says. Like all life.

Naveed's mind races again. Like us, he says. They need – others. Communication. Love, even . . .

Alex has a huge grin. Yes! he says. Exactly!

. . . and you and Nurul have been working on communication. And now Ameerah . . .

Alex nods vigorously. Yes!

Naveed's mouth is dry. Emotion has moved the moisture to his underarms and upper lip. His cheeks feel hot.

. . . she told me . . . task and trade . . . light, life . . .

. . . and love, says Alex. Yes. She has been wonderful. She is the – I don't know how to say this – it won't sound right. But she is the instrument our lab longs for but could never have. Because she's not an instrument. She is a person.

Naveed almost groans, his face is so hot. He is afraid he will cry. Something drips from the tip of his proudly hooked Persian nose.

You are talking to them, he says.

They have settled comfortably into a section of the lab Naveed has not seen before. The smell reminds him of the small patch of old-growth forest near his childhood home. The heat and the displacement of moisture in his body has receded. He has managed not to cry.

Alex has already changed the frame of my thinking radically, he thinks. Trees live longer and slower than we do. Insects faster. Communication has to bridge that gap, as well as the one of – call it language, he had said. But the frame has changed in another way as well. Making stuff is what trees do. Out of water and air and energy they make organic compounds. The building blocks of life. And not only that. When confronted with threat or change, they adapt. They invent stuff. They make new molecules to meet new needs.

Naveed has not taken his eyes off Alex. The latter is in full science mode, his brain a blur. It is fascinating. Alex continues his lesson.

See, Naveed, the problem is not so much communication as

timeline. Trees on Earth are dying because they cannot either move or change fast enough to survive climate change. And up here we need them desperately and we don't have time. We have to find a way to make a home for each other, and quickly.

Structure, thinks Naveed. Light, life, and love. New molecules. Timeline.

You are talking to trees, he says again. But trees speak slowly.

He notices what look like branches disappearing into the ship's structure. This is an outer wall, he realizes.

His mind comes to a halt, holding a hypothesis.

He nods at the branches. How fast do these grow? he asks.

Good question, says Alex. Trees adjust their growth rate to the environment, to the world they find themselves in.

And if they're happy?

Yes, says Alex. Times slows for them. Or they speed up. However you want to think of it.

So the timeline – maybe it's easier to communicate?

Yes, says Alex. Ameerah has helped us so much.

Naveed's cheeks are hot, but his mouth is not dry and his questioning, learning brain is running smoothly at speed.

If you love each other, you can communicate. If you have love, you have confidence to grow. He looks up at Alex. Even into structure?

Alex nods slowly, continuously, as if to conduct Naveed's thoughts.

The trees are learning to be in and out, says Naveed.

There is a long pause. Alex strokes some of the disappearing branches.

They are phototropic, says Naveed.

He reaches out as well and strokes one the branches. They are working on – not leaves . . .

No, not exactly, says Alex.

. . . but they want to photosynthesize – out there.

Alex looks like an eight-year-old boy who has just caught his first frog. He pats the disappearing branches.

I'm not sure even she knows exactly what she is making, he says. But it's new, and it's a product of photosynthesis. He points at the Ark's hull.

From out there.

•

Sometimes Isaac cracks me up.

What'd he say again?

You know dogs, Gramps. Just pant like a dog.

Ben and Colin share a chuckle.

Andrew looked so . . .

. . . lost?

I dunno. Admiral Andrew.

. . . looked like Ensign Andrew.

That cracks them both up. They guffaw, almost spilling their drinks, Colin steadies his, and takes another sip.

This is good stuff, Ben, he says.

Thanks. Thanks to this stuff, says Ben, gesturing at the surrounding vegetation.

They are seated in a cozy arbor in the midst of a field of barley. The verdure enclosing them could be grape vines, except the leaves are elm-shaped, not the vaguely maple shape of grape leaves. And the hanging fruit looks more like miniature green spruce cones.

Hops, says Ben. I put them on the list. With barley. Back when you and Alex and Nurul were organizing the life launches. You were pretty busy.

Yeah. Seeds out of the gravity well of Earth. Zillions of seeds. And lots of other tiny characters, too. Colin takes another sip. That citrusy bitterness. That's hops, right?

Ben reaches up and plucks a hop. Flower, cone, seed, he says. Whatever. He digs in a thumbnail and squeezes out a yellowish, waxy oil. Hold out a finger, he says. Smell that. Taste it, if you like.

Colin does. Lovely, he says, admiring his finger. By the way, we haven't had a drop in years. What's the percent in this batch?

About six. That's the way it came out. I didn't aim for high alcohol.

No wonder.

They sit, trying to be serious. It doesn't work.

Lamaze, says Colin. The stages of labour. He giggles. Admiral Andrew. I have never seen him so uncomfortable, says Ben.

They laugh.

I mean, me too, says Colin. I never expected to know anything about all those physical details. But Gramps – being dragged into that world – by his frickin' grandson . . .

He consults his beer. He is not sure what for. Wisdom? Stable reference? Sobriety?

. . . we're cheap drunks, Ben, he says. We'll have to be careful with this stuff.

That's why we're getting pissed today, says Ben. We are, as usual, part of the experiment.

Off duty, in a social setting, says Colin.

And we'd better hold off while the girls are pregnant, says Ben.

•

Andrew is putting on the charm, thinks Ameerah. But I will keep my mouth shut.

I guess I don't get it, says Andrew, radiating his smile over the seminar participants. I'm not the one in labour. Why do I have to learn the breathing?

Because it's an essential life skill, Gramps, says Isaac.

The room sags, as if gravity had suddenly doubled. That'll do it, thinks Ameerah.

But gravity or no, the room has not been emptied.

Isn't the breathing just a distraction, asks Niloofar. To keep me from feeling the pain?

Well, no, Honey, says Latifah. When you do the breathing, it is relaxing you and keeping you oxygenated. Same for your person. And Andrew, as we have been discussing . . .

Not only is it not a distraction . . . I don't know why I say these things, thinks Ameerah. . . . not only is it not a distraction, it creates a focus that shuts out other distractions that can take a woman away from the work of labour.

The gravity of the woman, the mother nursing two babies, fills the room. There will be no laughter, no smart riposte. No distraction.

Slow deep, says Latifah. It is the first stage of labour.

This is your work, sisters. And yours as well, men. Slow deep breathing. Breathe in through the nose. Shoulders relaxed. Feel the diaphragm pull down. Way down. Pause. Make a kissy face. Long, slow exhale through the mouth, like sending the air through a straw.

Her full lips make a circle, leaving another tiny circle of open space at its centre.

Hooooo. The long, slender column of air pushes into the space of the room.

With each breath, relax a hand or an arm, says Latifah. Concentrate on that one piece of you.

For a small girl, Nurul's exhalation is remarkably present, its tiny cyclone impossible to ignore.

Ben notices. On the next breath he tries to do what she does.

Good job, Ben, says Isaac.

Very like singing, says Ben.

Rachel Honey, you know your man tellin' it right, says Latifah.

Colin and Alex are also watching Nurul, imitating her. Latifah leads the group in a half-dozen more breaths, each one aimed at a new body part. She finishes the final exhalation with an audible huff.

Good, she says. Men, you don't know it yet, but you're gonna see how important you are. What does a woman in the work of labour – thank you for that, sister Ameerah – what does a woman in labour need?

Ameerah steps into the silence. Someone to hold your hand and wipe your brow, she says.

The silence returns. The hour is up. The class will reconvene tomorrow for more practice. There will be new knowledge, too.

But that is not the point. The skills are physical, and must be practiced every day.

Thank you, Latifah, says Ameerah. And not just for the class. And thank you Isaac.

She turns to the class. They held my hands and wiped my brow, she says. But that's not all a girl in labour needs. She needs people she loves and trusts. So, men – you are essential in giving her that space where she feels secure.

And women, girls, sisters, she says. This breathing, these techniques that will keep you focussed during the intensity of transition – they will work for you. They will make you able to do it. And nothing and no one can take them away from you.

●

How is he?

He's getting it on with the purple guy, Ben.

Oh. Yeah.

The leaves are moving, but birds are not in evidence. It is as quiet as the Ark gets. A whisper of air movement. The distant whine of a turbine. Or that baroque G sharp, or whatever it is, thinks Ben, when a high electrical load kicks in somewhere nearby.

Is he talking?

No.

Thanks to God, Nurul, and Alex, thinks Ben, the trees and flowers are thriving, beautiful, serene.

I prepared some Earth news for him, just in case, Wesley continues. Like it was old times. He always liked news from Earth.

Ben waits. There is something in Wesley's voice. An emptiness. Ben thinks of Wesley's bird friend, the triple-metre thrush. He would be welcome just now.

I'm still crying inside, says Wesley.

Ben inhales, testing the air. It is still there, pressure normal, he thinks. Why do I feel like I can't breathe?

Is it . . .?

The virus? Sure, says Wesley. Coming up on twenty-three million cases. And America accounts for twenty-five percent of that.

Oh, says Ben. What . . .

America has four percent of the world's population. It's barely fire season, but lightning has started fires all over California. Most of them are zero-percent contained.

And Noah? asks Ben.

He just shook his head, says Wesley. Didn't want to know any of it.

But it's getting to you, says Ben.

Wesley shakes his head, biting his lip. He closes his eyes.

Ben feels a wave of grief overtake him. Music fills his head. A single note, fortissimo, fading to piano. Not the 400 hertz of the wires, but a tritone lower. D.

Ben waits for it, listens. Pianissimo voices in six parts:

    re_qui_em ae_ter_nam

It is the Faure. That descending bass in low strings, bassoons, and horns will be heard again at the end of the Agnus Dei when the text repeats.

    D C

Many times Ben has tries to analyze how it works. Why it works.

    do_na e_is do_mi_ne

C B-flat

He doesn't do so now. Each descending full tone is the lub-dub of a giant heart. Ben's heart slows too, and follows in gut-wrenching, free-falling grief.

There is no analysis in free-fall. Only mercy. Only grace. A giant hand rescues his heart and lifts him up.

et lux per_pe_tu_a

His heart beats with the quarter-notes in the bass line. The choir, gathering strength, resolves the B-flat harmony into an open F chord which floats briefly over an A, a hint of happiness which immediately disappears. The A jumps up to F. The harmony is open again. Ambivalent. Heavenly. Eternal light.

There are tears streaming down Ben's cheeks.

Wesley's eyes open. It was a eulogy, he says.

A requiem.

You could say that, says Wesley. Not three weeks ago, the forty-fourth president gave the eulogy for one of our prophets. Yesterday, in the virtual convention, he gave one for the country.

Eulogy. For the country . . .

That's the way I saw it. What I took away emotionally. That it's not the election. It's the reason behind the last election. We the people have decided. Together, we have no agency.

So democracy . . .

Is dead, says Wesley. Like Noah. An hour ago.

●

Typhoon, Turk's look-alike, seems to be the convenor. He herds Ben and Wesley across the room to where his Mom and Dad sit with Sebastien and Ahiga.

Typhoon retains his puppy energy and flexibility, wagging

and wiggling as he works, tongue out, radiating the essence of *happy dog*. As they get closer Ben sees that he is already almost Turk's size. Not weight yet, though. He will probably fill out over the next year or two.

It's nice, thinks Ben. Typhoon is so pleased with himself.

His herding work complete, Typhoon presents himself to Ahiga for a two-handed head and ears massage. Before he sits, he rubs his beautiful soft muzzle against Ahiga's cheek. If there is any drool involved, Ahiga ignores it.

You want to know why, says Ahiga.

Ben nods. He is not surprised. After years on the belt ship with Ahiga he retains a feel for how he can be polite – if not in the Navajo way, at least respectful of it.

Wesley looks as if he is about to speak, perhaps because he expected Ahiga's statement to be a question. But he relaxes his face and keeps his peace.

The dogs lie down. Ahiga and Sebastien sit on the floor, cross-legged.

After a polite pause, Ben follows suit. There is another pause as Wesley sits next to Ben, likely as not because Wesley is testing his old body gently, easing it into a now-rare posture.

There is a Cleopatra air about Ahiga, he thinks, as the stiffness ebbs. It's Turk and Juno, flanking the throne, like – what was it? Jaguars? Panthers? But it's also his intense physical presence. He's magnificent. There's no other word for it.

Sebastien, slightly to one side, is the amanuensis. These two have been a team for years now, with Turk and Juno as their noses and ears.

Sebastien straightens his spine.

Wesley watches. These two don't speak much, he thinks. These five, for that matter. There is something else going on. As he watches Ahiga moves his body in a manner similar to Sebastien's straightening, but in another realm entirely. He is like a cobra, but without the menace. He is here not to pounce, but to dance.

The death was entirely natural, says Sebastien.

As Wesley watches out of the corner of his eye, Ben slowly nods.

And Rachel? asks Sebastien.

Yes, says Ben. From her perspective as well.

Slowly, so as not to startle the rhythm, Typhoon gets up and walks over to Wesley's side. With a sigh he lies down and parks his great head gently on Wesley's knee. Wesley feels a peace roll over him. I am blessed, he thinks. Among friends. Wedged, almost, between Ben and this dog. Not restrained, but couched. Loved.

I will be next, he thinks.

The thought patiently takes its place in his being and slowly expands. Do they know as well? flits through Wesley's mind and in an instant is displaced by Noah.

I did not know Noah well, Wesley realizes. Perhaps none of us did. We knew his blindingly independent mind. We knew his accomplishments – enough for many lifetimes. But who was he?

Wesley's awareness is suddenly occupied not by Noah but by Ben, at a recent gathering, telling stories of the deaths of two composers. Henry Purcell, who liked a pint or two at the pub with friends after supper. One cold night he came home to find the door locked. He spent the night on the stoop, caught pneumonia, and died. Jean-Baptiste Lully was the Royal Musician at the court of Louis XIV. In those days, and up until Handel's time, conductors used – not a baton, but a big, heavy staff to beat time on the stage floor. One evening, carried away by the music, Lully planted the staff on his big toe. It became infected, and he died.

Wesley struggles to get back to now. Why dead composers? he thinks. Where did Noah come from?

The room is quiet except for the Ark background sounds. Wesley can hear breathing. Ben, next to him. Ahiga doing what sounds like sleep breathing, where the long exhale is achieved by relaxation, and the sharp inhalation through the nostrils is prompted irregularly by a high carbon dioxide reading. Turk is the most audible, on the verge of a snore.

It's Ahiga, thinks Wesley. He pats Typhoon's head gently. The pup snuggles closer.

Wesley looks up at Ahiga, who is looking into his eyes. The feeling is that Ahiga is transmitting, not receiving. As Wesley hears Ahiga's next breath the gaze shifts slightly. To Ben, thinks Wesley. He watches through several breaths. The powerful gaze switches back and forth in the slow, irregular rhythm of Ahiga's breathing.

The *why* is on the way, thinks Wesley. He closes his eyes. Typhoon's head on his knee has relaxed him to the point where he can no longer move. He is hypnotized, open to suggestion. He goes with it.

Art was the only person Noah truly loved. Perhaps because Art loved him, in spite of his quixotic personality. Noah would rant, rave, and rage, changing course on a dime, and Art would smile and help him deal with the fallout. Especially with the women. They were the object of well-meant intent, but after a year or two wound up feeling like trophies. Noah would rush off to start a new business or to rescue one in crisis. Failure was not an option. For the most part, earlier businesses had to stay alive to feed their progeny.

So, it was Art's death, which hit him like a brick?

Not entirely. Noah was tough, and anyway he had always had

another new idea. Started another project. What happened this time?

Wesley looks up to see Ahiga's penetrating gaze focussed on him. Is he receiving now, too? Getting feedback?

In an instant Wesley knows why. He himself is complicit. It is their collective success, he realizes.

Noah's plan had been Mars. But our collective thinking started to change – as early as the mining near Moon's south pole. As we found we could get water and building materials out of a gravity well one-sixth as strong as Earth's, we changed course. All we needed to lift out of Earth was life.

So from Moon we got elements – the building blocks, forged in stars. And a bit of water, too. Wesley continues his meditation on what is needed to support that life lifted from Earth.

Water, of course. We didn't have enough. But the Belt Ship mission and Ceres fixed that.

And energy. Solar radiation. But here in an orbit like Earth's, at Earth's distance from Sun, the energy density is just right. There is enough to keep us warm and run our machines and make stuff.

What about food? You could just say we need life to support life, and leave it at that, thinks Wesley. And you would be right. But there is more to it. Alex and Nurul, and Colin and Dominic, have shown us how that works.

The energy animals use – all of it – comes from Sun, via photosynthesis. Plants make our food. They take the carbon dioxide we breathe out as exhaust, and add water. Chlorophyll absorbs light at the ends of the spectrum, but not at the middle. It reflects only green, the green of life. Absorbing and splitting Sun's energy leads – through a miraculous process – to the synthesis of carbohydrates, neutral hydrocarbons which have the same hydrogen/oxygen ratio as water: two to one. A by-product of this process is the release of molecular oxygen – O^2.

Animals are powered by these carbohydrates. They eat them, breathe in the O^2, and burn them for energy. Humans used to burn wood to stay warm – a similar reaction. The cellulose of the wood, in the presence of heat, breaks down into butane, pentane, octane, and the other -anes, which are essentially gasoline. Which of course burns very well indeed. That is what is happening when the wood fire *catches*.

Remember that you are dust, and to dust you shall return.

Wesley is thinking, again, of his own death. Not imminent, true. But next.

Dust and ashes. The universe forms itself in the eternal shifting of the balance between matter and energy. Einstein showed these are equivalent – manifestations of the same something. And in that point of balance lives life.

Wesley opens his eyes for a second at the thought of balance, the very balance we are trying to achieve here, he thinks. So that all life becomes one being, and for awhile, survives. He glances at Ben, who seems also to be in an Ahiga-induced state. Actually Ahiga and the dogs, he thinks. Typhoon cuddles closer and re-settles his head on Wesley's thigh. Wesley involuntarily closes his eyes again and surrenders to the relaxation. Or paralysis.

Plants and animals are both necessary to make a sustainable being. But even that is not enough. Animals and plants – but especially plants and especially trees – need other, tinier life to survive. We need our biome – the bacteria that live in our gut – to digest food. Trees need bacteria and fungi for everything, including communication. And with death we need the larvae of insects to break down the cellulose and the flesh into humus.

Ashes to ashes, dust to dust.

I will be next, and I am complicit.

Yes, it was Andrew who made the decision to cut loose. And

to forget Mars, at least for our lifetimes. Because we don't know Mars has water and we do know the solar flux is less than sixty percent of what we get here.

I am complicit because I agreed with Andrew and backed him up. And his decision – *our* decision, if you like – to cut loose from Moon also meant cutting loose from Earth, at least for now. So I am doubly complicit.

And the *why* is laid bare: Noah's work was done. To live, we need love and we need purpose.

Wesley emerges from his trance slowly, but already he is aware of why he is emerging. Typhoon has got to his feet and is licking his cheek. He makes a soft crying noise into Wesley's right ear, then rubs his soft muzzle against Wesley's face. Wesley turns toward the almost-grown pup and puts his arms around his neck. He buries his forehead in the pup's fur.

No more questions, he thinks. I have no more questions.

●

Your bread is wonderful, Dominic! Is it just me, or is it getting better and better?

Dominic looks down at his feet as he shuffles them.

I am still learning my trade, Ameerah.

As he looks up, Ameerah's smile takes him by the shoulders.

Isn't that right, Dominic? Right and good?

He has no words, until they suddenly appear in his mouth.

Learning things . . .

Yeesss.

One of the twins makes a sound. It is almost a word.

He's hungry, says Ameerah, as she lifts Jacob from the crib. As she starts to nurse him, Journey snuggles against her leg. The scene puts more words in Dominic's mouth.

Oh Ameerah – you speak of learning, and you – all your skills, and now motherhood, and . . .

Yeesss. Never mind, she says. She rocks Jacob gently. Husssh, she says. You know, Dominic, I have heard you, now and then, singing while you work.

He looks stricken. He wants to say something. Doesn't.

Nooo – Dominic, you have a nice voice. Would you like to join the choir?

She and Jacob rock sideways, forward and back, in a circle.

This is new for me, too, says Ameerah. I have hardly sung a note in my life. But Ben and Rachel – you have heard them; you know what musicians they are – we were talking after class yesterday. They want to get more of us involved in making music.

Oh, but I don't read . . .

Ameerah laughs, making music as she does. Neither do I, Dominic. But we can learn. Did you know that Pavarotti never learned to read music?

No – Pavarotti?

Yeesss. Ameerah nods as she moves Jacob to the other breast. He had to memorize everything. But that didn't slow him down, did it?

But . . .

And if we want to learn to read they will teach us. Naveed says he'll tell us about where harmony comes from. The physics of it. Ben will be our coach dond conductor. Rachel will teach us too, when she's not delivering!

Ameerah laughs her silvery laugh.

Tell me, Dominic. Did you have a sweetie? Back on Earth, I mean.

Dominic looks like he wants to run. Colour rises in his cheeks. He nods.

Here – hold Jacob for a minute, would you?

Dominic opens his hands to accept the baby as he would preparing to shape a loaf. With the bundle against his chest he sits, and Journey moves closer to him, brushing his leg with her body.

She married a guy with more money.

Jacob exercises his young neck and lifts his head to look at Dominic. Their eyes meet. Ameerah moves closer, patting Journey and scratching her behind the ears.

She liked me. But I am a tradesman. That's what she said.

Hmmph! You're a man who keeps learning.

Ameerah rises from her chair, using Dominic's steady shoulder as a handhold.

So we'll start with music. We'll learn together.

Dominic lifts Jacob, offering him back to Ameerah.

Nooo. Hold him a minute more, Dominic. You are good together. We'll make you a daddy yet. I'll talk to the girls. We'll make you a daddy yet. Maybe several times over.

●

Thank you all, says Latifah. You doin' great. And don't forget – in your exercises, include all the muscles around the perineum. You too, men! You gonna know what it feels like!

Latifah looks around at her class. They have been doing well. Even the skeptics are buying in.

Rachel Honey. You ready?

Rachel nods. Well, she says, you all – you let me know after class if you feel you need a break between classes. But for today we'll say a change is as good as a rest.

Latifah treats them to another gutsy laugh, holding her big belly so it will remain, at least for now, part of her body.

Rachel Honey, they all yours. I'm gonna learn how to read notes!

Rachel turns the light down a touch so the image from the projector takes life on the wall.

Don't worry about the notes today, she says. I'll play them, and you can watch them.

Rachel picks up her violin and bow.

Feel your pulse, she says. Find it in your wrist or neck, and keep a finger or thumb on it.

On the screen are three lines of music – single stave, treble clef.

With her bow, Rachel taps the wall in time with her own pulse, moving her bow-tip along the stave.

These are heartbeats, she says. This is time. Music exists in time as well as in pitch and space. She points to the left end of the first stave.

See this 3? she says. This is where I look first. It tells me the heart beats in groups of three. These threes are separated by bar lines – see these vertical lines? So if you count – one, two, three – you can keep up with me.

Don't worry – you won't get lost. At least if I succeed in starting the software Eric made for us. Then you'll see a vertical red line pulsing the heartbeat as it moves along.

She checks the tuning of her E string, and nods to Ben. With his nose and eyebrows, he conducts a bar and then starts Eric's red heartbeat. It appears to the left of the stave, moving right as it counts *one, two, three, one.*

On two, Rachel triple-stops the first notes of the D minor Chaconne.

●

I'm fieyiene, Wesley. Ameerah's *fine* is all diphthongs. I guess I just take to it naturally.

But Ameerah – you're still nursing the twins!

Yesss. But no harm in trying. You know?

Wesley laughs. This daughter-figure of his just gets sweeter as time goes by. Wasting no time with the covenant, huh?

Nooo, 'cause . . .

Ameerah's countenance and concentration take on a sudden abstraction as she looks for words.

. . . I think it's not best that just one of the boys is a father. Not for too long, anyway.

Wesley is whipsawed. I would never have had that thought, is what passes through his mind. Jealousy. Instability. Possible loss of purpose. She's right, bless her.

He smiles. But that's moot, now.

Yesss.

Does Youssef know?

The colour rises in Ameerah's cheeks. She has returned to herself, anchored in the here and now. Emphatically present.

Nooo. I wanted to see you, Wesley. You are the first person I have told.

Ameerah lets it sit. Journey gets to her feet and comes and puts her head on Ameerah's knee.

Wesley needs the time. The whipsaw feeling has blossomed. It is Einstein, Feynman, Newton. It is the Books of Moses, and his grandpa reciting the New Testament. It is his adopted daughter, with whom he has forged a covenant, reaching out to him.

Journey wiggles, insinuating herself between them, trying to make one body with them. Wesley can feel it happening.

I want you to be next, Wesley. I don't want you to be an orphan.

•

Great to see you, Naveed. It has been too long!

Well, I know you're busy, Ameerah.

Yesss. So come along with me. We'll be talking fungi.

Oh!

You will like this, Naveed. You're going to add a whole new compartment to your curiosity.

It is late October in his boyhood Persia. Photosynthesizing greens are growing dull or morphing into shades of brown and orange. But it is the smells that have transported Naveed. Delicious odours of decomposition, the partner of ripeness. He feels happy, even though the spectacle before him is one of decay.

Bean and tomato plants are the most recognizable in this jumbled scene. In his head Naveed backs them up to spring seedlings shyly pushing their way into the light. He sees the rush of growth in June, the flowering and fruiting, the harvest. Now, in the world of annuals, it is almost over.

Oohhh! Look here, Naveed! This is beautiful!

Ameerah squats beside a tomato plant, making a friend. You dear thing, she says. Look, Naveed!

Her nose is level with a small but green new shoot bearing three yellow flowers. It looks odd on the browning plant.

You know your life is over, sings Ameerah. And you make one last beautiful attempt at reproduction. Bless you!

Ameerah struggles to her feet, brushing the soil from her knees. C'mon, Naveed. Let's get to the main event. I see them. Over there!

It is a larger group than he expected. Ameerah has spoken of Alex and Nurul, but here are Colin and Ben with Alex looking down at what must be Nurul on her knees between the rows. Nurul looks up in time to see Ameerah.

Here, Ameerah. Take a look. See if you can see . . .

Naveed can't see. He sees the backs of the two women as they crouch over whatever it is, down in the dirt.

Fungi are the decomposers, says Alex. This is their season.

Naveed's mind races to catch up. I knew they were important, he thinks. But I don't know anything about them. Maybe Ben. He's a brewer. I think yeast are fungi. And mushrooms.

Alex is looking at him with a smile. How did they get up here?

Naveed can feel the blood rising to his cheeks. Yes. Exactly. Did you . . .

In the Life Lift. Yes. But it was close. You and Ben were gone.

The Belt Ship, says Ben.

Wesley and Noah formed a group, says Colin. Or maybe it was Andrew and Niloo. I think it was Andrew who pointed out that now life was the only thing we needed to lift out of Earth's gravity well. Anyway, they asked Alex and Nurul.

And you, says Alex.

And me, says Colin. And I asked Dominic.

Ben laughs. You knew what I wanted.

Sure, says Colin. You needed yeast. And barley and hops.

Naveed tries to follow. Wanted. Needed. What we need is to survive, he thinks. And these fungi are probably necessary for survival. The decomposers, Alex says they are . . .

We're still lifting human knowledge via the Spread Spectrum Protocol, aren't we?

Naveed hears himself asking the question before he realizes he was thinking about it.

Alex nods. Absolutely. There are still scientific papers being published. Old libraries being scanned.

And music being written, says Ben. And stories and novels. Noah's New Net is still working and we're trying to get as much as we can.

That takes energy, says Naveed, following his thoughts. Bandwidth. But nothing compared to lifting mass from Earth. And you . . .

He looks up to see Alex looking him in the eye. We lifted a lot of life, Alex says. Some of it very tiny. Was it enough?

Standing beside Naveed, Ben has begun feeling unwell. It is guilt, he realizes. It is his own selfishness. I wanted yeast, he thinks. I didn't need it. Or barley and hops. And I want all the new music and literature and art. But we need this incredible tiny life. And is it enough? Do we have enough to survive?

Alex hasn't finished his thought.

If it were just me up here working with fungi, he says, it wouldn't be enough for us to survive. That is clear to me. But I'm not alone.

He nods to the girls, still on their knees in the dirt.

When we see there is a fungus we need but we don't have – well, first Nurul tries to find it. We did manage to bring samples of the humus at three sites of old-growth forest. One in the Cascades east of Portland. The others from either side of the Strait of Georgia, north of Vancouver. So we have, literally, millions of species.

But, bless her, if she can't find what we need she persuades some we do have to reproduce and to morph into what we need.

There! Yes! Oh, I can see, Nurul. May I?

As Nurul nods, Ameerah gently fingers the loam, trying to trace, not break, the tendrils – the hyphae – of the fungus.

Yesss! It is faint. They are used to living in the dark. But they are sending light among themselves. And life! And love!

●

End Of Summer
Dream

Part VII

The Arkborn

Personae	Ark Year	Name
Eric Isaac Ameerahsson	5	One Ruler, First Twin
Jacob Isaac Ameerahsson	5	Second Twin
Benjamin Colin Latifahsson	5	Son of the Right Hand
Sarah Andrew Niloosdotter	5	Princess, Joy, Delight
Nadia Benjamin Rachelsdotter	5	Hope, Tender, Delicate
Estelle Alex Nurulsdotter	5	Star
Leila Youssef Ameerahsdotter	6	Night Beauty
Cassandra Wesley Ameerahsdotter	7	Helper of Humanity
Cyrus Naveed Ameerahsson	8	Far-sighted
Bidziil Ahiga Niloosson	9	He is strong
Mathieu Sebastien Latifahsson	9	Gift of the Lord
Mireille Dominic Nurulsdotter	9	Peace, Wonder
Nousha Naveed Ameerahsdotter	9	Kind-hearted
Bianca Benjamin Rachelsdotter	11	Stubborn, Sensitive, Happy, Zany
Joaquim Ferdinand Nurulsson	11	Established by God
Prisha Gopinath Latifahsdotter	11	Gift from Krishna
Shirin Naveed Ameerahsdotter	11	Kind and Sweet
Sami Omar Niloosson	11	Exalted

VII

End-of-Summer Dream

The course of true love never did run smooth . . .
Lysander, I, i

The moon, methinks, looks with a watering eye;
And when she weeps, weeps every little flower,
Lamenting some enforcèd chastity.
Titania, III, i

Lovers and madmen have such seething brains,
Such shaping fantasies, that apprehend
More than cool reason ever comprehends.
Theseus, V, i

~ Shakespeare – A Midsummer Night's Dream ~

Cassandra is taking notes. She is going to have to speak, and it is not something she relishes. She knows and understands that people don't like listening to her.

Heaven knows it is not her voice. She has inherited her mother's lovely, musical pipes. Unlike Mom she has sung from an early age. She loves music and has since birth. She has memorized whole libraries of it. That part is from Dad. Not the music, the memory . . .

She closes her eyes and drops her jaw as if to scream. She

tenses her singer's substantial crotch muscles, leaving the diaphragm and rib-cage muscles slack. It is an involuntary reaction to pain. Emotional pain which makes up a part of every day of her life. And now, with Dad gone, it has doubled in frequency and intensity. She beats back the pain with gratitude and thanksgiving. It seems to be the best remedy.

Ich esse mit Freuden mein weniges Brot
und göne dem Nächsten von Hertzen das Seine

With gladness I eat my morsel of bread
And wish for my neighbour the joy of his own

Cassandra is not singing out loud. Singing or speaking takes special permission because sometimes there is hurt. She plays it in her head. Something with words and music is best because it uses both hemispheres. Like this aria from a Bach cantata. It uses enough brain to partly block the pain.

The aria is over. It is as if she had been singing a high note but making no sound. When the gleuts and the perineals relax and her eyes open, she takes a deep breath with her diaphragm, keeping her shoulders relaxed.

Actually, singing has been a Godsend. But better in a group. And if by chance solo, better not improvisation. Better from one of the scores in her head.

Cassandra continues her note taking. She has to speak at Dad's funeral, his celebration of life. Mom will be there. Half-sisters and half-brothers. She mustn't screw up.

She is alone with no pencil, paper, or tablet. Not required. The list of safe topics is growing. What Dad means to her. What he taught her and shared with her. His love . . .

But no topic is entirely safe. Just about any thought has a side which causes pain. What she must for sure not talk about is what makes her different. Or what she thinks makes her different.

It has to do with how her two hemispheres are connected. Perhaps too connected, she has begun to realize. She read, not so long ago, about how the old bards would sing and rhyme – *arma virumque cano* – not I *tell* of arms and men, but I *sing* of arms and men. Homer. Virgil. Chaucer. Dante. It hit her like a clap of thunder. That's me. I always use both hemispheres. Every thought is there in two forms. Words and music. Reason and space. Logic and light.

People sometimes tell me how they search for meaning. I don't have to search. Meaning floods over me and wants to drown me if I don't speak of it. But I can't. What comforts me is anathema to others.

●

No, they don't confuse us, says Ben.

Cassandra laughs. It's rare for her, and it feels wonderful. She is glad Ben has dropped by.

It's not that I'm not smart, continues Ben. Or that I'm not a musician. He gives her a look. Because I'm both! It's just . . .

You're not old, though . . .

It is not quite a giggle, but Cassandra feels herself on the verge of one. Ben smiles at her, making her heart do a little jump.

. . . there is that, says Ben. But Uncle Ben, he's a bit too white, no?

That brings laughter again. Completely involuntary. Her chest feels warm and full.

Benjamin Colin Latifahsson! She blurts it out, still laughing. They have come upon this habit of addressing each other, in moments when there is a social pause, by their full, formal names.

Cassandra Wesley Ameerahsdotter! Ben laughs his deep baritone laugh.

The laugh reminds Cassandra of singing the Tallis *If Ye Love Me,* standing beside Ben, with Jacob Isaac Ameerahsson, her older half-brother, on the other side. They were centre stage, in the middle of a half-circle with the rest of the singers. She was singing soprano between Ben's rich baritone and Jacob's lovely tenor. That evening was one of those scenes you never forget, not ever.

It was not just a musical moment, thinks Cassandra. It was a life moment. On Jacob's other side was Nadia – Nadia Benjamin Rachelsdotter – Uncle Ben's daughter. She sings alto, just like her Mom. And where was Rachel? Holding down the stage-right end of the line.

> *. . . and he shall find you another comforter,*
> *that he may abide with you for ever, for ever*

It's in F, thinks Cassandra. And right there – *you for ever* – the harmony is suddenly II -V- I in C, Jacob singing that surprising and delightful B-natural into her ear, and Nadia and Rachel introducing the next line . . .

> *Ev'n the spirit of truth,*
> *That he may abide with you for ever*

There is nothing particularly remarkable about that alto line. But Nadia and her Mom were in a unison so close that it was a new voice. They had the same musical approach to the phrase, the same approach to the words. Like on that old blues album Uncle Ben gave me, when the horns, punching rhythm, turn into an electric guitar. I felt free of myself. I felt my hemispheres had become the music, I was floating, and I would never hurt again.

So, says Ben. You OK?

He can see it in her face as those crotch muscles clench.

No.

She is trying not to cry, but the tears are welling up.

You miss him. He puts his arms around her and squeezes. Squeezes the tears out onto her cheeks. She puts her arms around him and lets her head fall forward onto his chest.

It's day after tomorrow, she sobs. How am I going to do it?

Ben strokes her hair. She can feel his heart beating. Beating to the Tallis in her head.

You don't have to be alone, he says. She feels his voice rumbling in his chest. How about music? A few of us? I'll talk to Uncle Ben.

•

But I can't tell. Can't talk . . .

You have to, Sweetie, or the pain will kill you. Ameerah smiles. Puts her hands on Cassandra's bowed head. Tilts her chin up so they can look into each other's eyes. But we don't want that, do we?

Cassandra feels the force of her mother's love. Sees in her eyes what her mother sees. Ameerah, seer of light.

I remember . . .

Yesss. Everything. We need that, as a people.

And I can see – you know, ahead . . .

Yesss. And people are upset. They are not ready to accept . . .

Cassandra nods. I know . . .

And that hurts you. You can feel them not love you.

Ameerah has Cassandra's face in her two hands. There are tears. At first they slide like individuals gently down her daughter's cheeks. Then they run together, following in the wet stream bed of the pioneers, the first tears.

With her thumbs Ameerah lovingly re-directs the tiny streams into her palms.

You know, she says, twenty-five years ago I suddenly understood that there needed to be babies. Now those babies are grown and will have babies of their own.

Oh, Mommy . . .

Yesss, Sweetie. You too. Ben loves you. It will work out.

Cassandra sobs. Into her mother's hands. Into her mother's eyes.

But can I, Mommy? I don't want to hurt him. I don't want to hurt anyone! How can I not screw up?

Ameerah gently rocks her daughter's head. I see how you hurt, Sweetie. She waits until Cassandra looks up, into her eyes.

I just understood another thing. Twenty-five years later. Right now looking into your eyes. It's about you.

Cassandra has heard about her mom. How she helped Nurul and Alex. About how she can see life, light, and love. This is the first time she sees it for herself.

It starts as a flickering in her peripheral vision. Now she can see lines of white light between Ameerah's eyes and her own. It feels like music. Her hemispheres are floating, comfortable as clouds. They are becoming her mother's vision.

Like your Dad, says Ameerah, you have brilliant gifts. Different gifts, of course. We're all different and that is our gift to our people.

Different, whispers Cassandra. But gifts? Not . . .

Ameerah shakes her head slowly, holding the eye-lock and the pillars of light.

Nooo, she says. Not curses. Not if we use them right. Use the gifts.

Use … gifts … mouths Cassandra.

Ameerah can see the beginning of a smile. She knows her daughter's features are modest in repose.

Cassandra, she says.

Mommy …

Smile your beautiful smile. With that smile you can tell us thousands of stories about ourselves. Your stories will be beautiful. You will sing some of your stories. People will crowd around to hear.

Mommy … you are looking … ahead …

Ameerah laughs. Yesss. The bench …

They have met at Wesley's bench. It is autumn in this compartment. Cassandra has been kneeling in the leaves at her mother's feet. She hugs her mom as she gets to her feet, then sits next to her, cuddling as close as possible.

I can feel you worrying about the ceremony, says Ameerah. She takes Cassandra's hand and presses it to her breast. Your dad loves you, she says. Right here, on this bench, can you feel it? How Wesley loves you?

Now? There are tears, but Cassandra's smile is there still.

Yes, now, Sweetie.

He taught me so much …

Yesss. He is still with you. Think of him. Remember him.

The birds are largely silent now, but someone – no, there is more than one – they are making small peeping sounds. I don't know who that is, thinks Cassandra. I'll ask Uncle Naveed. Cyrus says his dad knows all the birds and their songs.

Cyrus Naveed Ameerahsson. And his little sisters Nousha and Shirin. My little sisters. Dad was older than Uncle Naveed. Quite a bit older.

Oh, Mommy. I remember something.

Something he told you? Taught you?

Yes. And you just told me the same thing.

Today, Sweetie?

Yes. Something I had forgotten. But you . . .

Cassandra sees her Mom's head turn and her eyebrows rise. There is laughter in her eyes.

I know, Mommy. I guess I hadn't forgotten. But it came flooding back into my head. How Daddy – you remember how he could quote things? – Daddy told me this one many times. I can still hear his voice . . .

Many times – like he wanted you to keep it. Keep it in you.

Ameerah picks up a yellow-brown leaf that has floated into her lap. Holding it by the stem, she turns it slowly, inspecting both sides.

And you have kept it, she continues. What is it?

It's from the *Gospel of Thomas*, says Cassandra.

The *New Testament*? I don't know much about it.

It's not in the *New Testament*. Athanasius – Christians call him the *Father of the Canon* – did not include it.

And what is the *Gospel of Thomas*? asks Ameerah. Is it like the other Gospels? The story of Jesus' life?

It appears to be sayings of Jesus.

So why did this *Father of the Canon* not include it? Do we know?

No. Not really.

Cassandra looks around, chewing absently on the nail of her right index finger.

Bishop Athanasius. Athanasius of Alexandria. St. Athanasius. We can't be too hard on him. He fought for the Holy Trinity. He spent his whole career discussing with other bishops what should be included.

Now the fingernail is vertical. Cassandra is polishing the nail edge with a lower incisor.

Elaine Pagels. She wrote a book about why. After they found the *Gospel of Thomas* in the 1940's. It had been buried.

Ameerah lays the leaf gently back onto her lap and turns to look at her daughter.

And what did Jesus say, according to this buried gospel?

Just what you told me today, Mommy. Maybe in different words, but it's just what you said.

> *If you bring forth what is within you, what you bring forth will save you.*
> *If you do not bring forth what is within you, what you do not bring forth will destroy you.*

Yesss. Ameerah picks up the leaf again. Yesss.

●

The ceremony is simple. Cassandra is singing Wesley's favourite hymn: *How Firm a Foundation.*

The words have been sent to the tablets and everyone is invited to join in.

> *How firm a foundation, ye saints of the Lord, is laid for your faith in his excellent word!*
>
> *What more can he say than to you he hath said, to you that for refuge to Jesus hath fled?*

The quirky but memorable melody, with its leaps of fourths and sixths, does not lend itself to harmony. But Uncle Ben on continuo and Rachel and Uncle Naveed on introduction and ostinato provide a harmonic context. Cyrus, beating a large bass tom-tom with one hand and shaking a tambourine with the other, makes strong the collective heartbeat.

As the hymn progresses so does the musical energy of the little band. Cyrus is singing, too – obviously from memory. His eyes are locked on Cassandra. His percussion plays with and to the words.

> *When through the deep waters . . .*
> *When through fiery trials . . .*

No one is immune. By the last verse this performance has achieved its aim and become a being unto itself, taking form in this time and space.

Great performances and great lives have something in common. They exist in time and end in silence. But they don't disappear. Since the beginning of the last verse, all have understood that the voice of the hymn has become Wesley:

> *The soul that to Jesus has fled for repose, I will not, I will not desert to its foes;*
>
> *That soul, though all hell shall endeavour to shake, I'll never, no, never, no, never forsake.*

The instrumentalists draw out the last note. Cyrus punctuates with a shake on his tambourine.

But Cassandra is still singing:

> *When my Dad was among us he urged us to know*
> *The home whence we come and the home hence we go.*
> *He bid us remember the wisdom of yore*
> *And to all pull together to that blissful shore.*

Cyrus is first to rejoin. The words are a surprise, but his tom-tom does its best to put them in relief. Then Naveed's violin, followed by Rachel's, takes up again the decorative obligato. By the last line the little band is at full strength.

> *My Dad was a teacher. He hoped we would learn*
> *And with curiosity we would discern*
> *Each one her own vision and version of life,*
> *Defending it always through change and through strife.*

Cyrus sees Cassandra is smiling. He has never seen his half-sister look so beautiful.

> *My Dad was a questioner. What's truth? he would ask.*
> *And what if the truth that you see wears a mask?*
> *If you walk over there and you get around back*
> *What you see might surprise you – but get you on track.*

> *The outline of Truth from this angle has changed,*
> *But you'll know in your heart that the object's the same.*
> *You'll discover that shape is just one way of seeing –*

Cassandra's voice, after the *ng* of believing, returns to the *ee* vowel. She nods at Cyrus. He punctuates with a tom-tom roll. The ee vowel opens into an *ah* vowel and fills, Cassandra's jaw low as she firms up her support and ends the note with a tiny glottal stop. It is a beautiful sound. The silence is absolute. As Cassandra relaxes her singer's posture her smile widens.

I love my Daddy, she says. He did so much for us.

She looks around, her newly revealed beauty holding the room's attention.

We have survived, she continues. The next generation is here. Let us keep Wesley in our hearts and keep learning from him. Let us keep learning from each other. Thank you. Thank you all.

From somewhere comes an alto howl. One of the new pups seems to have found her voice. From somewhere closer comes deep baritone laughter. Benjamin Colin Latifahsson is calling the room to order. To celebration.

•

Sarah has the con. She gazes out at the sea of stars in the black night sky.

She is not sight-seeing. Like a master on the quarter-deck, she is absorbing the condition and motion of her ship. She is looking for wobble and precession in her ship's spin.

Sarah Andrew Niloosdotter. Schooled by her dad and her half-brother, she is already quite good at attitude flying. Precession, she thinks. Pretty much right on track to keep my feet pointed at Sun as we orbit.

Hours of zero G in this cockpit have honed her physical skills. She cautiously extends her left arm to slow the slight spin remaining after she let go. Cutting loose, she calls it. Her extended but relaxed finger encounters an obstacle. Part of her chair, she thinks, as the spin stops.

Sarah enjoys floating. Tied to her chair, or moving across the deck in mag shoes, it is harder to tame the vestibular system and see – truly see – the stars. To patiently integrate their motion in her head. To model in four dimensions – because time is perhaps the important dimension – the visible universe and herself as a piece of it. *To hear the music of the spheres*, as her young friend Cassandra would say.

Four years younger, thinks Sarah. She has always seemed like my little sister. I have worried about her since I could worry. Her strangeness. Her brilliance. Her perplexity about what to make of herself. But lately . . .

Sarah has been floating, perfectly still, for several minutes. Her gaze has been steady, along the ship's axis. Her pilot's brain has been working hard, integrating the motions of the stars in her foveal vision. OK, she thinks. Wobble. Maybe one degree. Not bad, but worth a small correction sometime today. I'll go look at what the instruments say.

She puts a finger on her chair and pushes off with a deft little movement, which puts her on track for the screen where she can pull up a readout from the IRS setup Wesley installed before she was born. Zero-point-nine. Sarah pulls up the ship's log on the screen and writes:

2043 371 0947 WW 0.9. Calc and Sked Corr Today for 1300.

The date and time are already there. WW is for Wesley Wobble. Three seventy-one! she thinks. Four days until New Year's Day! Where does the time go?

Heck, I'm sounding like Dad. Except he's slowing down, if you want to know the truth. But we're still using Earth days because . . . because there are no days here. But we have a year. A little longer that Earth's. Because we're slightly outside and a bit slower. So we're a bit out of sync with Earth years . . .

Her mind drifts back to Cassandra. She's only 19, thinks Sarah. But since Wesley . . .

She cuts loose into a slow spin. From here she can see the whole night side of the ship. Her ship. Home. Heck. I can visualize the correction, she thinks. Why not?

It was Feynman, thinks Sarah. He said that the behaviour of rotating bodies seemed like a miracle. That some things can be deduced mathematically more rapidly than they can be explained in a fundamental, physical sense. That the Dirac Equation is a case in point.

Oh, my. I'm good at math, thinks Sarah. Angular momentum I can make into a picture in my head. I can integrate the movements of the infinite number of small bits of mass that is the Ark, and I can solve the problem. Predict the behaviour. But Dirac?

Sarah floats, relaxing her perception, losing focus, integrating her foveal and peripheral vision. Heck, rotating bodies are everywhere, she thinks. Ark, Moon, Earth. Electrons and quarks. All is spin and orbit.

Sarah is moving into that space she knows she should avoid while at the con. The world – solar system, galaxy and on out to wherever – has become beautiful. Void of meaning. Just *there*.

She thinks of her dear friend Cassandra. Of how her friend's mind is just . . . unique in the purest sense. None other like it. Cassandra is not going to reveal the mystery of Dirac's Equation. But what she will do is arguably more important.

Sarah allows herself to be moved. Beauty envelops her. I want to see the beauty of Dirac, she thinks. The superposition of an up-spin electron, a down-spin electron, an up-spin positron, and a down-spin-positron. Spinors. Belts like Möbius bands, changing sign as spacetime itself rotates. The implication of antimatter. Another universe? Part of our universe that so far we can't either see or interact with?

Maybe I'll see it and maybe I won't. Sarah climbs back into focused existence, getting her pilot scan going and her will purposed to the motion of her ship, for which she is responsible right now. The correction for this 0.9-degree wobble will involve a wave function firing of the axis-wise steam thrusters on the Ark's rim.

Sarah punches the buttons and turns her body to watch. A satisfying white plume starts out there on the black rim of the Ark. She watches a star over the plume. She swivels slowly to keep the star in view. So does the plume, switching to the next thruster on the rim. She knows that deep under her feet and behind her, 180 degrees or pi radians away, other thrusters are doing the symmetrical opposite on the day side of the Ark, but she checks the camera feed to be sure. Her head, the star, and the plumes have become the imaginary stationary axis of the Ark, independent of the Ark itself, which is turning beneath her feet. The force of the thrusters, applied 90 degrees or pi/2 radians early, have the effect of doing work on the Ark's axis of rotation, truing it up, reducing the size of the cones described by the imaginary extensions of the axis in both directions. Watching the steam plumes, she sees the wave function as they rise and fall.

The plumes stop. Steam. Throwing mass away to accelerate. Old stuff. Newton et al. But controlled by mathematics implemented in software.

Sarah cuts loose and stabilizes, watching the axis stars. Let's see how this settles down, she thinks. She drifts, watching her stars through two-and-a-half rotations of the Ark. Not bad, she thinks, and for less than a minute of steam.

The correction complete, her pilot mind relaxes into

surveillance mode. No, she thinks. It's not since Wesley died that she has noticed the change in Cassandra. It's since the celebration. When she sang. When she looked so beautiful.

Cassandra was smiling that day, Sarah realizes. She liked – no – she knew exactly what she was doing, and she loved it.

●

Hey, Little Sister!

Cassandra suppresses a giggle. Cyrus always calls Bianca Little Sister. I think he's sweet on her, she thinks as she looks around, searching for what the others are feeling, trying to catch the vibrations in the room. Cyrus isn't done.

Hey, it's your birthday, right? Fifteen?

Bianca Benjamin Rachelsdotter is blushing, but she has a saucy smile. She is clearly enjoying Cyrus' attention.

You gonna give me some percussion to mark the occasion?

Bianca, you are a woman now, says Leila. You are quinceañera. Hey, let's have a fiesta de quinceañera! Que le parece? Whaddaya say?

My big sister, thinks Cassandra. Leila the linguist. She realizes she is smiling, no longer searching the room for reactions. Just enjoying. Her hemispheres are humming with resonance as she considers the two women, their characters balanced like a dumbbell in her head.

This is supposed to be a musical meetup, a sopranos sectional rehearsal. But Bianca's first nature is more body than voice. Like dear quiet Uncle Ahiga, her physicality is inescapable. If she is no statue, it is only because that is an impossibility, even in sleep. As Cassandra's beauty emerges through her smile, Bianca's kindles through movement. Still – once noticed, her young body charms on its own.

Wow, that jumpsuit looks good on her, thinks Cassandra. The fit is perfect. Where did she get that? It doesn't exaggerate hips or bust. It says proportion and taste.

Cassandra stares, trying to get a freeze frame. It is not easy. It is going on a minute when she suddenly shuts her eyes, clicking the shutter. She studies Bianca's jumpsuit in a rare, relaxed pose. Alone for a moment with the image, she feels a welling of emotion. That time is over for me, she thinks. Why am I filled with joy? How blessed we are to see it emerging again! And Leila Youssef Ameerahsdotter, my big sister, is teaming up with Cyrus to bring it out.

Si! Cyrus sits, cross-legged. Let's party!

Oh my goodness, thinks Cassandra. Cyrus has brought his tabla. The foxy devil! The tabla are Cyrus' new preoccupation. I happened to be there when Uncle Gopinath proposed them to Cyrus. And it was not so long ago that he made this pair for Cyrus and taught him the rudiments of technique. I guess we are about to find out what he has learned.

With his left middle finger, Cyrus taps the small drum near the middle of its skin.

D! thinks Cassandra. And surprisingly loud and clear! She can feel the note occupy the room, whose dimensions and surfaces have been designed to be a part of whatever instrument is sounding here.

Cyrus is a leftie, she thinks. That's why the small drum is on the left. Its name means right, she remembers. This is going to be fun!

A rolling rhythm begins. Cyrus' hands are completely involved – palms, fingers, and fingertips making shifting and seemingly limitless combinations. His right hand is heartbeat and breathing, his left a ringing and clattering commentary.

Cassandra feels her Dad looking over her shoulder with

curiosity. Those pads near the centre of each drum's skin – they add mass, and change the skin's vibration. Like winding on a string. More mass per unit length. Or surface, in this case.

Oh, Dad! she thinks. But Cassandra doesn't lose her smile. How could she, with all this going on?

Some of those clear notes are changing pitch. Her questioning thought brings Dad back. His palms, says Wesley in her mind's ear. The boy is changing the tension of the skin.

Dad fades again as Bianca spins around to face them. Face me, thinks Cassandra. That saucy smile is still there, but with more intent. Her body is moving in beauty, an ode to the day. Or to the company, thinks Cassandra suddenly. This group is already one body. Something is happening.

She glances at Leila and catches her eye. This is a story, Cassandra is thinking. Cyrus' drumming is being fed by Bianca's dancing. Or is it the other way around?

That initial D has stayed with Cassandra. Now she is hearing it as the five in Mixolydian mode. Bits of melody are coalescing around the D, which still emerges from Cyrus' fingers, sometimes bent up a bit. Cassandra can feel the squeezed interval D-G in her body. That's what Raga is supposed to do, she thinks. Invoke a mood. Move you. Like all art is supposed to do. She hears the Mixolydian sharp sixth and flat seventh play in the squished fourth between D and G.

Suddenly Cassandra is singing.

> *Young love*
> *Beauty becoming*
> *Life emerging*

Cyrus' fingers furiously finish the verse. The D is very bent, twanging up and down. Leila joins it an octave above, hovering, bending with it.

> *Young love*

> *Beauty becoming*
> *Life emerging*

The repeat has two voices. Leila and Cassandra play within what is becoming their Raga, their set of restrictions which paradoxically multiply the manifold which contains their music. They are the chorus – the koros – singing the scene over and over, each time differently, each time within their Raga.

> *Oh lovely girl*
> *You play my heart*
> *Your instrument moves me*

Cyrus keeps his right hand moving as he sings, synchronizing the collective breathing and heartbeat. He is staying within our Raga, thinks Cassandra. How does he do it? How does it work?

Cyrus' left hand punctuates the verse, and a familiar sequence – like the double roll of a marching band – leads to only one place:

> *Young love*
> *Beauty becoming*
> *Life emerging*

Leila is still singing the upper voice. Her improvisations venture higher on the staff. This is fun, thinks Cassandra. We're telling a story together, and none of us knows exactly where it is going.

> *Oh Tabla Romeo*
> *My heart beats to you*
> *My body sings your song*

Singing as she dances, Bianca moves toward Cyrus, looking him in the eye. Somehow, he manages to lead them back into koros.

Leila and I are in a balcony in the church, thinks Cassandra. The one in Leipzig Uncle Ben told us about. The soloists are in an identical balcony, a mirror image, on the other side of the nave.

> *Young love*

Beauty becoming
Life emerging

As if reaching for the vaulted ceiling, Leila's improvisation dances up to the top of the staff, reaching a high G.

She did it! thinks Cassandra. I knew she would do it. That's her voice!

The story, the Raga, the dance, go on. Because story, song, life, are repetition. Theme and variation. No two lives the same.

That jumpsuit, thinks Cassandra suddenly. That's Ben's Mom. Aunt Tifah. She sews. That's her eye. That's Aunt Tifah letting us see.

●

Ooh! This beautiful, Sarah!

Have you spent much time in zero, Cassandra?

Wide-eyed, Cassandra shakes her head.

That's OK, says Sarah. That's why I asked you to come at the end of my watch. Eric, you have the con.

At 63, Eric still likes to show off. He pushes off from beside Cassandra in a left roll and forward somersault. Two-thirds of the way to the captain's chair, he spread-eagles, slowing the motions in roll and pitch. He grabs the top of the chair upside-down and with his left wrist stops the roll and completes the loop, dropping his butt in the seat and fastening his belt.

I have the con.

Cassandra laughs, shaking her head.

Good, says Sarah. You're going to be OK. I'm going to cut loose . . .

Cassandra's eyes speak panic.

Not like that, says Sarah, nodding at Eric. Gently. See?

Sarah lets go her hand hold. Hovers in front of Cassandra. Start like me. I'll help.

They float gently around the cockpit, staying right-side-up relative to Eric and his chair. They float slowly around the cockpit periphery, examining screens and controls.

How are you feeling, Cassandra?

This is beautiful! And congratulations, Sarah! I was so . . . I didn't realize you had made Master.

Of course you didn't. Thank you!

She's good stick, says Eric.

Cassandra waits for more. She sneaks a glance at Sarah, who smiles, shakes her head.

That's it, huh?

Sarah nods, lifts her eyebrows a hair.

Hey, you wanna try floating on the axis? Watching the axis stars?

Sure, says Cassandra. Where?

They float gently to the apex of the cockpit dome. The view is spectacular. They are still upright relative to the dome, the con, and Eric, but here, high above the consoles, they can see the whole of the night side of the Ark. Cassandra is staring at her feet and letting her body rotate slowly on its long axis.

You can see the five docks!

Sarah laughs. What's left of them. But you're right.

And those – tracks? And we're on them?

Sarah nods.

Cassandra completes another 180° of spin.

That's the Belt Ship!

Yeah. That's it.

Sarah tucks in her elbows to increase her spin rate and stay aligned with her friend. She turns her head, trying to see Cassandra's mind at work. She sees Cassandra gazing not at her feet, but just beyond, estimating their height above the night surface of the Ark.

We're on top of a tower, she says.

She points at the empty end of the track. We could move over there, she says. Then the Belt Ship could be here, on the axis.

Sarah smiles and moves her elbows out, slowing her rotation. As she and Cassandra come face to face, she gently extends her left hand and entwines her fingers with Cassandra's right. Sarah's right hand comes to rest on her friend's waist.

We're dancing! says Cassandra.

They have become one body, their masses linked, their inertias added.

This is fun! says Cassandra.

•

On Wesley's bench Fall has progressed into Winter. The deciduous trees are bare. The sweet rot of Autumn has given way to absence, a clarity which itself prepares the way for rebirth.

Cassandra has her legs crossed in a Buddha pose. Her eyes are closed as she summons stories from the past. From before she was born. From her Dad, Wesley, a young man on Earth. On the Earth Cassandra knows only as a blue and white sphere, and even that only now, as their orbits approach conjunction.

All that's missing here is snow, she thinks. Dad told me about snow. About the soft silence. About how the dogs love to frolic in it.

In recent days, the panic and pain of Cassandra's adolescence have eased. She has gained confidence in her ability to channel her Dad at will. Wesley being with her, and her Mom's love, let her get on with the job at hand. With memory and music she will be able to keep their collective story alive.

I don't know nearly enough about now, thinks Cassandra. Sarah is Master Sarah. We are a ship hurtling through space. Earth is passing us, Sunside. All our stories start there, even though we young were born here.

Hemispheres humming, Cassandra puts the problem into spatial terms. It's an hourglass, she thinks. That little neck that dribbles the sand is now. It regulates the flow, but other than that, it doesn't have much effect on those tiny rock particles. They fall where they fall. But Master Sarah would be the first to say you can't steer if you can't see where you are going. And I might add: if you can't imagine where you should be going.

Casandra opens her eyes. The sere simplicity of the winter compartment is like a blank canvas. Where destiny can be painted, she thinks. Where life can be painted.

Cassandra's gaze pans slowly, meditating on the dormant vegetation. This kind of seeing happens to be my job, she thinks, if for no reason other than that I can do it. Mommy says it's not a curse. I can feel Daddy comforting me, saying the same.

She closes her eyes again, maintaining the Buddha pose, listening to the silence, searching for clarity. She knows it can happen, because it does happen. Just not all the time. But maybe now, in winter . . .

The silence is not complete. Not soft, like outdoors in falling snow, as Dad told of it. It is an Ark silence – peaceful, but with low whooshes, whirs, and hums as Ark systems go about their business. I don't hear it because it's always there, thinks Cassandra.

For me, it has always been there. I have known nothing else.

Cassandra concentrates on this Ark silence as she would music, forming an edifice of structure in her imagination. There is more, she thinks. More than whooshes, whirs, and hums. Every once in a while, here or there, is a creak or a groan.

Expressing what? Structural stress? Expansion and contraction? Growth?

She searches her knowledge of Ark systems, probing for weak spots in her imagining of them, letting questions form in her hemispheres. Welcoming the questions that will lead to learning.

Yes, it's scary, thinks Cassandra. Probing and disturbing your image of existence. Those weak spots threaten you. You want to ignore them because they make you feel – diminished. Less capable. Not as smart as you thought you were.

Who are we, anyway? thinks Cassandra. Sure, we're characters from birth. We arrive with our gifts. We try to use them, because that makes us happy. Cyrus is left-handed, and really good at percussion. But is that it? The extent of his identity? Does fate then govern the rest of his life?

That could happen to anyone, thinks Cassandra. A static self-image becomes an unwitting handle for fate. That's tragedy. Macbeth. Lear.

But that's not Cyrus. He has just fallen in love. Not passively, either. He was wooing Bianca from the start. Leila realized it before I did. Romeo and Juliet . . .

Suddenly there is powerful music in Cassandra's head. Prokofiev. The March of the Capulets. The Montagues and the Capulets. Their teenage love is doomed from the start. Shit!

Cassandra opens her eyes. No! My little brother is too smart. There's no bad blood between the Rachelsdotters and the Ameerahs. No! It doesn't have to happen that way. It's beautiful and it can stay beautiful. It's possible. It *is* possible, dammit . . .

Where was I? thinks Cassandra. How did I get off on this tangent?

Identity. Learning as a threat to it. Growth . . .

Yes – that's a weak point in my image of the Ark. Growth. I know that much of our Sunside surface is alive and growing. I'll have to ask Stella and her Dad. That surface is really a tree. Or a new part of a tree. Alex calls it spaceleaf. It photosynthesizes, even though there's no air out there. And I don't know how it works.

Eyes still closed, Cassandra listens, trying to return from her digression on fate, focussing on Ark hums and their occasional punctuation with creaks or groans. She can feel a tension, as if waiting for a musical cadence. Maybe I'll hear spaceleaf growing, she thinks.

Instead what she hears is birds. A flock of tiny, fluttering birds, by the sound of it. Little squeaks. Peeps. Random percussion with long gaps.

She is on the same bench. Mom is here beside her. There are still autumn leaves everywhere underfoot. She was going to ask Uncle Naveed who they were, these birds. He would know.

Hello, Cassandra, says a soft voice.

Strangely, Cassandra doesn't startle. She opens her eyes slowly, and smiles.

Hello, Uncle Naveed. I think I felt you coming.

●

You look worried, Cassie.

They are emerging from a visit with Stella's parents. Cassandra breathes. Worried? she thinks. I'm worried?

Estelle Alexander Nurulsdotter watches patiently with her

surprising blue eyes. Blue eyes in a brown face.

A few weeks ago I would have probably denied being worried, thinks Cassandra. Yes, Stella, I think you're right, she says aloud. Only now I have to figure out what I'm worried about . . .

I hope it wasn't Mom and Dad. They're both pretty intense, and when you put them together . . .

. . . no, no, Stel. They're fantastic. And their projects are going well. Going so well it kind of boggles my mind.

Stella laughs. Your mind doesn't boggle, Cassie.

Cassandra can feel her body melt into warmth. It is like when Ben holds me, she thinks. Or Mom.

Still laughing, Stella watches Cassie's smile grow – first into beauty and then into laughter.

Thank you, Stel . . . manages Cassandra between gasps. I'm . . .

There is no need to say anything.

You want to keep walking, Cassie?

Sure.

They walk. Briskly, because it is winter in this park. Plant life is asleep. Cassandra always finds winter calming. Life pauses, takes a breath. Perhaps invents something new. Cassandra breathes deeply, enjoying the air, clearing her hemispheres. The path arrives at the partition and airlock between compartments.

What's next, Cassie? Do you know?

Spring.

The girls emerge from the airlock. The smell of new life is everywhere, bringing hope. They stroll slowly along the path. Suddenly there is a tune playing in Cassandra's head. It is *Quittez Pasteurs*, one of those quirky and lovely French folksong/carols whose provenance is uncertain. They follow the bells, thinks Cassandra. Dad said that. Dad said he was not a musician, but he could sing the bells to me: sol do re me, sometimes with a high sol on top. I have never seen bells, but I know about them. Churches, universities, clock towers. Some bells tell the time of day every fifteen minutes. Mi do re sol, then the same thing backwards. On the hour that pattern repeats twice, and then the low sol booms out the hour.

It's so weird I know that, she thinks. Dad told me when I was little. It was part of one of his stories. At bedtime he would tell me about life on Earth. And because I have sung *Il est né le Divin Enfant* and *Quittez Pasteurs*, I know they follow that 6/4 chord of the bells. Oh, thank you Daddy! Thank you for what I know from you, and not from our virtual archives! I can feel what it was like in a small French town, or an American college town. Or I think I can.

But yes, Daddy. Back to business. I understand what you're saying. This Ark life is as perilous as any life. I have to sing of Ark life, because stuff needs to get done if we want to survive. It is never guaranteed. We mustn't get . . .

What's that you're whistling, Cassie?

Cassandra feels her cheeks redden, but she smiles, because words are coming.

> *They crewed their ship*
> *And flew it off to Ceres*
> *They knew their stuff*
> *They'd done it once before,*
> *Just some of them –*
> *The others would rely on them to safely lead the way*
> *The way! The way!*
> *Through planet-slings and Belt debris*

> *The way! The way!*
> *Through planet-slings and Belt debris.*

Oh my, yes! says Estelle. That was when we were little! Is there more?

> *The dogs came too*
> *As they had done the last time*
> *They flew and flew*
> *So good at zero G!*
> *Ahiga led,*
> *But quietly with Sebastien and aided by the dogs*
> *The dogs! The dogs!*
> *As much by love as fearsome might,*
> *The dogs! The dogs!*
> *As much by love as fearsome might.*

Oh, you'll sing that for everyone, won't you, Cassie? You won't forget it?

This time it is Estelle's cheeks which are blushing in the face of Cassandra's smile.

No, of course you won't forget, Cassie . . .

Thank you, Stel.

. . . thank me?

You told me I looked worried. You have opened my eyes. I'm putting small things together. You know Sarah is now Master Sarah?

No. Wow! Good for her! When?

I don't know exactly. Ten days? It was five days ago she gave me a tour of the cockpit to celebrate. Or break it to me, or something.

Leaves are starting to emerge from tightly wound little buds. Birds are singing, and occasionally startling at the girls' progress and flitting to a further branch. Estelle breathes the air gratefully. She has inherited her dad's fascination with each small living thing. Dad grew up with Nature on Earth, she thinks. What a wonder we could bring so much of it with us!

There were small things, Stel, but they added up.

Estelle Alexander Nurulsdotter, Stel, Stella, returns smoothly from her reverie and rejoins Cassandra's train of thought. What a blessing Cassie and I can be peaceful together, she thinks. She walks a few more paces with Cassandra, and nods.

Small things. Sarah had just finished her watch. Eric – Uncle Eric – took the next watch. It's zero G up there, you know . . .

Yes. On the axis. Of course.

Well, Eric did one of those show-off moves of his to get to his seat. You know, tumbles and rolls and stuff.

And he's an old guy.

Yeah.

Then Sarah took me up high in the dome. I could see the whole night side of the Ark.

Wow!

Yes. It was . . . humbling, I guess. And I saw the Belt Ship. And the five docks. And Sarah was telling me how she can correct our wobble with the steam jets.

That must be something to see! Did you . . .

Glancing at Cassandra, Stella stops. Her friend's face has returned to worry. In the silence Cassandra turns to her and gives her a little smile.

It's OK, Stel. It's Dad. He's talking to me. He's saying, Yes, it is beautiful. I hope you get to see it sometime. Wave forms. Mathematics. But it's old-fashioned propulsion, because we have nothing else. Throwing away mass. Action and reaction. Newton's Third Law. And now in my head I'm looking around me, up in that dome. It's what I don't see.

Don't see, Cassie?

Ice. Ice, Stel.

Ice. Of course. The ice block.

It's almost gone, Stel. We need another Ceres mission.

●

Eric's my brother, you know. Even if his grandsons are my age. Right, Nephew?

Yes, Aunt Sarah.

Cassandra can't help it. She doubles over in a fit of laughter. Between gasps, she manages, And what are we, Isaac?

You're probably not my aunt, Cassie.

Cassandra knows her friend Sarah can manage a sharp turn of tongue when she feels the need. But Isaac has always seemed the quiet one. The reticent one.

What am I feeling? thinks Cassandra. I laugh, but I feel weak in the knees. Jacob's tenor voice is in my right ear. Singing that B-natural. His father is looking at me with those deep blue eyes. The spitting image. Lean, long, black-haired, and handsome. Beautiful, even. Just twenty year's difference in age.

Cassandra brings Jacob back as she looks at his father. Her hemispheres do a time-lapse change thing, watching Jacob's fresh youth promise slowly become Isaac's calm achievement. She can pick out one or two grey hairs at his temples.

Smiling at Isaac, Cassandra puts the crazy stack of the

generations of Andrew into some sort of structure, all the way down to Sarah and the twins, exactly Sarah's age but also Sarah's grandnephews. Well, according to lore, Andrew's deeds have always boggled the mind. And the twins are my half-brothers, she remembers.

Isaac, asks Cassandra, How is Short-V?

Cassandra studies the handsome face as a wave of emotion and recognition passes. She can hear Wesley. Like waves from a motorboat moving the lily pads, he says. Waves. She can feel Master Sarah stiffen slightly with their passing. But Sarah says nothing.

I haven't – Isaac's face is still in motion, twisting around the mouth as he thinks – I haven't seen Short-V in some time. In fact, I think moving us into Sun orbit was the last Short-V operation.

And Eric, says Sarah.

Eric, says Isaac.

Yeah. Not my brother. Not your son. Your father.

Yeah, maybe, says Isaac.

●

Naveed has suggested this late-spring compartment for their meeting. Here trees line a field of vegetables. The rich smell of tomatoes reaches them at their bench.

Of course you're right, Cassie. I can't believe I didn't see it before. I didn't see it because . . .

Cassandra hears the bees before she sees their fat yellow and black stripes buzz by like a formation of fighters.

Oh, good! says Naveed. Bees always make me happy. They mean pollination and new life. Like the kids, he continues. The kids have made me happy since the moment they arrived.

Naveed pauses and sniffs the rich air. I'm so grateful for you kids, he says.

There are shimmers floating up from the vegetables and wafting about, as if the tomato aroma were liquid and could twist the air.

I'm sorry, Cassie, continues Naveed. You're no longer a kid. Today you have made me see that. He turns and looks at Cassandra. No, Cassie. Not today. From when you sang and spoke at Wesley's . . .

He sighs. I'm a parent, Cassie. Cyrus. And the girls, Nousha and Shirin. I can't believe it. Shirin is almost fifteen. And Cyrus is wooing Bianca. It is so powerful, Cassie. Seeing the next generation coming of age. I see now, here with you, how parenthood has taken me over completely. If that's any excuse for forgetting the ice.

Naveed stops abruptly, as if regret had closed his throat. He swallows.

But – we have some time. The water – you know, where we swim. Under the parks. The source and destination of our water cycle. The level, the mass, is still nominal. We can easily work with thirty percent less. So there is some time.

Somewhere nearby a bird sings. Two notes, a descending full tone apart. The song seems to release something in Naveed.

Sometimes at night I'm suddenly afraid, he says. We are so vulnerable. If we had forgotten just one essential piece of life, or if that piece had died off. Or any of a million other . . .

Slow tears frame Naveed's proud Persian nose.

Oh, Uncle Naveed!

Cassandra gives him a hug. Her hemispheres fill with the essential pieces of life as she understands them. Tears are one of them, she thinks. Tears for us. She watches Naveed's proud nose as the tears slide. He is not afraid for himself, she thinks. He is afraid for his kids. For all of us. He feels responsible for more than . . .

Hands on his shoulders, she pushes herself back upright and irradiates Naveed with her smile. No one of us can do it all, she thinks.

Cassandra lets the silence shimmer. She feels her father close at hand, his hands on *her* shoulders. Is that why I put my hands on Naveed's?

I was an engineer, says Naveed. Your Dad taught me. Turned me into a physicist. I could never have dreamed of that. And then your mother . . .

In the shimmering light Cassandra feels that tingling in her peripheral vision, the precursor to her Mom's lines of light and love.

. . . I have always loved her, says Naveed. I never thought it could happen. Now we are together.

I feel Mom and Dad so strongly, thinks Cassandra. Dad is explaining entanglement, and why that and the mysteries of Paul Dirac could be unravelled and re-woven to secure our future. And Mom . . . Mom loves Naveed.

The bird sings again.

Who is that, Uncle Naveed?

Naveed laughs. Cassandra can feel gratitude emanating from him. That's the Black-Capped Chickadee, he says. Neat, huh? That full tone?

Naveed whistles the song.

Cassandra laughs. There's no mistaking that, she says.

Another bird sings:

Sol-sol-sol la fa do

The *do* is the high note.

And who is *that*? asks Cassandra.

Naveed blushes with pleasure. That's a thrush. He's new. I've never heard him before!

Cassandra's face pinches with playful doubt. But how . . .? she asks.

Oh – they're all different. They sing rhythmic motifs like that. But they're individual. Each one different. Naveed laughs. And they stick to the same tune all season!

The Passion Chorale, with one of the Bach harmonizations, starts in Cassandra's head. Words come, but she puts them on the shelf. She feels she has to sing about the Ceres Missions – both of them. And the next one. But she doesn't know enough. She knows nothing beyond the facts, the bare bones. She never knew Art, for example. But the others are still here.

You were there, Uncle Naveed. You were on the first Ceres Mission.

Yes.

It's so important, Uncle Naveed. Could you tell me about it? Tell me the story?

•

Rachel, Honey, you was the holdout!

The Original Ark Women are partying in an end-of-summer arbor. Even in the Eden of Ark's seasonal out-of-phase gardens, this setting is idyllic.

We all were, Tifah, including you, says Niloofar. C'mon!

I just wasn't getting pregnant, says Rachel.

Her observation produces fits of guffaw-giggles in Niloo and

Latifah. In truth, the mirth is partly explained by the batch of beer Ben has brought to the bower.

Honey, you was just doin' the same old thing and hoping for a different outcome, says Latifah. Meanwhile, Ameerah was in production. And not with just those first two boys.

Ameerah smiles, but keeps silence with her lovely voice, like a singer between phrases.

The occasion is the annual celebration of their first meeting. Way back then. Sebastien's recruiting was over. The Ark, in Moon orbit, was still two spokes and two gardens. It was before Wesley's Covenant ceremony, when the twins were just a gleam in Ameerah's eye.

Since then the Original Women have been busy with womanly things. Slowly at first, as after the twins Ameerah bore Leila and Cassandra and Cyrus. Then Ameerah settled with Naveed, and the others took up the baton.

Is that what changed for us? asks Nurul. That Ameerah and Naveed – well, it was more than – you said it, Latifah – production . . .

Latifah and Niloofar laugh again. With Niloo it is almost a cackle.

Yeah. Was time for us to get more men in our beds, says Latifah.

I felt bad for Dominic, says Nurul. It looked like he wasn't going to be a father. And Alex – he agreed it would be best for our collective future . . .

And we have Mireille, says Ameerah, breaking her silence. And she's a purrfect wonderr.

Eyes are on Nurul. A gentle breeze brings the smell of ripe tomatoes and incipient decay. The silence following Ameerah's observation is as rich and beautiful as her voice.

Dominic is such a good father to her, says Nurul. He has been with her from birth. All the time. Holding her. Talking to her. Encouraging her.

There are tears on Nurul's cheeks. Seeing them like that – even today – she's almost seventeen, says Nurul. Even today – I love them.

Yesss, says Ameerah, holding Nurul's gaze. Bless them. Bless you. *Mee-ray-yeh*, she says, pronouncing the French. *Peace. Prosperous. Admire. Wonderful.* She's a wonderful girl.

The breeze has shifted, bringing a new and powerful scent. Somewhere at the far end of the park someone is harvesting onions. Ameerah starts to salivate. Oh, for Heaven's Sake, she thinks.

We were all pregnant that year, says Niloofar. Oh – I don't regret that at all. Ahiga. Magnificent! There is no other word for him.

She is still beautiful, thinks Ameerah. Porcelain, perfect – and a bit saucy. Those lines radiating from her mouth when she smiles – they just make her *more* beautiful.

I looked it up, says Nurul. Ahiga means *He who fights*.

Now the cackle is Latifah's. Huh, she says. Yeah, maybe he fight. But it be silent and spiritual. And – her gaze sweeps the Original Women – I'm not gonna ask. She shakes her head with a sly smile. No way.

Nurul catches Rachel's eye. Rachel returns a shy smile.

And we have Bidziil, purrs Ameerah.

He is strong, says Nurul. I looked that up, too.

We'll see, says Niloofar. He's only seventeen.

End of summer. This batch of Ark-born is growing up, thinks

Ameerah. But we Originals have finished bearing fruit. It will be up to the New Women, bless them.

C'mon, Tifah, says Niloofar. You were pregnant too, that year.

Yes, Niloo. Sebastien. Latifah glances at Nurul. I feel a bit like you do, Nurul. Sebastien is sweet, but he's not one to woo. Make him a Papa, I thought. Be good for him.

And we have Mathieu. *Mathieu . . .* , says Ameerah, working for a good French *th* and tripthong.

Gift of the Lord, says Nurul.

Uh huh, says Latifah. Papa got himself a good little French Canadian black boy.

Not so little, Tifah, says Niloofar. Your boys aren't little.

Huh. Growin' up. Too quick.

But I still remember them as babies. Niloofar shoots Latifah a look. And Mathieu's not that dark, Tifah.

Uh huh. You want dark you take Ben.

Yes, Tifah, says Rachel. Ben is lovely. But frankly, Sweetie, he's not your darkest.

Latifah's laugh comes from her heart.

It is a church laugh, as when choral praise reaches a climax. It is a rush of emotion that takes her by surprise. Sure, it is for Prisha, born when Mathieu was two, her name meaning the same thing – *Gift from God*. But perhaps not exactly the same God. Krishna the Numerous, the Infinite, instead of the Blessed Trinity. But the emotion is also for Rachel – the love of her life, Latifah suddenly realizes. But that's OK. Rachel just called me *Sweetie*. And the kids also are the love of my life.

Oh, that handsome Gopi, says Niloofar. Tall, handsome, *dark* Gopi. And Prisha – long, tall, with her daddy's handsome long nose. And *dark* – wow!

Yes, says Nurul, brown eyes blinking in her brown face. She's gorgeous. And the darkest of us all.

Oh, my little Prisha, says Latifah. Now she's almost as tall as her Daddy. Time go by.

An invisible cardinal combines two of his crazy songs: burglar alarm, followed by

bairstow – bairstow – bairstow

Those birds are nuts, says Niloo. She laughs. That was a bumper year, the Prisha year. We were all pregnant. And we can't forget Ameerah and Naveed.

Huh, says Latifah. Three-in-a-row. She grunts out the words, one at a time, stressed.

That sets off Niloofar. She tosses her head and laughs, clutching the table for support.

Cyrus, Nousha, Shirin, says Rachel.

Far-sighted, Kind-hearted, Kind and sweet, says Nurul.

You looked it up!

This is choral speaking from the leading tipplers, who taper off into joyous cackles.

Oh, my! Omar! says Niloo, catching her breath. That was that year. The Prisha year.

And? says Latifah.

Oh yes! Says Niloo. Adonis. The perfect body. She smiles, and those lines appear like rays from the sun. For a guy, anyway, she adds.

And we have Sami, says Ameerah.

Exalted, says Nurul.

And? says Latifah, raising her eyebrows. Nurul?

Nurul's brown face darkens red. Oh! she says. Ferdinand.

And?

Perfect *little* body.

Rachel and Ameerah join the leading tipplers in their mirth. Even Nurul's blushing brown cheeks pinch into the beginning of a smile.

He's sweet, you know, says Nurul.

Yes, thinks Ameerah. And so is his son. Joaquim.

And so is our son, Joaquim, says Nurul. Established by God.

Joaquim, thinks Ameerah. Not quite fifteen. Like my Shirin. Heavens! It's her quinceañera. Soon! We were blinded by Bianca, by her powerful physical presence. And Cyrus is so stuck on her. Wonderful! It's wonderful. And Joaquim is a prodigy. He is already learning flying and physics from his father, from Sarah, even from me, a little. He soaks it up. He and Sarah and Ferdinand work together, running the Belt Ship Lander systems in simulator mode, like we did so long ago in Moon orbit . . .

Ameerah looks around at the table of tipsy mothers. They are gossiping, having fun, being themselves. She hears their voices, but the meaning is non-essential. Why do I feel so joyful when Joaquim comes around to ask me questions? thinks Ameerah. Why does it make me feel joyful now, just thinking about it?

There are rays of white and not-so-white light dancing among the Original Women. Rachel and Latifah. Niloo and me, thinks Ameerah, remembering the big party after the homecoming, when the twins were babies and she first saw the lights, even among the dogs.

Journey and Justice!

Ameerah realizes she is sitting with her arms out to each

side, as if to embrace two giant dogs. Her cheeks are wet with tears. The women's voices are still just a pleasant music with no rational content. But Niloofar catches her eye and smiles, becoming the sun, her energy sent to dry Ameerah's tears. She winks at Ameerah, a slow wink seen only by Ameerah, making its way to her through this yellow fog of beery chatter.

Journey and Justice!

Eric and Jacob. The twins. And through the injustice of canine life-span the dogs are gone and the twins are here and heading into their prime.

No, it's not injustice, thinks Ameerah. It is hurt. Injustice does not necessarily flow from hurt. Living and loving bring loss, and loss hurts. So we cry.

Ameerah sees a Mama Cardinal land on a nearby branch. Somewhere nearby her mate pumps out a new song. It is a one-second upward sweep – exactly the song of one black hole swallowing another. Exactly, because the first gravity waves detected in 2015 were audio frequency. Just like that. Like that note. As more were detected they became that song.

The girls are still discussing something-or-other but only the odd word gets through to Ameerah. Mama Cardinal, in Ameerah's line of sight but unseen by the others, holds fast as her branch sways in the breeze. She preens and dances in her fast bird rhythm, a private show for Ameerah. The fast bird rhythm is somehow connected to the slow swaying of the branch. Her muted colours stun the soul as well as the eye, bringing a rush of beauty. Her mate continues to evoke black hole cannibalism, his flashy brilliance unseen.

Joaquim.

The name pops out from the babble. Mama Cardinal's dance has helped keep Ameerah's hurt-beauty trance in place. Or spell. Or whatever it is that is stripping meaning from the women's conversation. But a word popped out. A name. Joaquim. They are talking about how good-looking he is.

Yes, thinks Ameerah. He is one of those genetic surprises. Good-looking would not be the first thought on encountering either of his parents. But Ferdinand's mother was Portuguese, and Nurul is South Asian. Joaquim is neither white nor black, nor any other known colour. He is just Joaquim, and his beauty is mesmerizing.

But not to him, thinks Ameerah gratefully. Mirrors – ponds of water – these have no effect on him. He looks at you with those eyes – what colour are they? They seem to change, so you can never remember – and asks questions. Tell me about that landing, Aunt Ameerah. What did you feel? What did you learn? Tell me the story!

I do, of course. And it makes me feel wonderful. I don't know why.

●●●